ALSO BY CAROL GILLIGAN

The Birth of Pleasure

In a Different Voice

Between Voice and Silence
(with Jill McLean Taylor and Amy M. Sullivan)

Meeting at the Crossroads
(with Lyn Mikel Brown)

EDITED BY CAROL GILLIGAN

Women, Girls, and Psychotherapy
(with Annie G. Rogers and Deborah L. Tolman)

Making Connections
(with Nona P. Lyons and Trudy J. Hanmer)

Mapping the Moral Domain
(with Janie Victoria Ward, Jill McLean Taylor,
and Betty Bardige)

KYRA

KYRA

A Novel

CAROL GILLIGAN

RANDOM HOUSE

NEW YORK

Published in the United States by Random House,
an imprint of The Random House Publishing Group,
a division of Random House, Inc., New York.

RANDOM HOUSE and colophon are
registered trademarks of Random House, Inc.

Grateful acknowledgment is made to the following for permission to
reprint previously published material:

HarperCollins Publishers: Excerpt from "Act IV, Sc. 1" from
The Dream of the Unified Field: Poems 1974–1994 by Jorie Graham,
copyright © 1995 by Jorie Graham. Reprinted by permission of
HarperCollins Publishers.

Hal Leonard Corporation: Excerpt from "Fields of Gold," music and
lyrics by Sting, copyright © 1993 by Steerpike Ltd. Administered by
EMI Music Publishing Limited. All rights reserved. International
copyright secured. Reprinted by permission of
Hal Leonard Corporation.

LIBRARY OF CONGRESS CATALOGING-IN-PUBLICATION DATA

Gilligan, Carol.
Kyra: a novel / Carol Gilligan.
p.   cm.
ISBN 978-1-4000-6175-4
1. Women designers—Fiction.   2. Man-woman relationships—
Fiction.   3. Loss (Psychology)—Fiction.   4. Psychotherapist and
patient—Fiction.   5. Psychological fiction.   I. Title.
PS3607.I4445K97 2008
813' .6—dc22   2007022205

Printed in the United States of America on acid-free paper

www.atrandom.com

2 4 6 8 9 7 5 3 1

First Edition

Book design by Katie Shaw

To Jim

And after the fire came a gentle whisper.

—1 Kings 19:12

PART ONE

1

WHAT IS THE OPPOSITE OF LOSING?

It was the Sunday after Thanksgiving, and we were playing chess. Felicia Blumenthal had invited the strays to her home on Francis Avenue—an old habit, hospitality to strangers, made urgent for her generation by the war. He was her cousin, "much removed," she said, laughing, as she brought him over to where I was standing in the blue dining room balancing a plate of turkey, and when I asked him what he was thankful for, his eyes registered surprise and he said, "This," meaning the lunch. He had come in from London the night before, he was leaving the next morning for Chicago. I had come from my studio wearing a long black skirt and white shirt. He stepped back and looked at me. "A flutist or an oboe player?" he asked. I had always wanted to play the oboe. He asked if I was cold, the dining room shaded on the north side of the house, Felicia too European to turn up the heat. We left our plates on the sideboard and crossed the hall into the living room, skirting the group standing around the fireplace— men in gray suits, a woman in a red sari—and gravitating instead to the sunny bay window. He sat on one antique blue-velvet chair, I sat on the other, the marble chessboard on the table between us.

I reached into the diagonal of sunlight, my hand momentarily translucent as I moved the white knight into position to capture the black bishop.

Andreas looked, saw, and moved his bishop away. The black bishop glided to safety, the inner recesses of black and white squares. Instead he would sacrifice a pawn: out of the many, this one.

"Your turn," he said, looking up, his eyes blue-gray, the color of river stones.

My half brother, Anton, had taught me to play, long afternoons at the table in front of the high window looking out to the sea, his face grim. He was the child of our mother's brief early marriage, the half in half brother a splinter under his skin. "Checkmate," he would say, explaining that it came from the Arabic *shāh māt,* meaning the king is dead. I said it meant he was her mate, the queen more elusive, more inventive, the one who moves freely in all directions. Who invented this game, I wondered, Andreas waiting. I touched the castle, its evenly chiseled turrets saying harmony, symmetry, even as its straight-line moves—up, down, across—concealed the darker purposes of alignment, the closing in of castle and knight on the unsuspecting (did she know, how did she know, why didn't she know) queen.

Andreas leaned forward, the lines of his face deepening in concentration, and then he swept his queen across the board. "Check."

The sun, horizontal now, ignited the yellow leaves on the maple tree outside the window.

He sat back, watching my face.

"Do you know how green your eyes are in this sun?" his voice quiet, as if to himself.

I looked at him, surprised, and at his hand at the edge of the board.

"What is the opposite of losing?" I asked him.

"Finding," he said.

And so it began.

The next morning it snowed, unexpectedly. Huge flakes hung suspended in a yellow-gray haze, revealing the air, its density, and also gravity, as tumbling slowly and then for a moment resisting, they were pulled inexorably down. The leaves of late fall mingled with the snow of oncoming winter as I crossed the yard holding the university buildings apart, each building standing alone, discrete. This was Puritan New England. No touching, no leaning on one another. It was more or less how I'd been living since Simon was killed, my husband shot by my half brother. I stared at the buildings, stony like Anton's face, memory rising, anger propelling me through the iron gates and out onto Quincy Street. The morning traffic was stalled, drivers peering through half-moons of windshield, marooned in their iron shells. I threaded my way between the cars, crossed Broadway, and headed for the concrete overhang of the Design School, my wet footsteps trailing me up the stairs to my office, where the phone was ringing.

"I found you," the voice triumphant.

It took me a moment: "My chess partner," I said, dropping my keys on the desk, my bag puddling on the floor beside me. Wasn't he going to Chicago?

We had left Felicia's together, he saying he wanted to walk, his legs still stiff from the overseas flight. He wanted to know how I knew Felicia, he wanted to know what I was doing. I told him I was an architect, working on a project to design a new city, on a small scale, on an island. It was something of an experiment, I said. He was trying to do operas in a new way, also on a small scale. He had trained as a conductor, was working mostly now as a director. The light faded across the river, the traffic picked up, people returning after the long weekend. We went into Harvard Square looking for coffee. Not much was open. We settled into the bar at Casablanca, at a table in the far corner, relieved to be out of the dankness that had set in with the end of the day.

We talked about our work, how we each were trying in our own way, he with operas, I with cities, to wrest a tradition into the unexpected, so people would actually see what they were seeing, hear what they were hearing. The island, Nashawena, off the coast of Massachusetts, was the site of my project. Richard Livingston, whose family owned it, had been taken by the idea that the structures people live in shape their lives. Andreas's face lit up, his dark hair and black sweater accentuating the color in his cheeks. I couldn't quite place him. Felicia was Viennese. He said he was Hungarian. Someone from the Lyric Opera had seen his production of *Lulu* in London, and he was on his way now to Chicago to meet with their board.

A loud noise from the kitchen. I jumped. I felt him watching me, puzzled. I looked around, no one seemed perturbed.

I told him I had been born on Cyprus, and except for university had lived there until the summer of '75. I left at the beginning of the civil war, I said, if such a term makes sense.

He raised his eyebrows. It doesn't, he said. He knew about war, he said.

Suddenly it was late. We ordered steak sandwiches from the bar menu.

Finally I said, "I really have to go." I stood up and reached for my coat. He stood as well. "It's been . . ." I began. Our eyes met. "Let's leave it there," he said softly, his long face creasing into a smile, then shadowed by a look of concern.

"I'll be fine," I said. He didn't know that a woman professor had been murdered in Longfellow Park, a few blocks away. Or that a graduate student in anthropology was killed just around the corner, in her apartment on Mount Auburn Street, red ochre on her body suggesting a ritual slaying. But I was going in the opposite direction, and anyway, in my life it wasn't the women who were slain.

I came back to the apartment, saw my face in the mirror, the flush on my cheeks, and said, "I'm not doing this." I threw my clothes in the hamper, showered quickly, turned off the light, and closed my eyes.

"Where are you?" I asked now, peering through the horizontal pane of plate glass that in this office passed for a window. The snow fell thickly.

"I'm at the airport," he said, "standing in a phone booth, calling you."

I retrieved the new drawings from the clutter on my desk and rolled them into a tube, cradling the phone.

"All the flights have been canceled," he said. "There is no way for me to get to Chicago in time for the meeting. So I was wondering. Do you want to play chess?"

Snow batted against the not-window. Who designed this Design School? A honeycomb of offices stretched out on either side of mine, the concrete walls radiating dampness. I had come in just to pick up the drawings, I was on my way to the island. I checked my watch: twenty to eight. I was wearing old jeans and a black sweater. I ran my fingers through my hair.

"Look," I said, "I have to meet the surveyor on Martha's Vineyard, and then we're going to Nashawena, but why don't you come. You can see the site, and then afterward, we can get oysters." What was I thinking? But the answer is, I was thinking just that. He was intrigued by the project, he would like the adventure, I was sure he liked oysters. Why not?

I picked him up at the Aquarium stop on the Blue Line, he wearing a leather jacket, Italian loafers, and gray slacks, his bag slung over his shoulder. He was born in Budapest, had lived with rivers, studied in conservatories, a tall man at ease in his body, impervious to the weather. He threw his bag in the backseat and folded his long frame into the front. The smell of leather infused the car.

We drove south along the expressway, snow gusting against the windshield, erasing everything except a small stretch of road. The intimacy of the car was unsettling, lending a gravity to what had seemed a lighthearted adventure. I turned on the radio— Mozart in the morning. The slow movement of a piano concerto vied with the whirr of the defroster. Andreas took out his hand-kerchief and wiped the windshield. "Can you see?"

"Much better." I found myself telling him my dream about driving blindly. In the dream, my eyes are literally shut, but my hands are on the steering wheel, my foot on the gas pedal, and the car is moving forward. I realize in the dream that this is wildly dangerous. I'm bound to hit something, kill someone. And yet nothing bad happens. The car moves ahead, the road goes uphill, the light is dim, sometimes it's night. Farmhouses line the road. It's somewhere in the country. I keep having this dream.

"Do you want to interpret it?" he asked, clearing the windshield again.

"Actually not."

The news came on. Snow light, snow bright, first snow—I decide it's a snow day, which made this all right.

We turned south onto Route 24 and then east on 25 heading toward the Cape, the sky lightening, gray arms of road surrounded by forest. As we approached the canal, the air became denser, snow drifting now through a haze of salt water, and then on the other side of the bridge the snow stopped.

Andreas took off his jacket and put it in back. I reached into my bag and retrieved an orange, handed it to him to peel.

"We had a lemon tree in our backyard," I said. "It's one of the things I miss about Cyprus, the taste of those lemons."

He placed a section in my mouth, a burst of sweetness.

Tall trees lined the road like sentinels. Beneath them, smaller ash and beech still held their leaves, white-brown, the color that chocolate turns when it's too hot, when it's too cold. I could never remember. Mid-morning sun flooded the car. I unzipped my coat, Andreas holding it as I freed my arms from its sleeves. A strand of hair fell across my face. I pushed it back; I felt him watching me. And then we were there.

He took his jacket and his bag, leaving his briefcase in the car. "Do you think it's safe?" he asked. I said sure.

We bought coffee in the lunchroom of the ferry and took it out on the deck as the boat headed through the channel into the Vineyard Sound. The line of the Cape receded to the left, the wind sweeping everything behind us. We rode in silence, standing at the rail.

As the string of islands appeared off to the right, he said, "Tell me about these islands." I turned, my hair blowing across my face. "Or tell me," his voice quiet, "is this as strange for you as it is for me?"

I didn't want to put it into words, this feeling of being carried, like a riptide sweeping you out from the shore, and if you grow up by the sea, you know to let it take you, and then when its force subsides, you can swim back to safety.

"Do you know the Beckett novel," he asked, seeing I could not respond, "where one character asks another, 'Do you feel like singing?' and the other says, 'Not that I know of'?" I laughed, and we split the turkey sandwich that Felicia had insisted I take home with me, the rye bread, only slightly stale, rescuing the turkey from blandness.

Kevin was waiting at the dock in his red truck, his face impassive as I introduced Andreas. Kevin glanced at him, but he wanted to talk about site lines and wetlands, the new restrictions passed by the commission having necessitated changes in the plans. The three of us crowded into the front seat, the gearshift pressing on my left, Andreas's leg on my right, my body registering his long bones, tensile muscles. I had grown up on Cyprus, where touching was commonplace. He was Hungarian. I rested my leg against his and talked with Kevin about the new location of the building at the north end of the site—an eddy where the design flowed back to the periphery. We stopped at his office, went over the wetland restrictions, examined the drawings to be sure they complied. Then we drove to Lake Tashmoo, where Frank, Kevin's assistant, was waiting, tripods and flags loaded into the Boston Whaler for the trip across the Sound.

The harbor on Nashawena is on the north side, shallow, rocky, facing the Massachusetts coast. A strip of farmland lines the shore, rising sharply to pastures with low stubby growth, boulders laced with lichen, meandering stone walls. I tell Andreas the history, how the islands, once part of the mainland, were separated when the Ice Age receded, inhabited by the Wampanoags, members of the great Algonquin nation, who called them *Nashanow,* meaning *between.* In 1602, Bartholomew Gosnold sailed into the Vineyard Sound. He named them the Elizabeth Islands for Queen Elizabeth, although some claimed it was for his sister. These small islands were included in the territorial grant of the king to the Council of New England. When the Council dissolved, Thomas Mayhew bought them, along with Nantucket and Martha's Vineyard. He paid two coats for Naushon, the island now owned by the Livingston family, who also own Nashawena and Pasque.

Andreas looked surprised. It had surprised me too, one family owning three islands right off the Massachusetts coast. But for me it had turned into a blessing, a minimum of permits and regulatory commissions. The Livingstons had built summer homes for themselves on Naushon. They used Nashawena, the next largest island, for livestock grazing and sheep farming.

We were approaching the Santoses' house, a red house on the hill, once the site of an old gray farmhouse. Emmanuel Santos had come to Nashawena at the age of seventeen and had stayed on to become caretaker, living there with Grace and their son, Luiz. When the Livingston family trust, persuaded by Richard, agreed to the use of Nashawena for my project, the family had stipulated that the Santoses would stay. They maintained a flourishing vegetable garden and cared for the farm animals and sheep. Their boat, the *Sarah Roon,* was the "highway" connecting Nashawena with Cuttyhunk and the mainland.

Luiz drove us to the project site, Andreas and I riding in front, Kevin and Frank in the open back with the equipment. We followed the track built by the army after Pearl Harbor when soldiers were stationed on the cliffs, patrolling the Vineyard Sound. Barracks, officers' quarters, a mess hall, and a water tower had been constructed and then torn down, carted away after the war. It was just after noon, the midday sun low in the sky. The surveyors set up their tripods and began taking their measurements, orange flags dotting the yellow-brown turf.

"There's not much to see," I said, aware of Andreas standing beside me, his collar turned up against the wind. I loved the land, quiet at this time of the year, the clusters of scrub oaks and pines.

I envisioned the settlement as a weave cast across the island, structures irregular in contours and height, though relatively low for the most part, like the hills. Some of the weave would be left open, some would be defined by surfaces that filtered light, shutters, scrims—porous to the open spaces. I tried to describe how transparency and translucency would be used not so much to manifest openness as to suggest its possibility, the feeling of openness alternating with a sense of enclosure, but I felt I was speaking a foreign language. What I am after, I said, is a fluidity of boundaries between inside and outside, private and public spaces. It wouldn't be a city in the usual sense, it couldn't be on this scale, but my hope was to discover if the architecture of a city can be reconceived in a way that shifts how people experience their identities and their interests, how they view themselves and one another, their society. Like spaces that flow into one another give an impression of continuity when one moves through a building.

I had approached a community of fishermen in New Bedford about moving their industry, met with the Wampanoags on Martha's Vineyard and the Cape, started discussions with the Wildlife Commission about deepening the harbor, talked with artists about the design of the studios. The land had perked surprisingly well, and the plans for sewage and water had been approved. Andreas looked at the land, squinting to envision how this spare earth could become a settlement.

The site hadn't been cleared yet for the outdoor theater, but I wanted him to look at the setting, the hill where the audience would sit, the area below which would become the stage, the sea in the distance. We climbed the rise and sat at the top. "Wait," he said, handing me his jacket. He bounded down the hill and stood, looking up at the sky: " '*Full thirty times hath Phoebus' cart gone round Neptune's salt wash and Tellus' orbed ground, and thirty moons with borrowed sheen. . . .*' " his voice rising through the trees, each word distinct, a grin on his face as he broke off and came back to join me. I had glimpsed the performer, felt the rhythm of the words pulsating through me. "It's the perfect place for a theater, Kyra," he said, retrieving his jacket.

A sadness came over me. It wasn't the sun or the sea, Poebus's cart or Neptune's salt wash, but the fullness of his response to my project. I thought about Simon. We had met at university when we were students in London, intent on creating a radical, restorative architecture. Simon had believed in the power of theater to bring people together. The Greeks were right, he said, theater is essential to the life of a city, revealing the conflicts and passions that drive human action. I looked at Andreas. Theater, he had said, had become his passion. Whatever second thoughts I had about bringing him to the island vanished.

I needed to talk with Kevin one last time. Andreas moved off to one side to give us space, sparing us from having to explain. Then Kevin and Frank returned to their measurements, and Andreas and I headed out to the cliffs.

The wind was blowing, cleaning the sky until it was all blue. We stood at the edge, looking out past Cuttyhunk to where the Sound flows into the ocean, the Texas tower in the distance, the land falling away at our feet.

"Do you like edges?" I asked him.

"Always," he said.

And that's how it was, that winter and spring. We lived like seabirds nesting high on a cliff, swooping down into our work, I into the new city project, he into his production of *Tosca,* which eventually became part of my project. When the long light of summer took over, it was as if we had deciphered the language of light, taking flight from a past that had become our winter haven. At night we left our clothes on the beach and swam in a cove, entrusting ourselves to the buoyancy of the sea, water falling from his body as we climbed back over the rocks and onto the sand, finding each other, each time with a sense of discovery, because the openness was so startling. I felt seen in a way I hadn't experienced before. He felt it too, he told me, his voice quiet. He touched my shoulder. I held my breath. "I hadn't imagined being joined so completely," he said. It was dark. I couldn't see his eyes.

I'm trying to brush away the ending, to remember how it was that summer, in the beginning, when the sky was clear as it was on that day when I first brought him to the island, and you could see for miles. Or when the tide goes out and you can walk seemingly forever over flats of wet sand.

A path led down from the cliffs, tufts of grass holding the dunes and the *Rosa rugosa,* the wild roses. The bay spread out leisurely on our left, the beach below a perfect half circle. The tide was going out, the waves tentative, entreating, retreating, each time a little more. Terns on stick legs chased the tide.

Andreas picked up a stone and threw it out across the water. It skipped once, twice, three times before it sank in a burst of rings.

"Here," he said, handing me a stone. I threw it out, and it sank right away. "Like this," he said, guiding my wrist, the stone skimming horizontally, a rolling stone. But I loved moss, the intensity of its green, its star-studded softness like a secret.

We were walking quickly now, falling into a rhythm, the wind behind us. I deliberately broke step. "I can't get involved," I said, turning to face him.

His eyes fell on the gold band on the chain around my throat. He looked at me, then off into the distance. The path had narrowed, bushes encroaching on either side, yellow changing to brown as we descended to the marsh.

A space had opened between us. I glanced at his face, his expression guarded, his mouth firm. I hesitated a moment, reluctant to say more. I was taking him into my world.

Two arms of land like crab claws reached into the bay, surrounding a body of water, which became a salt marsh washed twice daily by the tide. The sand was black, like silt from an antediluvian time, when carbon covered the earth. Exposed by the outgoing tide, it held the rhythm of the ocean, a faint recording of water moving, swaying around green, reedy anchors of eel grass. Shimmering blades of green-white light, vertical lines in this world of the horizontal.

For Andreas, it was the unexpected release from airports and meetings, a suddenly free day. For me, it was coming back to what had become my home. My sister, Anna, and I had lived at the edge of this marsh for seven years. Facing west, away from Cyprus, from memory, I could forget that the opposite of losing can also be winning, and that a stone without moss can signify freedom.

"Come," I said, "we have to hurry if we want to get oysters." The tide, I had noticed, was almost out.

He stood in the center of the living room taking in the house, his gaze lingering on the beams we had collected from the beach, washed up from ships, then following the rise of the ceiling where the house lifted, breathed. "The light here," he said, his voice hushed. The low sun bathed the room in November gold. The warmth was deceptive; it would be cold now out on the marsh. I checked the receding tide and heated water for tea. We would just have time before the tide turned.

A red Moroccan rug lay across the sofa. Andreas picked up the dark blue pillow with the red design, noticing everything, wanting to know.

"Where is it from?" he asked.

It was from home, one of the few things I had taken with me from Cyprus.

"My mother found it in a market," I said. "She loved the design, said it was ancient, like someone whispering in Aramaic. I always wondered what it was saying."

He looked at it steadily, then smiled.

"It's saying it loves this house."

I placed two cups on the table in front of the sofa. Outside, a pink glow hung over the marsh. The lines of the table ran back and forth between us—oak, the color of wheat. Our eyes met briefly, then moved away.

I went to change my clothes, putting on wet pants and boots to go into the places where the water pooled. I resisted the old questions: Did you take your, did you see my, where is the—the what? The ring, the talisman, the chalice, the clue, the opening.

We had built the house ourselves, my sister, Anna, and I. When we first came to Boston from London, where we had gone after Simon was killed, we stayed with Felicia in her house on Francis Avenue. She was a friend of Richard Livingston, whose family owned the islands. One night, we went with Felicia to Richard's home on Beacon Hill. It must have been around Christmas because there was a tree. I had admired the house, and after supper, Richard offered to show me around. We stood in the library, walls lined with books on history and nature. He knew about Cyprus. An English cousin had been stationed there during the war, had fought in the British army against the Germans. Like my father, I said. He was a refugee from Hamburg, fleeing Hitler, and like many Cypriots he fought along with the British. I told him that my parents had met on Cyprus, my mother also a refugee, from Vienna. They had married at the end of the war. It was after the war that the trouble on Cyprus began, constant strife, armed insurrection, first over independence from Britain, then over the question of union with Athens.

We had been talking about the coup against the archbishop, Makarios, then president of the republic, the civil war followed by the Turkish invasion, when Richard said, "Felicia told me your husband was killed in the conflict."

He added another log to the fire, and we settled into the worn armchairs.

"It wasn't really the political conflict," I said. "I mean, ostensibly it was, but that was a cover for jealousy and hatred. Simon, my husband, was loved by my father in a way that Anton, my half brother, was not, could not let himself be. Our mother had rejected Anton's father, the man whose name he bore, and maybe it was out of loyalty to him that he held himself apart. Bringing Simon into the family was like introducing a spark. Anton joined the radical EOKA B party, a right-wing terrorist group fighting for union with Athens. Simon and my father were on the left, working to create avenues of cooperation between Greek and Turkish Cypriots. The night Anton turned up in uniform, he accused Simon of being a traitor to the nationalist cause. There were men in Greek army officers' uniforms waiting outside. They took Simon out and shot him."

Richard's eyes clouded. He had lost his wife to cancer the previous year. He knew sadness, he had lost his lifetime companion, but they had lived miles away from anything like this.

I was fighting back tears. Richard got up to stir the fire.

"When did you leave Cyprus?" he asked quietly.

"The night Simon was killed, our parents insisted we go. Anna and I. They said they would join us. But then the Turkish army invaded the island, and they 'disappeared.' "

Richard turned to me, his blue eyes steady on my face. For a moment, neither of us said anything. Then, in a voice so understated that at first I didn't grasp what he was saying, he invited me to build a house on Nashawena for Anna and me. It was a gesture I will never forget: this quiet New Englander, an observer of nature, seeing that the only way forward was to build something new, after so much had been destroyed.

I picked up the silver barrette my mother had given me when I turned thirteen. On the night we left Cyprus, after Simon was murdered, I had vowed to live as if it hadn't happened. I would live for us both, as if he were still here. It was the only way I could make up for what my brother had done. I would carry on for both of us and work to realize the vision of the future we had shared. It would be dishonorable to let that go, disloyal to his spirit, to us, to myself. It was ten years now, and I had kept the vow.

I pulled back my hair, clasping it in the barrette. The blue of the bedspread caught my eye—sea blue, the blue of water in summer.

. . .

Andreas was talking on the phone. Standing by the counter, his thick hair darkening in the lowering angle of light, he looked like someone I had known for years. He drew idly with a pencil. No, he was not going to Chicago, no, he could not get there in time, all the planes had been grounded, there was no point now, the board would meet again in the spring, yes, he had spoken with the people at the Lyric Opera, yes, he would be back in Boston late tonight or tomorrow morning, yes, noon would be perfect, yes, thanks, "till soon then, *ciao.*"

The sand in the window glass bent the light coming in, fracturing it, filtering it, removing impurity. I had gone with my sister to see a film about a pastor who loses his faith, white light piercing, streaming through the side window of the church. *Winter Light,* the film was called. In winter, the light on the marsh hung suspended, clear and cold but containing life and color, reds and blues. Winter light, the light of winter that holds in light the promise of summer.

The lamp on the counter spread yellow light across the clay tiles, the light spilled onto the wide pine boards of the floor. In the window behind the counter, there were twelve panes, rectangles within rectangles.

We went out onto the marsh, the black sand making sucking noises under our feet. In the beginning, Anna and I had lived by the tide. We would wait each day for the low water and then search for the oysters that lay clustered in their ragged shells at the base of the eel grass. Washing away the black sand, we found the opening in the shell where you could insert a knife and then, by twisting, overcome the muscle that held the shell, concealing and protecting the oyster. Which is better, Anna would say, her dark hair glistening: to live forever closed up in darkness or to come into the light suddenly exposed?

Andreas stood on an edge of sand in the boots I had found for him, peering into the channel where the water was still rushing out to sea. "Where do you find them?" he asked, seeing nothing. The tines of my rake scraped a shell. I picked up the oyster and handed it to him, lifting one foot after the other, black muck dripping from my boots as I made my way farther into the stream, which was suddenly deepening as the tide turned.

The rhythm of the marshland had become familiar: filling, emptying, over and over, lunar rhythms, the lunacy of eternal return. To those who seek progress or direction, this life on the marsh makes no sense, its endless repetitions. Missing the edges of slight variation, they don't see that this year the birds have nested in different grasses and the oysters have mysteriously shifted their beds. Or notice that the water has turned a sudden emerald green.

We went back to the house, the oysters swaying in the net bag. It was almost dark. Trees spread their fingers against the deep red of the sky. I lit the lamp—marsh grasses on the table, the glass vase, the brass candleholders responded. We would have supper. I turned on the radio. They were playing Bach. Onions hung from a string above the counter, braided. An alto on the radio was singing an aria from the *St. John Passion*. Andreas joined in, *"Es ist vollbracht,"* his voice lifting, the melody suspended.

I stood quietly taking it in. It is over, it is finished, he said, translating the German to say what I had been feeling: it was as if we'd come to the end of a long journey, and had known each other for a long time.

Anna said that when she came back that evening and saw the note we had left on the table, the wineglasses in the sink, the shells resting against the lip of the colander, she knew. Even before we came back from the beach.

She had spent Thanksgiving on Nashawena, going over to Naushon to join Richard Livingston and his children for dinner, as we both had done the previous year. Then we had celebrated the start of what Richard had named the Carthage Project, after

the ancient city devoted to the arts and to commerce, the name itself meaning new city.

After our supper of oysters and wine, Andreas and I retraced our
steps, walking quickly, the moon lighting the path, the night surprisingly still. The tide coming in made a soft slapping sound,
slap, roll, slap, roll, kneading land and sea together until you
could no longer say for certain here is the land, here the sea. We
climbed the hill and walked to the site, the plot invisible, orange
flags swallowed by darkness. We sat on a rock at the center of the
site, the place where the design pattern would begin. I told him
about the Akha people in the mountains of Thailand, how they
carved their spirit world into the design of their villages.

On the way back to the house, we stopped on the beach. I drew
the plan of the city in the sand, the lines all fluid, a theme branch-
ing out. I told him that Richard had called it the Carthage Project,
to symbolize an alternative to Rome and what it stood for: empire
and war.

Andreas thought for a moment. He understood the need for
fortification, he said, the wish to pay homage to those who had
fallen, to find safety. "But, you know, *Roma* spelled backwards is
amor," he said. The words spun in my mind. He picked up a stick
and wrote them in the sand. "Think about it," he said.

I would think about it often, after what happened. *Amor* turning into *Roma,* or that's how it seemed to me at the time.

That night on the beach, I told him that Simon, my husband,
had been killed.

He started to say something, and then stopped.

The moon edged behind a cloud. Had he also seen how the
shadow of the ending can eclipse the beginning?

"Why did you come here?" I asked suddenly. "Today."

Why? Why really? Tag question of this psychological age. Why
really, really why? The question lay like a mantle around him.

"Let's go back," he said. "I can't tell you now, here, but I will tell you. Really." His face opened suddenly, like a camera. For a moment, I saw the sadness inside.

We left early the next morning. I had given him my room, I had slept with my sister. The day before had been a snow day, the world now reassembling. We took our boat over to Naushon and caught the small ferry to Wood's Hole. My sister, a psychotherapist, was going to see patients in Cambridge. Andreas was having lunch with Peter Maas, the person he had called on the phone. I knew Peter, he had started a small theater in Boston's South End. My design studio met at two, after that a faculty meeting. A morning stillness settled into the car.

I dropped Anna at her office, on Broadway near Central Square, and parked the car in the Everett Street garage. "It's been . . ." Andreas said, taking his briefcase, slinging his bag over his shoulder. We laughed. He put his hand on my arm. "Thank you," he said, the color of his eyes deepening. "It's been a gift, this time with you." He was leaving for London that night.

Anna is shorter than me, but I always forget this since she is older. Standing in the kitchen of our small Cambridge apartment, unpacking the vegetable drop from the co-op, she exuded an air of authority. She took the kale over to the sink and turned on the water. I dropped my things on the table and went to change. Out of deference to my colleagues, I had worn slacks and heels to the faculty meeting, to match their jackets and ties. Only David, my best friend on the faculty, a landscape architect whose work everyone admired, could get away with jeans. We taught a seminar together called Inside/Outside.

Anna was slicing the kale into shreds. I filled a pot of water for pasta.

"So what's happening?" she said, meaning with Andreas.

I put the pot on the stove and got out a board to chop the garlic.

"Isn't that a therapist's opening?" I said, cutting the garlic cloves into rough pieces. "I thought you were leaving all that behind."

She had said that she was closing her practice. The day she saw herself walking by the musicians in Harvard Square without stopping had clinched it. It was a long time since I'd heard her play her guitar.

She put the kale in the wire basket and swung it, showering me.

"Actually I am, but just for the record, the orthodox therapist says nothing and waits to see what the patient brings up."

I dipped my fingers in the pot and sprinkled water back at her.

"If you want to know what I would bring up, it's that lecture on architecture and psychology we agreed to give." Some students had organized a series of talks on crossing disciplinary boundaries. They had approached us last April, convinced us to do one together. We had chosen the slot in December. At that time, it had seemed a long time away.

Anna brought the kale to the stove, put olive oil in the pan, and turned on the heat. I threw in the garlic.

"Look," she said. "Let's make a deal. I won't ask you about Andreas if you won't talk about the lecture."

I laughed, went over to the fridge, took out a bottle of Pinot Grigio, and poured two glasses. "It's a deal. Let's put on some music and eat in the living room." The kitchen table was buried under papers and mail.

She added the kale, turned up the heat, waited for it to wilt, and then lowered the flame. "*Salud,*" she said, clinking my glass, and went to choose a record. The sound of classical guitar preceded her as she came back holding the cover—a photograph of Segovia, a heavyset man with jowls, smoking a pipe. "Does he remind you of Papa?"

"Let me see." I added the pasta to the boiling water along with a handful of salt. He did. I turned over the cover and discovered that "Lilliburlero," a song our mother used to sing to us, was an Irish revolutionary song.

The spirit of our parents came into the room. They would have liked this, the two of us together, no revolution in sight.

I drained the pasta, added the kale and some Parmesan, and carried it out, the Tuesday night special. Anna brought the salad and bread. She looked tired. I turned the music down.

"I dreamed about Papa last night," she said, pushing away her plate. I got up to fill a pitcher of water. She waited. "I haven't done that for a long time," she said. She studied her hand. "We were in the kitchen, sitting at the long table, you and me and the two of them. In the dream, the ceiling of the room was low. Friends started coming in, Yoni with his green shorts and sandals, and Elektra, elegant in a long skirt. Papa was telling one of his stories." She looked across the room.

I remembered those summer evenings, the windows open, the stories, the friends. But something in the dream was troubling Anna. I poured water into her glass.

"I took a spoon from the cup on the table, one of those mismatched silver spoons that Mommy picked up at flea markets. I looked into the bowl of the spoon, and it began to tarnish until I couldn't see anything. Then we were outside, standing by the sea. The water was rising, someone was missing, and Papa was looking up and down the beach. He said 'We have to get a boat.' There was more, but I can't remember the rest."

"Who was missing?"

"Maybe that boy, whatever his name was, who came that summer with Mommy's friends from Vienna, the one Anton must have picked on or something because he took off down the beach and it was a long time before we found him. I think the dream was about Anton, how I couldn't see what was coming. And I should have seen it. The signs were all there. I of all people should have known."

I knew she had tormented herself over this. I looked across the table at Anna, her face taut. She had always looked out for me, and at times I had resented this, found it patronizing. I liked to think now we looked out for each other.

"Mommy always worried about Anton," I said, "but then Papa would reassure her, 'It's just a phase, Katya, he'll get over it, our marriage, it's hard for him. Give it time,' he'd say. But it wasn't a question of time."

"But it was Papa who insisted we get a boat," Anna said. "He must have had a premonition."

Segovia was playing "Lilliburlero." We listened to the song.

"Such a sweet song for a revolution," I said, getting up to clear the table.

"If only we had photographs from that time," Anna said, "then we could see from the faces."

"See what?"

"Who knew."

I plunged into the corridor between Thanksgiving and Christmas, the tunnel of time leading to the end of classes, then winter break, followed by reading period and exams. Going in, there were leaves on the ground, brown and crisp, picked up by the wind, and in the late afternoons, a startling light. Coming out, there was the solstice, the pastels of winter taking over the sky, red-pinks and streaky yellow-greens against the inky blue.

I looked out the window one afternoon and saw the ash tree bare across the street. I remembered the chess game, the yellow leaves of the maple tree, the blue-gray of his eyes, and wondered if mine were still green. Otherwise, I didn't think much about him, or if I did, I was careful to redirect my thoughts. He had left. In a way I was relieved. I was on leave that spring. I had a small grant to go to Thailand with Randy, my anthropologist friend, who was studying the Akha. He was the one who had told me about the design of their villages. I wanted to see them for myself.

Faculty meetings were consumed by fights over appointments, arguments about curriculum. For my colleagues, I was something of a conflict-free zone, an academic not seeking tenure, a woman not looking for commitment. The age of anxiety had followed the age of Aquarius, a virus having put a stop to free love. And maybe

Freud was right about sublimation, the advantages of channeling unruly desires into something socially constructive. Sex went underground, people talked about publishing. "Lover" had given way to "partner." Reagan was in the White House. What could you say?

Anna and I had agreed to meet at Cafe Pamplona on the Thursday before we were to give the talk. We had exactly one week to prepare, which underscored the gravity of the situation. A reddish-gray haze hung low in the sky, blurring edges, the straight black lines of the wrought-iron fence outside the café came as a surprise. I looked up, wondering if it was going to snow again, and I thought of Andreas. What was he doing now? The air held a feeling of expectation. I headed down the stone steps into the steamy interior.

Anna was sitting at the table below the high window. She had her back to me, her green sweater, her dark hair absorbing the light. She had cut her hair short to signal her intention to change her life. It changed her face, her features at once sharper and more delicate.

She took out her knitting, a wildly colored sock, spools of color dangling from the needles. She was making the pattern up as she went along.

"Next Thursday is the ides of December. It's a bad omen. We probably should cancel," she had said that morning.

Yet here she was, at the table, my sister, the rebel, sitting with her knitting, in a steamy café.

The lecture series was called In Tandem. The idea was to bring faculty from different fields together and hear how they would converse. We had decided to talk about Gothic cathedrals and psychology as the twelfth and the twentieth century's answers to the problem of mystery—how to reveal the presence of the invisible.

"I don't know," Anna said, "I don't know about this. Both the spiritual world and the psyche are in trouble but I've forgotten how to speak psychologese. They say if you don't learn a language early, it doesn't stick. I clearly learned psychology too late." She turned the heel of the sock.

A waiter in jeans and a black turtleneck appeared at our table, pencil and pad in hand.

"Let's have tea," I said. "Do you have any scones?"

He shook his head.

There was a vast array of teas to choose from, a new addition to the espresso and caffe latte that were the staples of the Pamplona crowd.

"Do you have Typhoo?" Anna asked. She knew you could only get Typhoo tea in England. She really did not want to do this—that much was clear.

On the ides of December, at five o'clock on the following Thursday, a crowd gathered in Boylston Hall. People stomped in in winter coats and boots, leaving a trail of slush down each of the aisles. Like snails, said my friend David, the architect of outdoors who had come to provide moral support. He followed me in and to the front, his bushy hair ensconced in a voluminous hood. It had snowed again the week before, and the thinnest of paths were shoveled, as if the local inhabitants had given up on clearing the sidewalks, even before winter really began. The Christmas hum was in the air—"Good King Wenceslas" on constant replay. Homeless people lined streets filled with Christmas shoppers.

"I was right," Anna said. "This sister show is irresistible. It hardly matters what we say. Just appearing together is like proving the existence of God—it shows that sisterhood exists."

Divisions among women had begun to appear like cracks in a new building. A majority had turned into minorities, seemingly overnight, the seventies giving way to the eighties. Who engineered this, I wondered, I who lived with my sister, for whom sisterhood was a fact of life.

We tuned to each other, affinity flowing wordlessly between us. The student organizer climbed the steps to the platform and began her introduction. I liked her earrings, made of stained glass, perfect for the occasion, one with a long silver thread hanging down, a blue bead at the end.

"Whatever you can say," I whispered as the introduction ended, "this has not been overplanned."

We stood together at the podium; we had worked out a counterpoint. We would go back and forth rather than following each other like buses. I began with a slide of the Abbey of St.-Denis, followed by one of Chartres. I would take this audience out of words, into the realm of shape and space. Anna began with a metaphor: therapy is a cloud chamber, the psyche revealed through free association. I talked about light, its use in cathedrals, the unique relationship between structure and appearance, the decision to turn walls into windows. Stained glass showed that the windows were intended not to see through but to reveal the relationship between inside and outside, light filtering in as the spiritual world enters the material world, a revelation of the divine.

The Gothic builders had made the cathedrals porous, and this was Anna's point: the psyche is porous, permeable, in a constant relationship of exchange with the world. The transparency of the spiritual world, the transparency of the psyche, unseen but manifest, essential to life.

I glanced at my sister, we had found a rhythm. The tightness was gone from her voice. She glanced at me, I took the cue.

The cathedrals were built in a way that seemed to reverse the force of gravity, the verticalism startling. Light became the active principle. I cited the scholar Von Simson, who had described it as transparent, diaphanous architecture, and showed more slides of Chartres. Then Anna reminded us that we are breathing air that Cleopatra exhaled: we live in a state of constant exchange. I can't remember now if she actually used the example of the placenta to convey the psychic filtering of the world around us, like breathing in and out. The psyche, she said, depends on this ongoing process of exchange between inner and outer worlds, and trouble comes when people start, psychologically speaking, holding their breath. When they cannot take in what is going on around them or let out what is inside them.

I wondered how people were taking this in, given that we were in the world of "good fences make good neighbors." I flashed a slide of a Romanesque church on the screen, relying on the academic staple of compare and contrast. Thick walls covered with murals were intended to distract attention from the weight of the building and remind the faithful of the existence of a world beyond this one. The mosaics in Byzantine churches did the same thing. But with the Gothic, the form of the building was integral to the religious experience. Anna said that the therapy relationship also dissolves form and function. The relationship is not a container for healing but is in itself therapeutic. At least that's the ideal. With the therapist, people enact the problems of relationship that brought them into therapy, but if the therapy relationship itself is problematic, then therapy only compounds the problem.

I showed architectural drawings from the thirteenth century, the Reims palimpsest, a drawing made over a partially erased older drawing, revealing the underlying geometric pattern, lines ordered according to true measure, a geometry based on the proportions of the human body. Villard de Honnecourt had taught people how to halve the square for the purpose of determining the proportions of a building, and the façade of Notre Dame was composed of four squares, developed according to true measure. It was a science of modulation, a system of proportions translated by purely geometrical means.

Anna raised the question: What was true measure within the therapeutic situation, is there a good measure of relationship? Was there an underlying geometry, so to speak, of relationship that bridged architecture and psychology, the outer and inner structures of human life?

Because that really was the question: What was the relationship between inner and outer worlds? The Gothic cathedral had emerged from the religious experience, the metaphysical speculations, and also the political and physical realities of twelfth-century France. It reflected the cult of Mary, *notre dame.*

Psychoanalysis and its offshoots in the twentieth century, said Anna, originated in the psychological experiences and the culture of late-nineteenth-century Vienna—they came out of the study of hysteria, inspired by a woman, Anna O.

Was there a clue here, Anna asked, in the link between Gothic architecture and the cult of Mary on the one hand and psycho-analysis and the study of hysterical women on the other? Had a new spiritual or psychological connection with women spurred a new understanding of the relationship between inner and outer worlds? I ended with a question: Does the exploration of the relationship between the visible and the invisible, the seen and the felt presence, hinge on men coming into a new spiritual or psychological relationship with women?

The audience seemed in shock. They had expected a lecture on architecture and psychology. Who knows what they thought we would say. The organizer with the stained-glass earrings couldn't contain her delight.

A biologist stood up to ask the first question, but instead he began a mini-lecture on the correspondence between the ground plan of the cathedral and the proportions of the human body. I decided to treat it as a question and said that I wondered whether this grounding in the body and its proportions was partly what had sustained people in building cathedrals over generations. Since life, although contained in the body, continues through time, the cells of one generation forming another.

A historian got up and said that his specialty was the tenth century. Prior to that time, people all over Europe had lived in mud huts, except of course that then there wasn't anything we would now recognize as Europe. In the twelfth century, people were building Gothic cathedrals in a Europe that is recognizable. His question was: Could anyone tell him anything that had happened in the intervening century to bring this about, or did the cathedrals just come out of nowhere?

"Out of nowhere?" Anna said, her voice rising. Hadn't we just suggested that they had come out of a new relationship with women, the cult of Mary, *notre dame*? As psychoanalysis would come from the study of hysteria, Anna O.?

"I think we have time for one more question," the organizer said, her face tight, tension building in the room. I watched her look for a woman's hand, a futile search. Not a single woman had raised her hand.

She settled for Sandro, who taught Roman architecture. A good choice, in my book, and he asked a real question. Given the contrast between the Romanesque churches with thick walls you couldn't see through and the way Gothic architects had used line and light to dissolve the true volume of the supports into bundles of frail, soaring shafts, did I see a correspondence between these two religious visions and the different visions of cities represented by Rome and Carthage?

It was right up my alley, I said. I spoke for a few moments about the contrast between imperial Rome, eight hundred years of nearly uninterrupted war, and Carthage, which at least in the beginning represented a frail, soaring possibility, a city devoted to arts and commerce rather than to conquest and imperialism. Then I concluded by saying that this was the subject for a new talk.

There was wine and cheese. Friends and colleagues had come, along with students and the anonymous crowd that shows up at five in the afternoon for the free buffet of education, the array endless at a university of this size. Now the silent women came up to speak. "You know," one said, "even in that last question the connection with women was implicit, because Carthage, you know, was ruled by a queen."

I found myself wishing Andreas had been there. I thought he would have loved it, thick walls turning into *Notre Dame,* like *Roma* turning into *amor.*

Afterward we went to a restaurant in the North End. A friend of Anna's knew the owner and had reserved a small room. David and Sarah came, he from the north of England, she from South Africa, as black as he was pale. His bushy hair, released from the hood, exuded warmth, her gold hoop earrings accentuated her beauty. They had met in London, where he was teaching landscape architecture and she was studying set design. She came over to where I was sitting. "Chekhov said that the artist's task is to state the problem correctly, and you did that brilliantly," she said, her accent lilting, her smile conspiratorial. A sisterly act. Relief pulsed through my body. I caught Anna's eye across the table. It had been fine.

———

That Saturday the Design School students held their annual masked ball. Two members of my studio class headed the committee and I had promised I would come, forgetting until the last moment that this meant finding a costume, one more thing to do before classes ended. Reading period began after the holiday break, exams didn't start until mid-January. For the students, it was a moment of elation. I found the darkness of December oppressive. I rummaged through my closet, irritation mounting. "No" was a one-word sentence I thought I had mastered, but students were my soft spot. I fished out a long white dress and a pair of gold sandals. Anna had found a Venetian mask for me at a shop in the North End. I put it on, looked in the mirror. I could have been anyone. I stared at the white *commedia* face and found the anonymity enticing. I had become someone I never intended to be.

Torches lit the steps of the Fogg Museum. Inside, a band was playing. I hung my cape in the coatroom and walked through the Renaissance arches into the interior courtyard, turned into a forest for the occasion—a respite from Christmas decorations. Tree branches hung from the pillars, yellow and green lights dappled the paper leaves. David was playing the drums, and I headed over to him, straightening the mask over my eyes. People were dancing, some shapes recognizable, but for the most part the costumes held. Good. If you couldn't see, did that mean you couldn't be seen? Child logic. The music took over—the unmistakable sound of the Beatles, "Octopus's Garden." I noticed the sea creatures climbing the walls. The students had done a terrific job.

I made my way through the dancers and stood just below David, his burly frame hunched over the drums. He looked quizzically in my direction and I lifted my mask for a second. He played a flourish, his face absorbed, turning inward into the rhythm that flowed through his body, downward and out through his arms, into the sticks, onto the hide of the drums, through the skins of animals, into the stone floor, and underneath, the earth.

My friend David, my pal, my anchor of sanity in this university. We were the outposts, urban design and landscape design, in the world of the monumental. No one in the architecture school had taken my design ideas seriously until Richard Livingston entered the picture, and then nobody took him seriously, except for the fact that he was paying for the construction. Whatever they thought about the new city project, the money was substantial.

"Did Sarah come?" I mouthed the question. David nodded, and I turned to look for her.

A child was standing by my side, staring up at the band.

"Do you want to see the drums?" I asked, bending down to speak to him so he could hear me under the music.

He drew back instinctively, and I remembered my mask.

"Here," I said, pulling it down so he could see my face. His face clouded, then cleared, curiosity trumping shyness.

"Would you like me to lift you up?"

He nodded. He was about five.

David, pushing his hat back on his head, took his sticks, hit the cymbal and handed one to the child.

"Go on, hit it," he said, holding the other ready.

The child was wearing a costume of sorts—high boots, a sword attached to his belt. He was getting heavy. After he had struck the cymbal a few times and tried one of the drums, I put him down. He reached back, I held out my hands, and we turned in a circle, spinning faster as the music picked up. Soon others came over and joined us. When the song ended, the band rose to take a break. I noticed an elderly man with a kind face standing against the wall, beaming at the child, who darted over to him.

I was heading out to the lobby to get a drink when I saw Peter Maas, my theater producer friend, coming toward me, and I realized I had forgotten to replace my mask.

"I was looking for you," he said. "But now I've lost the chance to show you that I know you through any disguise." I liked Peter's quirky, offbeat manner, his late-night phone calls. You just jumped into my mind, he would say, wanting to talk, assuming that everyone slept until noon.

I started to pull up my mask.

"Too late," he said. "I need to ask you a favor and you can't escape me." I owed him a hundred favors.

"I want you to meet a friend—actually you know him." He gave me his most winning look, the one I recognized as the look he reserved for donors and for the officials who granted the permits he needed for his theater. I picked up a glass of punch and followed him to the far corner. Andreas was standing next to a pillar.

"You're here," I said, the words sounding childish and hopeful. Heat rose through my body and settled in my face.

He started to say something but the boy came running over to him. My stomach lurched. The pieces fell into place, the expression on his face that day on Nashawena when I told him I couldn't be involved. Obviously he couldn't either.

I stepped back.

He looked at me steadily. "This is Jesse, my son. And this is my father, Abraham," he said, turning to the man who had joined us. He smiled. "And this is Kyra Levin, the one with the island."

"It's not mine exactly," I said, and laughed to cover the sensation of feeling foolish.

"We really do need your help," Peter said. "We're going to do *Tosca* in the Counterpoint Theater. The space is small. We want you to help us with the design."

"I don't know anything about theater," I said, my voice sounding stilted. "But," I added, "there's someone here who might be able to help." I looked around for Sarah. I wanted to leave.

"I was at your lecture," Peter persisted. "That gave me the idea of asking you. What you said about inner and outer worlds is what we're looking for. The opera is set in Rome, the city is essential to the story. But it's a psychological drama, a love story, and what we're hoping to achieve is . . ."

But now it was impossible to hear, the band had resumed. Jesse tugged at my hand. "Follow me," he said, pulling me in the direction of the drums.

"We really must go now," Andreas said, taking Jesse's hand from mine, "but I'll phone you tomorrow at the university. May I?" He looked at me, a light in his eyes. I put the mask back on my face and nodded.

He called on Monday, late in the afternoon. I was in the middle of office hours.

"Look," I said, "I can't talk now," as if he could see that this was impossible, one student sitting in front of me, a line snaking down the hall. "I'll call you back later." I fished a pencil out from the mound on my desk.

"It's not possible," he said, a formality in his voice. I wondered who was with him. "I'm in the middle of auditions, we're just on break. But why don't we set up a time for later this week. Or," he paused, his voice shifting, "why don't we have dinner tonight, if you're free? I have to be in Cambridge later. I could meet you at eight, wherever you suggest."

The student was trying to look like a person not listening. I reached for my book. "Fine," I said. "I'll meet you at the Harvest in Harvard Square."

I turned back to the student, a new animation in my voice as I picked up our conversation, our discussion of her studio project.

———

Through the window of the café, I saw him sitting in one of the booths, a score open on the table in front of him, a glass of red wine to one side. I stood for a moment, noting his absorption. He was like a continent entire to himself. He looked up. I wrapped my coat around me and went in, sliding into the bench across from him. The restaurant was crowded, the café and bar off to one side.

The warmth of his greeting disarmed me. "I'm so pleased this worked out. It makes me happy to see you." His face lightened.

"Red or white?" he asked, signaling for the waiter. "White," I said. He closed the score and placed it on the bench beside him.

"Thank you for being kind to my son," he said. "My father told me."

"He's a beautiful child," I said. "I love the openness of his face."

"He's had a hard time, losing his mother," Andreas said. He paused to watch the waiter walk by. "But my father," he said, the look on his face suddenly unguarded, "he would talk with him when I couldn't speak about it, play with him when I couldn't bring myself to play."

That night on the beach, when his face had opened, this was the sadness I had seen. I had a sense now of why he had come with me to the island. Loss was something we had in common, like animals picking up a scent.

The waiter brought the wine, and Andreas lifted his glass. "To you," he said. "To life."

He drank, put the glass down, and looked at me.

"There's something I want to tell you," he said, "but it's not easy for me to talk about it. I usually can't talk about it. Which has made it hard for me. With Jesse. But when you told me that night that your husband had been killed, I started to tell you then, and then I thought to myself, we'd just met, why should I burden you with more sorrow. I don't know if I can tell you this without . . ." He glanced away. "But I think you will understand."

He paused, closed his eyes for a moment. I moved my glass to one side and leaned on my elbow, my fingers cold against the side of my face.

"My wife, Irina, she was a singer, a soprano. Beautiful voice. I fell in love with her voice, and then with her. She was the soloist in a concert I was conducting. At the time I was touring Hungary with a small orchestra."

He picked up his spoon and twirled it, the metal reflecting the light.

"It was the 1970s. Things in Hungary had loosened up. I had the idea of starting a small opera company. We would do the standard repertory. I also wanted to do something more daring— Menotti's *The Consul*. Irina would sing Magda, a simple, good woman who married a freedom fighter. In many ways, it was like us."

He put the spoon down.

"What happened was that after one performance, the officials shut us down. They saw what the opera was about. 'My name is a number, my story's a case,' Magda sings. It was about what was going on, the lies, the indifference. Irina was enraged on my behalf. 'Is there nothing they won't touch?' she asked."

Anger sharpened his face.

"She believed in the sanctity of art, she wanted me to be able to do my work. She joined the dissidents who were regrouping at the time. I thought she would be safe. My mother, a painter, had been active in the resistance to the Nazis during the war. My father always said she was a goddess, and as a child I had believed him. I thought she would protect us, and she had, then."

He stopped abruptly.

"Why am I telling you this?" It was a question for himself.

I looked out the window. A scatter of people walking along the passageway next to the restaurant, seemingly oblivious to this history. Or maybe not.

"Are you hungry?" he asked. "We can order."

I shook my head. "Later."

"Then let's have another glass of wine." He held up his glass for the waiter, who came over, looked disapprovingly at the unopened menus. "Soon," Andreas said.

"When you told me about your husband," he said, "I felt I could understand you, your feelings, what you were doing with your life. I . . ." He looked away and then back. "There's something about you, about being with you. When I came here tonight, I wasn't planning to talk about this. But I look at you, and I want you to understand me. Why I'm doing what I'm doing."

I did not take my eyes away.

"The day it happened, Jesse was with my mother. I was to meet Irina at the conservatory at five. She didn't show up. I went to my parents' house and told my father, who was alarmed. He said we had to leave at once. With Jesse, we couldn't take a chance. I went out to look for Irina, but I couldn't find her. Nobody knew anything. My mother said she would stay and wait in case Irina came. She had contacts in the resistance, she would find out what happened and then join us. I knew Irina would want me to go with Jesse, not let him out of my sight. So I went."

He picked up the candle in the small glass on the table and stared into the flame. When he continued, his voice was hollow.

"We left," he said. "My father, Jesse, and I. We went back to the farm family that had hidden us in '44. The farmer was old, his sons had taken over. We waited. A few days. Then my mother sent us a message. Irina had been arrested, the Russians were involved. It was too dangerous now for us to go back or to stay in Hungary. One of the sons led us across the border."

He looked at me.

Forlorn. To be bereft, to walk around with a hole in your heart. An odd word—forlorn. A clutch in the chest. Before—forewarned. And then after, forlonged, forlonging, longing without end.

I looked at his hands, his fingers long, elegant, the hands of a conductor. They had commanded attention, power, and yet they had been utterly useless. "To leave without her, without knowing . . ." I said, my eyes blurring with tears.

He said he really didn't know what had happened to Irina. Everyone assumed—he assumed—she was dead.

We were silent for a while.

"With Simon," I said, "I saw it."

"You saw it?" he said, his face alert.

I found myself telling the part of the story I never tell, thinking it was too much, yet something impelled me to tell him. How that night, we were having supper at my parents' house. Anton must have known Simon would be there. Tensions had been building on Cyprus, there were kidnappings and assassinations. Our neighbor had been shot one morning on the way to the bank. It was right before the coup. But this was our family. I knew Anton was jealous of Simon, angry at my father. Still, I didn't think Anton would betray us, or not in this way. Then I saw the coldness in his eyes, the look of uncertainty gone from his face. Inside me, everything stopped.

Andreas leaned toward me, his eyes on my face. And maybe for both of us it was a relief, finding ourselves no longer alone in something that had left such a shocking sense of aloneness. Now the words were coming back, words I didn't think I could ever bring myself to say, the scene happening again, as if right before my eyes.

"I assumed at first that Anton was after the money. It was what my father thought. He said, 'Anton, put down the gun. If it's money you want . . .' Anton laughed. 'There's nothing I want from you now.' He turned to Simon. 'It's you we've come for.' We? There were others? It was surreal. This couldn't be happening. I looked at Simon and saw him panic. I'd never seen him panic before. I looked at my mother, her face ghost-white. I looked at my father, his whole face had gone slack. Then I heard myself say, 'Someone do something.' As if there were anything any of us could do.

"I must have screamed," I said, "because Anton turned to me. 'Stop screaming,' he said, speaking to me as though I were a stranger. Simon made a grab for Anton's gun. At the sound of the scuffle, the others came in, Greek army officers, all of them armed. It was hopeless."

I looked at Andreas. That night after Felicia's party, when we were at Casablanca and the noise from the kitchen made me jump, he didn't know why. It had sounded like a shot.

"It happened just outside the house," I said. "We saw it through the window."

I picked up the knife, put it back on the table. I had wanted to do something, there was nothing I could do. He had wanted to do something, he couldn't do anything. It was a powerlessness we both understood.

Andreas reached for my hand, enclosing it in his. "It's a nightmare," he said.

The waiter brought fresh glasses of wine, and we ordered the special, some kind of fish.

I told him that when I met Simon, he was an architecture student, interested in psychology like my sister, but he said you had to start at the foundation. To change the structure of people's inner lives, you had to change the outer structures as well. It was a bold vision. "I don't think you can fall in love with a man unless you fall in love with his work."

Andreas looked thoughtful.

"What are you thinking?" I asked.

"About what you said. I don't know that I'd ever thought about it like that, but it would be hard for me to love someone who didn't have a passion in life. With Irina, it was singing."

He took a deep breath, exhaling slowly.

"Music was my life," he said. "It has become my refuge. I want to do *Tosca* now because in that opera, you can see what was coming. The history of Europe in the twentieth century. Fascism. Secret police. Tosca is a singer. Her lover, Cavaradossi, is a painter. *Vissi d'arte, vissi d'amore,* I lived for art, I lived for love, Tosca sings. But the fact is she cannot live once her lover is shot. He is executed, a victim of jealousy and political terror."

Like Simon, I thought.

"Do you know the opening of the second act?" he asked, and I shook my head. I knew almost nothing about opera.

"It's set in the Farnese Palace. Scarpia, the chief of police, is waiting for Tosca. A table is set for supper. Tosca is to sing a concert at the queen's apartment below. Afterward, Scarpia is planning to seduce her. He is impatient for her to come. He orders his assistant to open the window to hear if the concert has begun. Music comes into the room. The orchestra is playing a gavotte. The tune simple, exquisite, a dance rhythm. Music from another time. Suddenly there is beauty in the midst of such terror. For a moment, we hold our breath. In this instant, everything could change. And then the window is shut.

"In a very quiet way, it's the most emotional moment in the opera. For a minute, we have hope. Otherwise it's all about fear and betrayal, the defeat of art and love and freedom. But in the midst of it, there's a beautiful, complicated love story, impassioned arias, which is why people come to this opera. I want them to hear the whole story, the love and also what destroys it. I want them to see into the emotional heart of terror. You can do that with opera. You have the words, and you have the music."

The fish came, and we ate quickly.

"When I called you," he said, putting his plate to one side, "I wanted to ask you if you would come and look at the space in Peter's theater with me. The sets are a problem. I was hoping you might help me think about them. I know you haven't worked in the theater, but in this case that's beside the point because there isn't room for sets in the usual sense. I believe you will see what I am looking for. What you said that day on the island about the mix of transparency and enclosure is precisely what I'm after. There's an emotional porosity, the psychology is completely exposed, and then there's a sense in which everyone in the opera is trapped. We'll bring in someone to deal with the technical specifications. It's your sensibility I want, your understanding of space." He paused, and then with a sense of gathering up the entire conversation, he said, "And I would like to work with you."

The thought crossed my mind, maybe we could become partners, not lovers. I smiled to myself. I said I would come.

The waiter brought coffee, and Andreas asked for the check.

I had wanted him to look at the amphitheater with me. I would look at Peter's theater with him. I told myself it was a simple request.

The next afternoon he was waiting for me in the lobby of the Design School. It was four o'clock, and he was holding a cup of coffee and a pear and smiling. Like my mother with food, I thought. She would always bring something when she met me, chicken livers wrapped in waxed paper, thick slices of Turkish delight, the rounds of apricot paste studded with walnuts or pistachios, coated with a skin of powdered sugar. It was not something I associated with men, not something my friend David would have thought of, or Randy, kind and thoughtful though they both were. I had just taught my last class, and I took the coffee, grateful for the caffeine. "I thought you'd be tired," he said. He checked his watch. It would be nine o'clock now in London, darkness trailing him across the ocean on this, the solstice, the shortest day of the year. We stood out on the steps while I finished the coffee, students filing out of the building. "Have a good break, Professor Levin." "Happy solstice," they called over their shoulders, students heading home. I bit into the pear, unripe but crisp, the way I liked it. We walked into the Square and got into a taxi.

Daylight was evaporating as we left Cambridge and crossed the river. He put his arm around my shoulder. "Tell me what you thought after last night," he said, rearranging his legs in the tight space. Spurts of indecipherable speech blurted out of the taxi's two-way radio. "I kept thinking about Irina, that she had done this for you, and you, having to leave without her. And then that night with Simon coming back. I don't know if it's worse to see it or to imagine it—the terror, someone you love. The shock, it never goes away."

I leaned back against his arm and looked out the window. He put his hand on my shoulder, the feelings strange after so long. The thought occurred to me: We are both exiles, strangers in this city, the desperation of Europe in our blood. I'd lived here now for a number of years, and Boston was said by some to be the most European of American cities. It didn't feel European to me. I liked the wooden clapboard houses, but they were American. I stared at the deserted streets, the rows of nondescript shops, and felt happy to be in this taxi with him. Run-down brownstones signaled that we had reached the South End.

Suddenly I sat up. It was obvious that this cabbie was lost. The address had seemed simple enough, a number and a street, but he lacked "the knowledge"; unlike London cabdrivers, he hadn't internalized the map.

Andreas drew out the paper with the address from his wallet, as if looking at it would produce the place by magic. And it did. After circling around what had seemed a hopeless maze of streets, we stopped next to a church, a Gothic building rising airily from the midst of tenements.

"This must be it," the cabbie said, barely concealing his astonishment at having found the place against all odds. Like a winning lottery ticket, the number he had been given matched those on the iron gate beside us. Andreas paid him, and we walked through the gate into the sweet evening smell of box hedges. The light, reflected off the surfaces of the stained-glass windows, rallied against the darkening sky. I could just make out the jagged edges of holly leaves and the softer shape of the ivy that trailed up the stone walls. A single yellow bulb shone over a wooden door at the end of the diagonal arm of the path. Andreas bent his head as we walked through, his hand on my elbow.

The door opened into a large room, linoleum on the floor. This was America. Pillars held up the ceiling in a frank, palms-up manner. Peter came out—long, lean in his brown corduroy pants, his glasses reflecting the light, his straight hair falling over his face. The impresario, this was his theater.

"Kyra," he said, kissing both cheeks, "you're an angel to come."

He led us into the theater and disappeared to turn on more lights. The emptiness was palpable, creating a feeling of suspension. We stood together in the semidarkness, neither of us speaking, the air ionizing between us, the molecules taking on an electric charge, as if registering the new closeness and physical ease between us. This time, I reminded myself, he wasn't leaving town.

I walked away, crossed the center aisle, and headed to the back, to sit in the last row and get the feel of the space. Andreas came and sat beside me. Seats faced the stage on three sides, a gallery running around the back, columns measuring the space underneath the balcony. I turned to him. "You know, it's odd but I have the same feeling here as I do in Rome. It's claustrophobic."

I felt him watching me quietly, listening.

"In *Tosca*," he said, "everyone feels trapped. You are the one to do this."

The lights came up, and we moved to the stage.

"Here's the challenge," Andreas said. "The first act is set in a church, the second in the Farnese Palace, the third on the battlements of the Castel Sant Angelo. Each place contributes to a sense of the monolithic, the alliance of church and state. We're in a reign of terror, the police chief joins in the singing of *Te Deum*. Nothing is sacred, humanity is crushed. And we're in it with two artists, a painter and a singer, both passionate, sensitive souls."

His mother was a painter, his wife a singer. It was the story of his life.

"Conventional sets won't work," he said. "I'm looking for something spare and suggestive to convey the intensity of the situation, both the emotional drama and the political—the gravity of what the lovers are up against."

An opera meant musicians and singers. I looked at the stage: it was small. The whole project was quixotic, impractical.

But Andreas deflected the concerns I raised. Everything would be scaled down, only a handful of singer/actors, no choruses, a small chamber orchestra and a piano.

Peter, the producer, took over.

"I realize this is not exactly what you had in mind, Kyra, when you gave that talk, but I'm convinced from what you said about the relation of the seen and felt presence that you can help us arrive at an approach to design that will convey the atmosphere of Rome at that time, and of the story itself, which is timeless."

"What we are hoping," Andreas said simply, "is that you will say yes."

Our eyes met briefly. I said, "Look, I haven't worked in the theater. I know nothing about set design. I don't know opera."

They wanted a fresh eye, they said.

I would want to bring in Sarah. She knew how to improvise. In South Africa, they had taken plays into the townships.

Andreas and Peter agreed.

I had completed the drawings for the first phase of the project on Nashawena. Now that winter had set in, construction there had stopped. The university term was ending. I was going on leave but I wouldn't actually be leaving Cambridge until March. I had thought of taking a watercolor class. I wanted to do something different. Why not this?

Why not work with this man?

"Then you'll do it?" Andreas said, reading something in my face.

"Good," Peter said, and went to turn out the lights.

"I'll make some sketches, and you can see what you think," I said. Andreas raised his eyebrows, thick as hedgerows, as if to say, why would there be a question? He had trained as a conductor, he was working as a director. His impulse was to move forward, not wait and see.

Outside, the night was surprisingly cold. The breeze, gentle earlier, had picked up. Branches swayed across the streetlights, making shadows on the sidewalk. Andreas took my hand. Peter suggested getting dinner at a new place that had opened on Columbus Avenue, but Andreas needed to get back to Brookline, where he and Jesse and Abe were staying with Abe's sister, Edith, and I wanted to go home and have a bath. He said he had promised Jesse he would read to him before he went to bed. While we were standing on the steps outside the Design School, he had shown me the book he had bought for Jesse at the Coop, the illustrations striking—an arctic landscape, the snow red in the late afternoon sun. In the story, a boy sets out to hunt the wolf who killed his dog, but by the end, he realizes that killing the wolf would not bring his dog back. Profoundly simple, the logic impeccable. How does this clarity get lost? We had walked to Peter's car. The alarm release made its three beeping sounds. All clear.

2

DAVID'S DOOR WAS OPEN THE NEXT MORNING WHEN I CAME INTO school. He was sitting at his desk, hunched over, typing.

"What are you writing?" I asked, sinking into the relic of an armchair he had rescued from Goodwill.

He swiveled around.

"It's a fellowship application," he said, his fingers tapping the edge of the chair. "It's for the American Academy in Rome. It has to be mailed by midnight tonight."

Even when he was frazzled, there was a solidity to David. As a landscape architect, he worked with the earth and had a yeoman's body, I thought, looking at his arms. Extending from the pushed-up sleeves of his charcoal-gray sweater, they exuded strength.

It was David I sought out when I got stuck, when I needed to discover where I was going with my island project. We talked mostly about work, but there also were times when we talked about our lives, when one of us needed an outside ear. I knew about Sarah, he knew about Simon. When Sarah was talking last winter about moving back to Cape Town, he had asked me what he should do. Listen, I said.

"I don't want to interrupt you," I said, thinking of leaving. To be in his presence was to expose myself to his eye, and I wasn't sure I was up for that. David was someone who said what he saw.

And on those days when he told me I looked tired or upset, I resented it, even when it was true.

"Just give me a minute to finish this paragraph," he said, "or I'll forget what I was going to say."

I stared at the photographs of plants lining the wall over his desk, a birthday gift from Sarah. The marsh grasses from the Fenway were my favorites.

"Okay," David said, typing a few more words, "I could use a break."

He turned to face me and pulled down the sleeves of his sweater.

"Guess what?" I said.

He took off his glasses and studied my face. "I give up."

"I've been asked to design sets for *Tosca*."

"You're kidding," he said. "I thought you were building Carthage. So now you're going to build Rome too?"

I took off my coat. "It's for the theater. This man . . . Do you know Felicia Blumenthal?" David shook his head. "Well, her cousin, Andreas, is directing *Tosca* in the Counterpoint Theater, the one Peter Maas started in the South End. They've asked me to design the sets—or the not-sets. The problem is the space is small."

"Sounds like a good project for students," David said, swiveling back to his desk, "the never-say-never crowd." He turned back. "Why would you do it?"

Suddenly it didn't seem like a good idea.

"Kyra, we're friends," David said quietly.

My eyes teared unexpectedly.

Outside, the steady beeps of a truck backing up.

Was it the conversation in the restaurant, Andreas's wife disappearing? Or was it simply David's offer of friendship? Friends can tell each other anything. Yet something held me back.

David shifted his body in the chair, his glasses reflected the light coming in through the window, the gray, December sky. He waited.

"It's the director," I said finally. "He intrigues me."

David's face lightened. "That's lovely, Kyra," he said. "It doesn't happen often." I brushed away the tears.

"There's really not much more to say at this point," I said. Still I lingered. Something wasn't finished, something more I wanted to say, or hear.

He typed a few words and bent down to lace up his boots. "Let's get out of here, get coffee, go for a walk. I've been here an hour and I already have a headache. This is what the Dutch call a sick building. No fresh air. We have our predecessors to thank for that."

I had a million things to do. Anna was leaving that night for London to spend the holiday with our aunt and uncle. It would be a large family gathering. I had decided not to go, but I wanted to send gifts with her. "Let's go to the Square," I said.

David took his coat from the hook behind the door and switched off the light. The definitiveness of the gesture reminded me of Martin, our English uncle. The difference between Europeans and Americans, Martin would say, is that Europeans turn off the lights when they leave a room and put on a sweater when they're cold. I noticed a postcard on the wall, tacked up near the door, a photograph of red and gold grasses. "That's new," I said.

"It's from Anglesey Abbey," David said. "After Kew Gardens, my favorite place."

I told him that Martin had taken us to the abbey the first winter Anna and I were in London. He wanted us to see the winter garden. "I remember those grasses, the small trees standing among them, their bark stark white, the deep red stems of the plants. When we came to the grove of white birches planted in lines, I burst into tears. It was like entering a city of ghosts."

And then I was sorry I had said that.

We were standing by the door, the room dim.

"How long are you going to live among ghosts?" he asked.

We walked out into the corridor, David's arm around me, firm.

I spent the holiday break on Nashawena, grateful for the quiet, the presence of the sea. David had given me a book with photographs of Rome, and I leafed through the pages, stopping to study the Farnese Palace, the Castel Sant Angelo, the church of Sant Andrea della Valle, places where the scenes in *Tosca* take place. I got ideas for the sets, did a few drawings. Then one afternoon I went for a long walk on the beach and thought, This is not what I want to do. I was involved in building something new, first it had been the house, now it was the island project. It was a relief to be here on Nashawena, by myself.

When I got back to the house, the message light on the phone was flashing. The call was from Andreas, the number he left was in Vermont. I brought in more logs for the woodstove and heated up the sorrel soup I had made. It was a childhood favorite, and I'd finally figured out my mother's secret, adding the yolk of an egg. I'd call him after supper. On the message, he said he was with Jesse and Peter, staying in a friend's cabin, teaching Jesse to ski.

When I called, he answered the phone on the first ring. "I was hoping it was you," he said. He was calling to invite me to dinner at Felicia's. She was giving a dinner for the cast, right after the new year. "I'd love it if you could come," he said. I surprised myself by saying I would.

It was a perfect Italian supper, good salami in the antipasto, handmade pasta. Andreas met me at the door. He looked happy, a little distracted. "Come, I want to introduce you to the singers." He led me over to the Israeli soprano, the one whose voice he had raved about. She was tall, sensual, dark hair cascading around her shoulders. I wasn't prepared for her, her easy physicality. My body stiffened. They were musicians, but still . . . I turned to the tenor standing beside her. His name was Dan, the corner of his mouth flickered, a gesture I would find riveting through the long days of rehearsals. He wore a black *Abbey Road* T-shirt.

Felicia came up. "Kyra, darling, how was your break?" She placed her arm around my shoulder. I noticed Dan, the tenor, watching us closely. The soprano was talking to Andreas. I felt drab by comparison. "This cold," Felicia said, "it does something

to the body. You should try the beets in the antipasto—root vegetables store the energy the body needs in winter." I saw Andreas
move to greet a new arrival, a small, dark-haired man who turned
out to be another of the tenors. Because the opera was to run
every night like a play, the principal roles had been triple-cast.

Supper was followed by introductions, starting with the lead
singers. In addition to the Israeli soprano, whose name was Tali,
there was Alice, an Asian soprano, and a redhead named Karen
who had grown up on a farm in Iowa. They would all play Tosca.
Dan, who was blond and stocky, would play Cavaradossi, Tosca's
lover, as would the small, dark-haired tenor, and Paul, tall and
black. I tried to imagine the pairings. Tali and Dan, for sure. They
had the same energy. The three Scarpias, the villain, were all
heavyset. To play the chief of police in a reign of terror clearly required heft.

Afterward, Peter, as the artistic director of the theater, spoke
briefly, thanking the benefactors who were there. They commanded the sofa and chairs. The singers and actors chose the rug
in front of the fire, the tech crew leaned against the walls. Andreas, standing beside the mantel, welcomed us, his face alive
with expectation. "We are embarking together on an experiment,
to do *Tosca* not as a spectacle but as intimate theater." He had a
vision; my shoulders released. I had confidence in art, he would
find the form.

I remembered the night on the beach, his body lithe as he bent
down to draw the words *amor* and *Roma* in the sand, the smell of
the sea, the tide coming in.

I scanned the faces of the singers. Whatever apprehension they
may have felt seemed assuaged by Andreas's assurance, his promise to accompany them. We will find our way together, he said,
there will be ample time to prepare. Rehearsals would start at ten
the next morning. He wished everyone a good night's sleep.

He came across the room to join me.

"Can I give you a lift?" he asked.

I looked around, delighted to be singled out.

"How do you think it went?" he asked, as we waited for the engine to warm up.

"It went beautifully, I could feel the group drawing together as you spoke."

He told me he was grateful to these young singers, their willingness to work for practically nothing. Otherwise, it would be impossible to have three casts.

I told him that Dan had said it was a great opportunity for them to work with him.

Andreas smiled and shifted into gear.

"Let's go out for a glass of wine to celebrate. I'm so glad, so happy you're doing this with me."

Happy . . . a major key. I smiled in the dark car, noticing that music was creeping into my vocabulary. C major. Keep it simple. No flats or sharps.

The Harvest was closing, so we went to the Charles Hotel, the bar dim, plush chairs circling small tables. We chose a corner and sat looking out into the courtyard, trees strung with white lights.

I asked about the ski trip, and he said that Jesse had been apprehensive at first, but once he caught on, he insisted on going to the top. "There was a cart road down, an easy trail, but it was long and Jesse was cold. I skied him down between my legs," Andreas said. "I can still feel it in my shoulders." He reached back under his collar and massaged his shoulder blades, elbows bent, like the wings of a bird. "Jesse's really growing up now," he said. He shook the tension out of his neck. "And you?"

"Me too," I laughed. Maybe we all were. That night it seemed clear that we each had our own lives, and we would work together. Maybe it was less fraught than I had feared. The opera was a story, it was only a story, and perhaps it was important to remind people how easily people can be trapped, how easily freedom can be lost. The glow on his face from skiing matched the calm I had found on Nashawena. When he dropped me in front of my apartment building on Dana Street we kissed on both cheeks. Friends.

The next morning, rehearsals started with a collective warm-up. We were in the large reception hall of the church, above the theater. Andreas was across the room from me. He had told me to wear loose clothes, said I would be expected to participate. Mika, the voice coach, led us—her hair in a buzz cut, black and white strands standing straight up on her head. With her turned-up nose, she reminded me of a porcupine. Her earrings were dangling strands, streaked red and blue, hanging from silver stars, dazzling. We gathered in a circle. She started with breath.

"Let the breath fall in," she said. She scanned the room, her eye exact. "Listen to the words I say. I didn't say breathe. I said let the breath fall in." She moved through the room, placing her hand on bellies, waiting for the muscles to release. "Your body knows what to do. Trust it." My muscles tensed. Her hand was on my stomach, her gaze steady, patient. Let the breath fall in. My belly expanded. The muscles had relaxed under her hand. Air rushed in. I suddenly felt dizzy. "It's the oxygen," she explained, "you'll get used to it." She moved off, her authority easy, sure. The warm-up continued. She added sound to breath, we rolled up and down our spines, vertebra after vertebra. Suppleness rippled through my back. "And now, a totally pleasurable sigh of relief." Sound filled the room. My concentration settled. Vowels came next, each with its distinctive coloring, the room awash with the sound of emotion. It felt like a perfect way to start the day.

At the end of the hour, following the pee break, Andreas took over. The cast moved into theater exercises and games. I retrieved my sweater and sat on one of the folding chairs against the wall, a fleeting regret at being outside the circle. I had liked the sensation of relinquishing control to Mika. Let the breath fall in, I repeated the mantra, my eyes surveying the cast. Tali, the tall Israeli soprano in loose gray pants and a fuchsia shirt, Alice, the Asian soprano, energy coiled in her body, releasing into the room, her movements precise, like a dancer. Dan and Paul, two of the tenors, also a study in contrast. They passed gestures from one to the other, adding rhythms and sounds, reversing directions. One of the Scarpias, Steve, asked a question. A rule was proposed: do first, try the exercise, discussion afterward. I made a mental note, do this with my students.

I stayed for the first part of the read-through. They were taking the score—both text and music—at face value. I found it hard to leave, but I had to get back to school. There were no classes in reading period, only office hours and committee meetings, scheduled for the most part in the afternoons. I was bridging two worlds, the South End and Cambridge, theater and university. In the committee meeting that afternoon, I practiced my breathing; I wondered if anyone noticed. It was a dangerous place to let go of control.

Anna came to a rehearsal one day when they were well into the work. I wanted her to see Andreas again. In some way I couldn't articulate, I wanted her to watch him working, to see how he worked with the singers.

The pianist was playing through the music when we came in. I recognized the melody of the gavotte, delicate, lilting. We sat down quietly near the front. Andreas noticed us and explained they were starting with Act Two. He turned back to the singers who were scattered around the stage. They formed a group around him. "Why is it that in this opera every time someone comes close to someone else, it's fatal?" he asked. "Here is where you really start to sense it, at the beginning of Act Two. You know the theme, the Scarpia motif—the three descending chords, E major, D major, B-flat major. But then something new happens, something you haven't heard before." He turned to the pianist. "Would you play just the three chords for us."

The room seemed different. Maybe it was Andreas's question: why in this opera is intimacy fatal? A shudder ran through me. I turned to Anna. She felt it as well.

Andreas nodded to the pianist. "Now if you would start at the beginning again and just go on, ignore us. Scarpia"—he motioned to Steve, round, sweet face above a too-big body—"you begin." The rest of the cast moved to the edge of the stage. I watched an invisible circle form around Andreas and the baritone.

"Tosca is a good falcon," Steve sang.

"Good, continue . . ."

"Surely by this time my hounds have fallen on their double prey. And tomorrow's dawn will see Angelotti on the scaffold and the fine Mario hanging from a noose."

I whispered to Anna: "Angelotti is the escaped freedom fighter Scarpia is hunting, and Mario is Tosca's lover. Mario has hidden Angelotti in his villa."

"All right. Let's stop here." The piano stopped. Andreas moved closer to Steve. "Can you picture them, Angelotti and Mario, as you say the words *double prey*?"

Steve closed his eyes. Andreas motioned to the singers playing Angelotti and Mario. They stood. He turned back to Steve.

"Now look at them. You have played on Tosca's jealousy. She had seen another woman's face in her lover Cavaradossi's painting of the Magdalene. You have fueled her suspicions. You suspect that Cavaradossi is hiding Angelotti, the political fugitive. You want Tosca to lead you to them. She is your falcon, they are your prey. Tosca," he motioned to Alice, "come and stand in front of Scarpia. Now, Steve, look at Tosca and say it. 'Tosca's my good falcon.' "

I felt intensity mounting, the concentration seemed palpable.

Steve tried again.

"Much better," Andreas said. "I can see them now, feel them."

I could feel Andreas moving in.

"Falcon?" he asked Steve. "What is a falcon?"

"Watch this," I whispered to Anna.

"A bird of prey."

"Have you ever seen a falcon?"

Steve shook his head.

"They are very fast and powerful. They can catch birds as they fly. Now think about *prey*. In English, the word has two meanings."

I glanced at Anna. She was riveted.

"*Prey* as in bird of prey, and *pray*." He steepled his hands. "The opera opens in a church. We are in Rome, near the Vatican. We see Scarpia first in church. He was praying. And now he is preying. Can you feel the alliance of church and state closing in? There is no sanctuary, no escape."

He glanced at the pianist. "From the beginning again, please."

Steve, the round-faced choirboy, disappeared. Scarpia had taken his place.

I saw Andreas let out his breath.

"It's so explicit," Anna whispered, "calling her his falcon. And the double meaning of *prey*. Why are they doing it in English?"

"It's like translating the Bible into English, so people can understand it for themselves, bringing it into a language they speak every day."

Andreas turned to us and said, "Please." We stopped talking.

He turned back to Scarpia.

"What do you do next?"

Steve cleared his throat.

"Forget the music for now."

Anna sat forward in her seat.

"I ring for my assistant," Steve said.

Andreas picked up his score. "I'll read the assistant Sciarrone's part for now. You begin, Scarpia."

"*Is Tosca in the palace?*" Steve says.

"*A chamberlain has just gone to look for her,*" Andreas replies.

"*Open the window. It is late. The Diva's still missing from the concert, and they strum gavottes.*"

"Okay." Andreas stepped back. "Now we need to hear the music."

The pianist plays the gavotte, the music we heard when we came in.

"What happens to you when you hear this?" Andreas asks. "Listen for a moment, take it in."

"I think of Tosca," Steve's voice as Scarpia, almost inaudible.

The other Scarpias lean forward, straining to hear.

"As your falcon?" Andreas asks. There's something about his manner that allows him to move in like this without crowding, a curiosity, a questioning so genuine it contains no judgment. He has the pacing of a musician, as if he were conducting beat by beat, but it's the emotional rhythm he's following. I was seeing something in this man that I had not seen before, a passion checked, coming out in art. I saw him turn now to the other Scarpias, his face taut, his absorption total. "I want you to stay with him here. I want to feel you feeling this with him, and later, you'll do it yourselves."

"What do you feel in this moment?" Andreas says to Steve. "It's a question. See what you find. Take your time."

The muscles in Steve's face twitch. He shakes his head. Lets out a long breath. "I feel . . ." He stops. Swallows hard. "I feel desire."

The room is still.

"I want to be her lover."

Andreas stays with him. "What do you do?"

"I instruct Sciarrone to wait for her, to say that I shall expect her after the concert. Then it occurs to me how I can make her come. I write a note, appealing to her love for Mario." Steve covers his face with his hands.

"And here," Andreas said, "we descend into hell."

I looked at Anna, she looked at me. We had seen the descent with Anton. He had wanted our father to love him, not Simon.

"What do you say?" Andreas continues.

"*For love of Mario, she will yield to my pleasure.*"

"So it isn't really you she will come to. And the truth is, you know it. The psychology here is clearly spelled out. Go on."

Steve as Scarpia continues: "*For myself the violent conquest has stronger relish than the soft surrender. I know not how to draw harmony from guitars, I crave, I pursue the craved thing, sate myself, and cast it by, and seek new bait.*"

"You, Scarpia, have become a falcon," Andreas says. "And why? Because for a brief moment, you felt desire, maybe even tenderness. It's in the music. Scarpia cannot bear to feel these feelings. So he will turn her into bait, not a person but a craved thing. This is what evil does. It goes after and tries to destroy what is most human in us. Now Scarpia will prey on Tosca's love."

They took a break.

"It's incredible," Anna said as we left. "So clear. As he said, the psychology is all laid out. You see how desire can create an unbearable vulnerability, which people then cover by trying to destroy the very thing or person who has provoked or inspired these feelings. And then they feel strong again in their own eyes, and invulnerable. It's how a person becomes a monster, seemingly without feelings. No wonder people love opera."

I knew she was also thinking, What's wrong with Kyra? Seeing Andreas working would have clinched it: he was amazing. She understood about Simon, how, feeling guilty about Anton, I felt responsible for what had happened to Simon, or the other way around, how, feeling responsible for Anton, I felt guilty toward Simon. We had been over and over this. None of it brought Simon back. It was like Jesse's book about the dog and the wolf. "You have to live," Anna would say. "You're not a nun."

We had reached Huntington Avenue. Anna wanted to take the subway. It was cold, and she didn't want to be late for her one o'clock patient. I wanted to walk. Maybe it was the image of the falcon. I wanted to move, to get away. I looked at my watch. If I walked fast, and if I was alone I would, I might have time to pick up some lunch and still get to my office before my first appointment.

Low gray clouds hung in a fleetingly blue sky. The sun went in and out, but even when it was out, the light seemed strained. I passed Symphony Hall, the posters announcing upcoming concerts. I read the words without taking them in. He seemed to be everywhere.

Across the street, Horticultural Hall—what was it doing in the middle of the city? A shelter for plants, plants in captivity. I pulled up the hood of my duffle coat, took my scarf out and wrapped it around to hold the hood. The street was crammed with delivery trucks, meter maids circled like sharks. When I reached the bridge, the sun came out steadily for a moment. The water looked completely opaque.

I came up with three reasons to dismiss him. One was Simon. That spoke for itself. A commitment for life. Two, I had seen Andreas come forward and then recede, become self-enclosed. The third reason slipped my mind.

I looked up into the sky, shading my eyes against the weak sun. Gulls were circling. How far up the river did they go? They looked so innocent. I was trying to clear my head, get rid of the falcon. Using a woman as a falcon? To capture her lover, his prey? Was it worse that Scarpia desires her? But then the falconer does love the falcon. In the opera, her prey is him. The falcon turning on the falconer. She kills Scarpia.

The wind was behind me, carrying me across the river into Cambridge. I checked my watch. I could stop and pick up a sandwich and a cappuccino from the Italian store if I cut through Putnam Avenue. The thought of food was a relief. My mood brightened. I was glad to be away.

Eva, the first student, knocked on my door as I unwrapped the sandwich and took a bite. She was one of the talented ones; I liked the boldness of her work. Office hours had begun. "Come in," I said through provolone and turkey.

She entered, hesitant. "Are you sure you're ready? I can wait in the hall."

I motioned her to one of the chairs next to the round table and picked up my sandwich and coffee to join her.

"Do you mind if I eat my lunch while we talk?"

"No, really, no," she said. Well, really, what else could she say? She bent down to fish her notebook out of her book bag, her neck long, slender. She was taking my urban design studio and had brought a list of questions having to do with the development of her project. The students were each doing a design for the reuse of the High Line, the abandoned stretch of elevated tracks that run through Chelsea in lower Manhattan. Their projects would be juried the following week.

"Would you like a little cappuccino?" I asked.

She looked at the cup.

"I'll get another cup and we can split it," I said, going over to the shelf where several mugs and an electric kettle stood in front of a row of books.

"Yes, I'd love some," she leaned back, relaxed a little.

I had brought a rocking chair into my office, like John F. Kennedy, I told myself, and a Danish sofa I had acquired from Felicia, covered in apricot corduroy. Shades of the sixties, one of my students said, vintage Howard Johnson, but they preferred it to the Harvard chairs. I actually liked those chairs—their sleek black arms, *veritas* embossed on the back. Speak the truth. They ringed the table, chastising equivocators.

Eva came to the end of her questions, her face flushed. I encouraged the ambition of what she was attempting. It could be really good. She looked at me for a moment, as if uncertain. She was about to ask another question, but then changed her mind and left. The next student came in.

Outside, the afternoon grew bleaker. I rode the caffeine high of the half-cappuccino until about four o'clock, when the energy suddenly drained out of me. I had a committee meeting at four-thirty. The subject was appointments, the fight would be bitter. I looked at the stack of pink phone messages on my desk. It was hopeless. I put on my coat. I would go for a walk. I thought of walking through the woods behind the American Academy, but instead I found myself heading for the river. The motion of the water, there would be more air.

I passed the Catholic church at the intersection of Bow and Arrow streets, the sun behind the church, the front in shadow. A woman was sitting on the stone steps, wrapped in loose garments, holding a baby. "Please," she said, "can you help me?" She shifted the baby to one arm and held out her hand. I reached into my coat pocket and found a few dollars and some coins—the change from lunch. Her eyes were coal, the bones of her face sharply etched. "God bless you," she said.

At the committee meeting it soon became clear that the work of the meeting had been done before the meeting. The meeting itself was like a show trial. Three finalists for the faculty position had been culled from a long list of applicants: Kristin, the insider, the darling, the protégé of one of our colleagues, and two who had come from afar to give their talks. Our former student was by any "objective" criterion the star, the winner of coveted prizes in fierce competitions judged by names that gave everyone pause. It was her undoing.

Somewhere, sometime before the meeting, an agreement had been arrived at. Anyone but her. The motivation wasn't hard to fathom. Envy was involved, but also resentment. Her mentor was already too powerful, his work the focus of media attention. Hiring Kristin would slant the department in the direction of his work, a move my colleagues abhorred. The other two finalists, both competent, posed no threat.

Ballots were cast, votes were counted. With few exceptions, they split between the two not-Kristins. On the spot, a motion was made to hire both. I was stunned when it passed. Was the budget suddenly no consideration, had a windfall landed on the table? Someone said something about classes being oversubscribed, but the intention in hiring both, I suspected, was to deflect attention from the limitations of either one. "You would think," I began, and then stopped myself. I was about to say it was obvious what had happened. I looked around the room. No sign of a falcon. Outside the window, light slanting against roofs.

The meeting ended with a cheery collegiality that belied what had just taken place. Kristin had been sacrificed, in the name of seeking excellence. Nobody made eye contact. The two students on the committee looked confused.

My thoughts kept drifting to Andreas. He wanted to take *Tosca* into the schools, to invite people from the neighborhood to the final rehearsal, people we had passed on the streets, seen in the shops. One night we had gone out for Chinese food, wrapping shreds of pork and cabbage in paper-thin pancakes, hoisin sauce dripping from the ends. The energy of the opera was in his body, and I was in it with him. I told him it was like working in a holy space. He smiled. "It is a holy space." He reached across the table and brushed a wisp of hair from my face. I said I'd been talking with the lighting designer about how much could be done simply with lights. We could use a column to suggest the thickness of the walls, and then darkness to create the feeling of enclosure.

It had been late when he drove me back to Cambridge. There was a parking space in front of my building. We sat in the car listening to the all-night jazz program. "I'll walk you in," he said. We stood in the entry between the outer and inner doors, ceiling light glancing off the glass in the doors, the brass rows of mailboxes and buzzers, landing on the dirty white tiles. I searched for my keys. "Can I hold something?" he asked, moving closer, and then his arms were around me and we were kissing. With the unfamiliar sensation of my body softening, releasing, I must have leaned back against the buzzers, because suddenly there was a cacophony of voices, irritated and abrasive, asking, Who is it? Who is it? Who's there? We both started laughing. I caught my reflection in one of the mailboxes, my face looking guilty, flustered. Had whatever gods, Chinese or otherwise, who were presiding over the evening sent us a signal? Stop?

But the kiss left an impression. In that moment I felt how easy it would be to give myself over to this, to him. A rush had gone through me, compelling, impelling. I felt light-headed. Upstairs, in my apartment, I sat in the living room, on the sofa, waiting for the room to settle. I had seen him give himself over to his work. I found it very beautiful, arresting. Would we do that now with each other as well?

After the committee meeting, I went home to have a bath. The design crew was meeting for dinner, and since the lighting person was working on a play at a church in Central Square, we had decided to meet at a restaurant on Mass. Avenue, around the corner from the church. I put sea salts in the bathwater. It turned green, like photographs of the Caribbean, the white porcelain a stand-in for sand. I stretched out in the tub and closed my eyes. If I were on a beach, waves lapping. If we were on a beach. I opened my eyes abruptly. In the fantasy, I was with Andreas, not Simon. I got out of the tub.

My hair was darkening now. It was winter. I brushed it, starting at the nape of my neck, my head down around my knees, dropping down, vertebra after vertebra, fifty strokes. I rolled up my spine. Fifty more, from the forehead now. I watched my face in the steamy mirror. I looked like a person emerging from a fog.

The bedroom was cold. I put on jeans and a black sweater. Added red beads, they picked up the lamp, shone with a far-off wisdom. Randy had given them to me, a gift from Thailand, in anticipation of the trip we would make there in March. I was looking forward to that, to experiencing what I had read about, a world where everything was permeable. Randy had said the Akha had no concept of the self. I looked at the beads under the light. Someone had seen that red, chosen that red. The necklace was made by the Akha.

Boots or sneakers? The lighting person always wore black. Mika led the warm-up in red high-top sneakers she bought in London. I opted for the boots, the ones that folded down around the ankle.

Anna had gone directly to Nashawena after her last patient. Since I had committed myself to *Tosca,* we were spending less time together. She and Tony, one of the construction workers who lived on the Vineyard, had been talking about starting an oyster farm. Tony was a dreamer, his love was the sea. His thin, wiry body sprang something loose in Anna, the sternness leaving her face. She was less judgmental, less the older sister. When the two of us were together, it was easier to talk.

We had spent an evening talking, finally, about Andreas. The way he had worked with the singers fascinated Anna, the intense contact he made with people, the way he zeroed in, and yet there was also something remote about him. She wondered about his relationship with Jesse. It was complicated, I said. Aside from the color of his eyes, Jesse looked like his mother. Have you seen her picture? Anna asked. I hadn't, but Andreas had commented on the resemblance, same hair color, reddish-brown. "It's been over three years now," I said, "since she disappeared." Jesse had been two. Presumably she was dead. Anna said it takes at least two years to get over a death, and with something that shocking it can take much longer. I waited, but the comment wasn't pointed at me. Simon had been dead for over ten years.

I liked the way Anna and Tony were together, their calm assurance with each other. It brought out a side of Anna I hadn't seen in years, a buoyancy I remembered from when we played together as children, the way she would cast herself into a game. She was doing that now with the oyster farm. She and Tony were moving ahead, planning to seed oysters in the spring. With their hair the same dark brown, their bodies approximately the same size, I thought they could have been twins.

Otto von Simson's *The Gothic Cathedral* sat on the table next to our front door. If it were a homing pigeon, it would take off for the library by itself. The cover was black with a row of cloverleaf windows, two in red, two in blue, underneath, a sudden light—gray-white stone and the curve of arches. I opened the cover and read the subtitle: "Origins of Gothic Architecture and the Medieval Concept of Order." I put the book back on the table and went out the door.

This sounds ordinary. I mean, in a way it was. I'm an architect, an urban designer. Through a piece of good luck I became involved in a project to design a new city, albeit on a small scale. But mostly I was teaching at university, working with students, writing papers, going to meetings, making a living, more money than most people on this earth, not much by some people's standards. I was living with my sister—which is unusual these days, but my husband had been killed, murdered by our half brother, which would be unusual except that many people's lives have been shattered in this century. I'm asking myself how it was that I didn't see it coming. They say you can always go back and find the beginning, recognize the theme the first time it comes in. Like the Scarpia theme. Like *Peter and the Wolf*. Every life has its leitmotif, its distinctive whorl. And you could also say that in every life there is a potential for disintegration. The keystone dislodges and the arch collapses.

———

The studio projects were juried the third week in January. The constant was the elevated tracks of the High Line, rusty now and clotted with weeds. Architects in New York had petitioned against the High Line's destruction, the plan for its restoration remained an open question, giving the students' imaginations free rein. They had been working on their projects all semester, now was the moment of evaluation. It was something they would face in the future; here was a test.

We gathered in the windowless classroom, the students with their models and drawings, the jurors a mix of faculty and guest critics. Sandro and Hakim were there from architecture. Erik and Craig from my department. Sid Winter, my pal, came up from New York, an architect involved in the campaign to save the High Line. Sid was tough, but I knew the students would love him because he fit their image of the successful young architect, cool and sexy, which was mostly not the case.

The afternoon got off to a good start. My edginess subsided, I too was being judged, but the students' projects were inventive and for the most part well executed. They presented them well, despite the fact that the room was freezing; something was wrong with the heat. The concrete exuded dankness; outside it was beginning to snow. The jurors drank coffee and huddled in their coats.

When Eva got up to present, it was toward the end of the review. She had studied in Geneva, and her manner was diffident, Europeans would say restrained. She wore a gray skirt and a light blue blouse, her hair prim around her face. And maybe it was that her appearance belied the ambition of her project, or maybe it was the ambition itself, but something bothered the jurors. It may have been just the cold, but they were not receptive. I could see she was not making contact. She soldiered on, but as the critical queries mounted, she faltered and began to cry. I looked around the room. The faces of the other students were frozen; the jurors continued their conversation about the project as if nothing were happening, shifting slightly to soft-pedal their comments. Eva collected herself and finished her review, but without receiving the recognition I thought the project deserved. The next student got up.

I had been spending my days with actors and singers, tears part of the daily rhythm of emotion, often the gateway into a break-through. Culture shock fused with concern for my student. Eva's project was exceptional, delicate and bold at the same time, but now her wings had been clipped. Where were my colleagues? I should have invited David. I had forgotten the academic distrust of emotion, the association of tears with breaking down. I sus-pected something more was involved. Envy perhaps, or in-credulity that someone who looked and acted like Eva could be brilliant. If she looked like Tali, the Israeli soprano, or had the earnestness of a Japanese student, or was a regular guy like Sid, they might have spotted the brilliance, even though the presenta-tion was flawed.

I knew that the jurors' comments would not be held against her, but I worried about how she would integrate the experience.

Sid used the meager honorarium the Design School paid him to take me to dinner. We had worked together often when he was in Cambridge, not seen each other much since he went to New York. He had wanted me to go with him, start a firm together. His wed-ding ring was still shiny. They were expecting a baby. He was not the domestic type. Still, he looked happy.

I brought up the subject of Eva. He didn't have much to say.

He felt sorry for her, it was a difficult review, but she's got to learn how to take criticism and use it to move ahead. We've all been raked over the coals. I swallowed my distaste at cliché. He picked up his glass of wine. "To friendship," he said, closing the conversation.

I said I was doing the design for a production of *Tosca*. "That's a shift," he said. I said I was finding it challenging, like learning a new language. He had worked with a director in Paris, he loved the theater and especially opera. He offered to come with me the next day and look at the space before he left for New York.

When Sid and I arrived, the cast was in a meeting. "Have you seen the church?" Sid asked. Somehow I hadn't. We went in. It was quietly beautiful, simple Gothic, nave and transept, stained-glass windows. The blue in the rose window reminded me of Chartres. A piece of the twelfth century in this desolate part of Boston. Who built it, Sid wondered, and when? We sat in a pew, my mind floating, and suddenly the idea came to me: wouldn't this be the perfect place for *Tosca*? I could see it, the lines of the walls soaring, the structure majestic, the intrigue of the drama set off by contrast to the spare elegance of the space. Lighting poles could be brought in. My mind was racing. I turned to Sid. He thought it was a fabulous idea. For the second act in the Farnese Palace, he said, a Persian carpet could be spread over the floor. The director he had worked with in Paris had come upon that as a simple solution to the problem of staging.

We went to find Andreas. His face lit up at the idea. He had never liked the proscenium stage, felt it defeated his efforts to create an intimate relation between the performers and the audience. He had gotten to know some of the priests, had gone out drinking with them. One in particular had come back from Ecuador, bringing the message of liberation theology. Here in the South End, they were ministering to the poor in a seemingly godforsaken neighborhood in the midst of a city increasingly affluent. The priests had welcomed Peter's idea for theater to take place in their building. Why not bring it into the church proper? It was in the spirit of Vatican II. Andreas said he would broach the idea, see what they thought, his enthusiasm only slightly dimmed by the realization that they could say no.

Belatedly, I introduced Sid to Andreas. "We were almost partners," I explained. Andreas looked puzzled. "I mean, we had thought of starting a design firm together." Rehearsal was beginning. "Can you stay?" Andreas asked. "I'd love to," Sid said. We were standing in the lobby outside the theater. Andreas put his arm around my shoulder as we walked through the door.

"We're starting with the third act, Cavaradossi's act," Andreas said, sizing up Sid. Did Sid know that Cavaradossi was Tosca's lover, Mario, the painter? "It has two of my favorite tenor arias," Sid said, passing the ball back. Andreas caught it, nodded.

We sat in the third row, and Sid turned to me: "It breaks my heart. Just when Cavaradossi finally has what he most wanted in life, his dream of love, he has to die. That's the aria that kills me. It's where you hear the poetry of Puccini. Did you know he wrote some of the lines himself?"

I realized I had missed Sid's energy, his impetuousness, his loose-limbed body. He could have been a basketball player. There had always been a tension between us, a question as to whether we would become lovers, but I had said I couldn't. Still, the frisson was in the air. I remembered the fissure in his voice when he called up to say, "I'm getting married." He had moved on, but we remained friends.

Tali and Dan moved to the stage. I watched Sid's eyes follow Tali. She was wearing white pants and a long green shirt, which set off her dark hair. Dan wore jeans and a black soccer shirt with a red stripe down the arms, his shoes picking up the motif— brown with a white stripe at the side. He looked like a dolphin with his expanded chest, thin hips, his body shimmering, his motions lithe. The other two sopranos and tenors would be called upon later in an exercise that was one of Andreas's favorites: a Tosca and a Mario singing while two others did the acting, to free the body's movement from operatic conventions, to separate the dramatic from the musical line, or delineate as he would say, his British English softened by Hungarian cadence.

Joel, the music director, led a boy to the stage. He was around nine or ten, his face impassive. He would sing the Shepherd's song, which opens the third act. Andreas bent down to speak with the boy, who looked at the floor. The pianist began the Lydian melody. Suddenly, out of that dark, quiet boy's face, a voice clear as the dawn. "Bravo," Andreas said after, and got a shy smile in response. "Thank you," Joel said, leading the boy back to his teacher, the priest who had started the choir school.

The jailer entered, Cavaradossi was brought in by guards. The sergeant handed a note to the jailer, who opened his book to register the prisoner. You have one hour, he tells Cavaradossi, a priest awaits your call. Cavaradossi refuses the priest, asks for a favor. He wants to write a letter to Tosca. He offers the jailer his ring, if he will promise to deliver the letter. The jailer hesitates, then accepts and motions Cavaradossi to the chair at the table.

Andreas stopped them.

"Dan, if you sing a closed vowel in the prefix of *deliver,* it sounds like *de-liver,* to take out the liver." Everyone laughed. "Otherwise it's beautiful, but follow the line of the music, where it's going." He repeated the words *"Would you give me leave to write her a letter,"* placing the stress on *leave* and then on *letter.* "Listen to the pulse under the line." Dan, the Cavaradossi paired with Tali's Tosca, took the pencil from behind his ear and made a note in his score.

"Go on," Andreas said quietly.

Sid turned to me. "Now, here it comes: '*E lucevan le stelle,* by the light of the stars.' "

Dan closed his eyes. The room became still. When he opened his eyes and began to sing, his voice was gorgeous, fluent, simple. There was nothing operatic about his delivery. He is a man, writing his farewell to his beloved, remembering her footstep in the garden, her fragrance, the feel of her in his arms, soft kisses, sweet abandon. It's his dream of love, and he must give it up. At the very moment when he could live most intensely, he is going to die. He bursts into sobs.

"I love it, I love it, Dan," Andreas said. "That's it, that's all I'm asking you to do. Go on."

"That's the aria that totally breaks me up," Sid whispered.

Tosca arrives, a flurry of activity. She shows Cavaradossi the note of safe conduct, tells him he is free. She describes the bargain Scarpia had made, either she yields to him or Cavaradossi dies, the terrible decision, how Scarpia had then given the order for a simulated execution, fake bullets, how she extracted the free conduct pass. She is a religious woman, but she had taken a knife from the table, and when Scarpia came to claim the horrible embrace, she plunged the knife into his heart. "My hands were reeking in blood," she says.

I waited for Andreas. "Do you see it, do you smell it, the blood on your hands?"

Tali nods. Andreas turns back to Dan. "I'm thinking we might do this next aria a cappella, or accompanied by solo piano." He looks for Joel, in charge of the music: "What do you think?" Joel likes the idea.

Sid turns to me. "He's fantastic, this director friend of yours. Are you an item? He's just your type, serious, funny, a little lost in himself."

I do not want to answer. "And the soprano?" I say. "Isn't she yours?"

"You bet, but now that I'm married, I've given that up."

"Me too."

"There's a difference, Kyra, between alive and dead."

Andreas turned to us. "Please," he said. I felt like I was in high school, but Sid's words echoed through the afternoon. Was this something I would later regret, giving this up?

Andreas returned to the singers. He took Tali's hands and looked at Dan. "She has just said that her hands are reeking in blood. You realize that with these hands, she has killed Scarpia. Take her hands, touch them. What do you feel? Listen to the music. What do you hear?"

"It's just incredibly tender," Dan said. A shiver visibly ran through his body.

"*O dolci mani, mansuete e pure.*" Andreas held Tali's hands and sang the words, his voice soft, the phrasing supple. I watched her return his gaze, and then he dropped her hands. "Let's do it in Italian for now, those *m* sounds are gorgeous, it's what Puccini set. Once you put it into English—'Oh sweet hands, pure and gentle'—it sounds like a soap ad."

Sid had to leave. I walked out with him. The air was heavy with snow. "What a winter," I said. "It seems pretty good to me," he said, raising his eyebrows. He checked his watch and looked at the sky. "If I can get to the airport before it starts, there's a chance I will get to New York." There wasn't a cab in sight.

Was it Sid? His lingering tinge of regret? Or the tenor aria? Simon too had been shot just when he held his dream in his hands. Or was it Andreas, as he was that afternoon—the precision of his ear, his gentle humor, his total presence, and the generosity of his emotional response—that caused something in me to dislodge? Walking back into the church, I felt giddy. As if I were going into free fall, or giving myself over to the fall line, as you do in skiing. It's when you hold back that you get into trouble.

It wasn't that I didn't know that Andreas, like all conductors and directors, traveled. I also knew the meaning to him of his work. It was something we shared, a sense of total devotion, even mission you could say. I was prepared for what happened after I came back from Thailand. It's just that I wasn't prepared for what happened after that.

There was a month still before previews. The rehearsals had entered a new phase. I was to leave for Thailand right after the opening, to spend two months with the Akha. The tickets had been bought, but I had done nothing to get ready. Randy called to remind me about shots. For anthropologists, this was routine. I balked at the thought of introducing toxins into my body. The alternative was worse. He gave me the number of the travel clinic. I put off calling. I was reluctant to leave. Still, I couldn't pass up the opportunity to go with Randy, who spoke the Akha language, who knew the people. I wanted to see the Akha villages, to experience the fluidity of center and periphery, the permeability of the boundaries between inside and outside. It had seemed essential to my work.

"So you're really going?" Anna looked up from her book.

"I just can't pass it up, the chance to go there with Randy. I would always regret it if I didn't go." She gave me a skeptical look and returned to her book. It wasn't what she was really asking. She knew I knew this. I had avoided the question: Did I really want to go? The answer was yes and no.

The church fathers agreed to the idea of doing *Tosca* in the church. "The spirit of Vatican II lives," Andreas said. "If Constantine won't give the church back to the people, the people will take it back." It was his dream, to bring opera into the places where people live, to bring the stories into their lives so they would hear them, learn from them, instead of repeating these tragedies, instead of turning away from facing such intense feelings. It was why he was doing *Tosca* in English. He didn't want spectacle, he was suspicious of the word *awe*. He took off his sweater and tied the arms around his shoulders.

"What I want," I said, leaning toward him, "is to create spaces that will bring people into harmony with their inner rhythms, where the language of building is in scale with their lives."

We were sitting in an alcove of the church, patterns of colored light falling on the stone. I needed to talk about the sets. Sarah was helping me. She had found a large, beautiful Persian carpet that was perfect for Act Two. But Act Three was a challenge: how to turn the church into a castle. I had brought drawings. I leaned down, retrieved them from my bag, and handed them to Andreas, the church still, the windows turning black, the end of the day.

"What do you think?"

"Let's look," he said, getting up, taking the drawings to the front and spreading them on the floor. There was a section of casement wall, a battlement abstractly rendered, a ramp to convey elevation.

I stood beside him, our shadows falling over the paper. A priest came in, noticed us, nodded, retrieved a book from the altar table, and left.

"I'm thinking that the parapet will be on the audience's right," I said, taking a clasp from my bag. I gathered my hair away from my face. "The eye, reading from left to right, will fill in the continuation of the battlement. The ramp on the opposite side of the stage will pick up the diagonal line of the casement wall and extend the elevation." I sounded like someone giving a lecture. I removed the clasp.

What's a parapet? Tali had asked in rehearsal one day.

"I'll do a model, then you can see it before the sets move into construction. The height of the ramp should conceal the mattress or whatever it is Tosca lands on. I'd like your take on this before we move ahead."

He stood back, squinting to visualize the forms in three dimensions. He glanced at me, the expression on his face startled, then looked back at the drawings.

"I think it's brilliant." He folded his arms, leaned back, one foot out in front of him. "You are." He was staring ahead as if viewing the set itself. "I don't need a model. I love the abstraction of the wall. Menacing without being literal, or trivial. It conveys the ambiguity, will this execution be real or fake?"

He picked up the drawings and handed them to me with a look of what I might have called awe, had he not just said he was suspicious of the word.

"It's beautiful, Kyra."

We gathered our coats and started to leave. "The third act," Andreas said, "it always surprises me. For the first time in this so-enclosed opera, we are outdoors. We are reminded there is still nature, shepherds, the dawn. Suddenly we taste the possibility of freedom, a world beyond the rim of terror, but then the net closes in. And the music . . ." His eyes brightened, a flush on his face.

"Sing it," I said, "the aria about hands."

He sang, his voice fluid, the melody drifting through the hushed church. Running through me after we left.

In the week before previews began, there was an argument over a flag. The sets had been constructed, the window and the doors for Act Two. Sarah brought in the carpet, and the performers loved working on it, the Toscas in particular since it invited their aria about art and love. The proponents of the flag argued that we needed something to symbolize the presence of the state, especially now that we were performing in a church. I worried it would detract from the effect of the wall, reduce the monumental to the tawdry. It was the feeling of Rome I was after, not the literal sign. The cast was divided, Sarah was adamant, no. Andreas voted yes. We already have a crucifix, he said, to stand for the church. Peter said that was specified in Puccini's stage directions. Peter read from his score to make his point: "A crucifix hangs on one of the casement walls." I waited for Tali: "What's a casement?" she asked.

"What do you think?" Andreas turned to me, his face serious, his voice conveying new deference.

"As long as the crucifix and flag do not distract from the emotional statement, as long as they don't function like neon signs, here's the church, here's the state, get it?"

Andreas nodded. "We'll try it and see."

The musicians arrived, a small chamber orchestra seated around the performers, the pianist off to one side. On the Thursday before previews, the neighbors came, families with children, the homeless, the shopkeepers. Word had gotten out. The sparsely attended church was filled. They cheered, booed, wept, applauded at the end of every aria. The cast was buoyant.

Andreas was keeping his mind in tight focus. The atmosphere around him was tense. He wanted a tightening here, an adjustment there, his eye always on the dynamic, the relentless move forward of the drama. Usually the conductor directs this; here, he reminded the cast, everyone is responsible for the pace.

Anna came with me to the opening, or, as Andreas would say, the first of the three openings, the three casts performing on three nights in succession. Tali and Dan sang Tosca and Cavaradossi the first night, along with Steve, the Scarpia of their trio. Again the church was filled, but now it was largely the Cambridge crowd, heads buried in programs reading assiduously, waiting to be convinced. Boston was a music city. This wasn't the right way to do opera. We'll see, tight faces said. I turned to Anna. "Opening night is always tough," I said. I wanted her to like it, to see it at its best. Scattered through the audience, the critics sat in their carefully chosen seats. The danger was that their presence would draw the ear of the performers outward in an effort to glean the response, distracting them from the emotional pulse. I took off my coat. Andreas had worked hard to create an ensemble— would it hold? When I was concerned about last-minute changes in the sets, he reassured me. "Given the kind of work we have done, it doesn't pose any substantial problems." He had once changed an entire mise-en-scène at the last moment, the actors terrified that they wouldn't remember, but in fact there were no difficulties. He looked at me and smiled. I thought of Tali, what's a mise-en-scène? I picked up my program and saw my name listed. Set designer. I liked the sound.

The musicians took their places, the oboe gave the A, the instruments tuned, church lights went down, stage lights came up. With the three descending chords of the Scarpia theme, the performance was under way. I sat forward in my seat, my attention gripped. The singing was inspired, the movement at once stark and fluid, the sets worked, adding without distracting. Tension left my shoulders, my heartbeat slowed, and I gave myself over to the music and the story, as if I were hearing it for the first time.

Afterward, Anna said it was the first time she had liked opera. She found it mesmerizing, terrifying, too close to home. She liked the sets and the sexy young cast. The singing had been exquisite. Peter came over and gave me a hug. "See, our intuition was brilliant. I adore you." I was in a daze. I was used to working in isolation, long hours alone at the drawing table, followed by meetings with clients, contractors, zoning boards, stretches of time between conception and completion. This had had a dreamlike intensity.

The cast party took place on the third night, after all three casts had performed. The *Globe* critic wrote, "My one reservation about Mr. Verban's *Tosca* is that its lessons are destined to be misapplied for years to come." Andreas worked to keep the focus inward. In the short speech he made at the party, he quoted Peter Brook: "We are a small group of human beings. If our way of living and working is infused with a certain quality, this quality will be perceived by the audience, who will leave the theater subliminally colored by the working experience we have lived together. Perhaps that is the small contribution we can make, the only thing we have to convey to other human beings." In a drawing class once, the teacher had addressed us simply as "humans."

Before I left for Thailand, he took me out to dinner. "There's so much I want to say to you, so many things I have wanted to say through this time of working together," he said. His eyes found mine across the table. A shiver ran through my body. Breathe, I remembered, let the breath fall in. I placed my hand on the flat surface of table, my fingers splayed across the wood. The blue lapis in the ring Simon had given me absorbed the light. I looked toward the window. I didn't want to think about leaving. I told him that Sid had said that this theater experience might prove fruitful in ways I could not anticipate. It already had, I said. Solutions to problems about the sets had spurred ideas for other projects. Andreas's way of working was more center-oriented than bounded. No orchestra pit, no clear demarcation between musicians and singers, no raised podium, the impulse coming from the singers themselves, everything starting from and flowing back into a circle.

I looked at his face. He placed his hand over mine, fingers interlacing, a Braille conversation. Neither of us looked away.

When the plates were cleared and two small cups of espresso set before us, I said, "I'm so glad we did this."

Outside the restaurant, the street was quiet. I turned my collar up against the wind, tree branches swaying, patterning the sidewalk under the light. He didn't ask when I was coming back. Superstition maybe. Not to tempt fate. I didn't ask about his plans. Faith was unreliable. We both knew that. "Safe journey," he said, sadness in his eyes. Travel safely, God be with you. I didn't believe in God anymore, after Simon. "You have to live life," as Anna would say. To do otherwise made no sense. Let the dead bury the dead. That didn't make sense either. "It's been . . ." I said, and smiled, remembering, past now turning into present, the future indefinite. I held out my hand. He kissed it softly, three times, like a stone skipping across the water. "Come back soon."

I walked unsteadily to my car.

3

I GOT BACK FROM THAILAND IN LATE APRIL AND WENT DIRECTLY to Woods Hole. Anna was waiting at the dock, her face glowing. "You," she said. Joy rushed through me. We hugged, stood back, looked at each other, then hugged again. "I see it in your face," Anna said. "It must have been amazing." I said that it was, truly amazing, living in the Akha world. We climbed into the boat, the sea rocking. I had been on solid ground for two months, high in the mountains, in literally thin air. I breathed in the moisture, spray on my face, the taste of salt. Home.

Anna had roasted a chicken, charred onions on top. She made a green salad and we sat down to supper. "Tell me everything," she said, but with the twelve-hour time difference, it was morning now in Thailand, and I had in effect been up all night. She told me that the weather had been mild on the island, spring had come early, construction had started in sooner than planned. She said she had closed her therapy practice in Cambridge. I said that with me on leave, we'd be together on the island, in the way that we were when we first came. I felt her hesitation and wondered about Tony. I had been away for two months, and as the Akha would say, nothing stays put.

I woke at four the next morning, and at first light took my jacket and went to the site. The framers had come, the lines elegant, the fir beams gold in the early sun. I watched the color change with the light. I wanted Andreas to see it this way with me, light and airy, the open structures shaping vistas of sea and sky. It would never be this magical again. In Thailand, I had felt myself letting go of my memories, not thinking much about Simon. The thing with Andreas had receded. Now I wondered where he was.

The south side of the site was filling in so quickly, it might be ready for habitation by summer. Some of the enclosures, fluid in concept if not in contour, could expand and contract depending on the activities that people imagine for them. On the hill, the terracing was under way. Turf had been turned up, stone risers set. I imagined Grant, the head of the construction crew, smiling. This was his gift to me. I was thrilled, a little taken aback by how much they had done in my absence.

The sun was up, and suddenly I was hungry. The Akha would be eating their evening meal, rice in a bowl, steamed in the right way. I went back to the house, boiled an egg and made a fresh pot of tea. Anna was still sleeping. She had left a manila envelope addressed to me on the counter. It was my mail, forwarded by Hannah, the department assistant. The university world now had become remote. I shuffled through the envelopes and took the blue airmail letter along with my tea into the living room and settled onto the sofa. Morning light filled the room. I slit the flap.

Dearest Kyra,

I'm thinking of you, imagining you in Thailand, ringed by mountains, surrounded by gentle people. Has it been all that you hoped?

I'm in Barcelona for two months working with a small, experimental opera company on a contemporary opera that you would hate. I'll be back at the beginning of June, and then I'm hoping to stay. Jesse and Abe have settled in with Edith, and Peter has plans for a new season. We're thinking of doing Pelleas and Melisande.

I could go on, but there's an urgency to this letter. Peter, ever the impresario, and your pal Richard Livingston, who doesn't miss a chance to call attention to your project, have cooked up a plan. They want to bring Tosca *to Nashawena this summer (the Boston run sold out!).*

I told them that before I could say anything, I needed to know if this is something you want. I know you're on leave and protecting your time, and this may be the opposite of what you had in mind. Tell me what you think, but more to the point, Peter and Richard are like runaway trains. It's hard to stop them once under way. For me, the question is whether enough of the singers would be available. For us, it's a chance to work together again, and I would love that. But it's your island, your project, and if this doesn't work for you, we'll find something else to do.

I realize that you will have just gotten back and may want time to think it over. The whole idea may be impractical from your end, but for whatever reason, Richard thinks it's not. For the moment, I've managed to hold them back, but there is a need to act quickly now if you want to stop it. Peter knows you'll be back at the end of April. I told him to wait for you to call him.

Let me know if there's something you want me to do. I'm eager to hear about your trip. About this, it's really up to you, and I'll do whatever you wish. Till soon, A.

I had read about divers getting the bends when they come up too quickly, decompression overtaking them. This was the opposite, everything suddenly felt compressed. I had visions of boatloads of people landing on Nashawena, the sheep looking up in alarm. This image crowded out the prospect of Andreas being here for the summer.

Anna stood in the doorway in her silk bathrobe, a lightness to her presence, the silk falling gently, her morning face quizzical. "What's up?" she asked.

The Akha speak of *zang*, meaning their way of living, their way of doing things: how you honor your ancestors, how you boil eggs, how you take rice out of the steamer, how you speak to your father, how you don't have intercourse in another person's house. Randy was right. It had taken two months, but by the end I could feel it: the *Akhazang*. A different way of life. To these mountain people of Thailand, life was unbounded, inside and outside flowed into each other, like a street running through a building, but with them, there was even less demarcation between where one thing ended and another began. This was true with people as well. It was the hardest part to grasp. No self, no individual. Randy had told me a story that made my mind swirl. A woman had said that when she and her husband and children lived with his brother, they had raised pigs. But once they were living as only one person, she said, meaning herself and her husband and their children, they no longer raised pigs. What we call a family was to them one person.

I had always appreciated Randy's calm, his patience with students and with colleagues. I had liked his skepticism about the term *cross-cultural,* the bemused look on his face as to who was doing the crossing, and on whose terms. In Thailand, among these quiet mountain people, he had taken on an aura of grace. Like water finding its level. His private life had always been private. What I did experience with him was a remarkable perceptiveness and a kindness that seemed without limit. We had arrived after the rice harvest, during the dry season, which the Akha called the "people's season." The rainy season belonged to the spirits. He wanted me to see the village replacement ceremony that ushered in the claiming or clearing of new fields, the restoration or building of new homes, depending on whether the tribe was migrating or staying put, and the construction or restoration of the three gates that marked the entrance to the village. He helped me to struggle with the question of how you could have boundaries without having barriers. Think about encompassment, he said, the sense of being surrounded, protected rather than kept out or hemmed in. Everything is porous, he said, his face tanned by the sun. There is always a center in every house, every village, and yet the center can shift, just as there is a sense of being at once in motion and still. Like a dancer, I thought, beginning to grasp it not as a concept but in my body. My inner compass reset and I found myself walking more freely, speaking more slowly, feeling less guarded, more sure.

I handed Anna the letter. "Here, read this." She had settled on the sofa beside me, her feet tucked under her, her robe flowing over her knees. She picked up my tea and took a sip, her eyes scanning the lines on the page. She read it twice and then looked up, hesitant, I could see, to place her hand on the scale. "They might have asked you first," she said, "but then you were away." A far-off look in her eyes. I started to say something but then she said, "Why not give yourself a week. Wait until your body has landed."

I looked at the phone poised on the wall in the kitchen, as if ready to spring into action at any moment. I was grateful Andreas had told Peter to wait for my call.

Back at sea level now, on an island surrounded by water, the cells of my body registered the change. Walking on the beach one morning, my thoughts drifted to the Akha word *nyma*. It means "heart-mind," the center of the body to which the soul is connected. When the soul wanders off, the Akha have a ritual for calling it back. They believe that when one heart joins with another, in friendship or love, the souls also join.

Like with Simon, I thought.

I knew Anna saw a problem with this idea, but to me it made sense. Simon and I had been nested, like person and household, lined up with the cosmos. When that happens, the *nyma*, the heart-mind, is *jo sha*, meaning level, and then one is contented, at ease. It was important for people's heart-minds to be at ease rather than unsettled. In the village, discussions would continue until everyone's *nyma* was *jo sha*. If a child cried a lot or demanded too much of others or did what he or she was not supposed to do, their *nyma* was said to be too big. But a person with a large *nyma* would not be afraid of others, would not frighten quickly. Being a migratory people, the Akha always saw the potential for shift— what was too big in one place might be advantageous in another.

I tried to explain this to Anna. I assumed she would understand. She was shifting her life, but she was also distracted. Her mind was on oysters, she was working with Tony. I watched her carefully, wondering, as she would say, what's up.

The first time I saw Simon, he was wearing sandals, blond curls wreathing his face. I had transferred into the architecture program, abandoning biology with its endless classification. I had signed up for a seminar on the city. He had come in late, folded his body over the long table, and begun writing furiously in his notebook. Then he'd looked up with a wonder or curiosity so radiant that he looked like an angel. An annunciation had come into my life.

We fell in love quickly. For both of us, it was the first time. I had had boyfriends, crushes, some that lasted for months, one for over a year. But this was like the once in once upon a time. We felt no two people had ever experienced what we did—our souls, our bodies, were joined. There were the inevitable conflicts and tensions, but neither of us ever turned back. And now he was gone, and I . . . I was not going to turn back. I would move forward, but with him, as if he were still here, our heart-minds joined. Without him, I would be a half-soul.

Felicia called a few days after I got back. "Darling," she said, her Viennese accent recalling a world I had let go. "How was your trip?" She wasn't interested in hearing about the Akha. After the minimal politeness of a few questions, she could no longer contain herself. "I have news for you, actually two messages. My cousin, you know, your friend Andreas, is in Barcelona doing this fantastic new opera about Nixon, but he's coming back in June. The second, but perhaps someone has already told you." She didn't pause to find out. "Richard Livingston is bringing your *Tosca* to . . ."—she never could quite manage *Nashawena*—"to your island. This summer. He loved it. It's a marvelous way to let people know about your project."

I hadn't called Peter yet. I wasn't sure what I thought about *Tosca* on Nashawena. I was uneasy about Andreas coming.

"Richard might have asked me," I said.

"He was planning to," Felicia countered, "but he thought you'd be pleased. And as for my cousin, I know you like Andreas. Now you'll have him for the summer."

"*Tosca* is an indoor opera," I said. "I'm surprised Andreas is willing to do it outside."

"He said he would if the cast was willing. Like your city, it will be an experiment. He could not start now again with new singers. But he was waiting also to know what you thought."

There was silence on the line.

I thought of the island protecting new growth. It wasn't really the moment to draw attention to the project, nowhere near done. Still. The train had already left the station, it would take a boulder now to derail it. Richard would have raised the money, not hard after the rave reviews, and knowing him, he probably had contacted a ferry service about bringing people over for the performances. A vision of Glyndebourne, people in evening dress, picnics in wicker baskets. But this was New England, and as it turned out they came in summer dresses and shorts. Andreas's stipulation was met, two of the trios were available, and they adjusted the schedule accordingly. They would perform on Saturdays and Sundays, weather permitting.

"Come see me, sweetheart," Felicia said, closing the conversation. I resisted the order, wondering what Andreas thought I thought.

A knot formed in my stomach. They might have contacted me. There were ways, even in Thailand. I replaced the phone and steadied myself against the counter. I went to the sink and ran the water, staring at the pine outside the window, its branches studded with new yellow-green cones. I filled a glass, took a sip, and carried it across the room.

The tide was coming in, the marsh filling. There were the practical questions: would the buildings be ready to accommodate the performers, would the amphitheater be finished. There were other questions too. Where would he stay, would he be bringing his father and son? The problem with Felicia is . . . I stopped. Everyone means well, Anna would say. I took a long drink, the well water sweet, an aftertaste of iron. To the Akha, one's *zang* may be different from another's, but not better in the sense of truer. It's just a different type of *zang*. They have a phrase for this, Randy had told me one day when we were sitting outside the hut they had built for him, his arms freckled from the sun. "To each his own." I had said it sounded Western. He had looked at me skeptically. "In the West, you can't say *different* without saying *better* or *worse*. To the Akha, when one spirit priest chants with a different verse from another spirit priest, he is viewed as practicing a different type of *zang*, not a true or false version of it," he had said. I had said, "Come off it, Randy, I get it." Still, with Felicia, she assumed her way was right. It's the Viennese-*zang*, I told myself, wondering what else Andreas had said to her. I picked up the pillow with the Aramaic design. Speak to me, I said.

That evening, I called Peter and said it was okay with me. "I knew it would be," he said, which I found irritating. But construction was moving fast, I was busy with the project, there were decisions to be made each day, so I let it go. And now that I think about it, what it really boiled down to was the theater was ready and I wanted to see him.

Days of misty fog alternated with days of sun. The beach plums blossomed, and the Gulf Stream must have come nearer to the shore because by mid-June the water was warm. Anna and Tony were together much of the time, busy with their oyster hatchery, going over to the Vineyard to learn how to do it from the oyster farm on Tisbury Great Pond. In the evenings, they pored over books and catalogues. Tony would leave late, steering his boat back to the Vineyard across the Sound. I wondered why he didn't stay over, whether he had stayed over while I was away. Our household was beginning to encompass his lithe body, his restless energy, his eyes searching the sea. I shrouded myself in my leave, rearranged my room, and tried to give them space.

I had left a message on my office phone saying that I was away. I ignored the paper on Akha settlement structure I had promised to write for a journal on urban design. In the mornings, I would check in with construction and then head off with my watercolors, taking a sandwich and a thermos of tea. I was trying to capture the shifts in light and color. When it rained, I spent the days reading, curled up on my bed.

If someone asked what I was doing, I would say "not much," meaning nothing that registered on the Cambridge Richter scale. With her therapy practice closed, Anna was also off the chart. When I asked her what was happening with Tony, she shrugged me off. "I'll let you know when I know."

They came in mid-June, Andreas, the performers, the technical crew. I went to meet the boat at the dock. I had moved into the theater, his space, but he had invited me in. This wasn't my idea. That freed me from responsibility. Perhaps it was fate, whatever that meant, I told myself, as I watched Andreas climb onto the pier. Our eyes met, questioning, and suddenly we laughed. Here we were, but it was as if we had been moved by forces beyond our control.

Enough of the housing was ready, thanks to a great spurt at the end on the part of Grant and his crew. I had set aside one of the cottages for Andreas, with room for Jesse and Abe, who would be coming at the end of June. I was grateful for this time alone with Andreas.

It had been two months, we'd been in different parts of the world. There was a lot to talk about, including the plans for the summer. He said that he worried that this was an imposition, an intrusion on my leave. I said it was. I thought it was presumptuous on everyone's part. He didn't disagree. I felt him listening, his face attentive, waiting. I said I wanted to write about my experiences in Thailand while they were still fresh, before I lost the feel of it. The life there was so different from this life. I had thought I needed quiet, which was difficult at best with the ongoing construction. I worried about inviting the public into what was still a construction site. But the theater was at the far end of the site, away from where they were working, and the performances would only be on the weekends. Andreas's interest in what I had experienced might spur me to actually do the writing. As for my leave, it had been extended. A faculty grant I had applied for came through. My chairman was pleased, and thanks to his flexibility I wouldn't be teaching again until February. By the end of the conversation, I felt we had aired everything and moved on.

Rehearsals began, the design questions were minimal. There was no church, no walls, only trees and a stage with several levels. We were back to the challenge of creating an intimacy between performers and audience, now outdoors. The darkness will do it, Andreas said. But darkness came late in June.

"Let's go and sit in the space," I said.

We went at night to get the feel of how it would be and so Andreas could check the acoustics in the night air.

It was the last week of June, just after the solstice. I don't know if it was the light or the feel of summer in the air, or whether the *Akhazang* was still with me, but all the spaces felt new—as if a wind or a tide had swept through. With the Akha, there was no word for *forever*.

Patches of clover dotted the grass, white against the green.

It was hard to sort out my feelings; everything was changing, the earth was shifting, swelling into summer, and my body—I had been living at such a high altitude. Now I felt the sea—my body pulsing with its rhythms.

We were sitting on one of the risers that had been sunk into the ground, stone holding the earth that rose now in steps from the performance space up the side of the hill. The top buttons of his shirt were open, the arms of his sweater tied around his shoulders in a knot. I watched the knot rise and fall with his breathing.

It was not that anything special happened that night. We talked about the opera, checked out the acoustics, he told me what had happened in Boston, the performances growing through the run. The success had made him edgy. He wanted to go further, strip the performance down more. I thought he was totally absorbed by his work, but then he turned to me and said, "I've missed you."

And it was different. At that moment. I mean, it didn't sound different from other things we had said to each other. Working together, we had become friends. The first time I brought him to Nashawena, when we threw stones into the sea, I thought he was a playful man. That night at the Harvest when he told me about his life, I thought he was courageous, as one thinks of people who have lived through great suffering. But there was also a gentleness to him. He was used to picking up subtle shifts in emotion. It's what made him such a good director. I had seen it in his work with actors, and also with me.

"What?" he said, the trees slowly absorbing the light.

I had been thinking about the look of solemnity on Simon's face the night he was shot. There was something else, something I had forgotten. Anton's betrayal had been so shocking that I had blocked it out. But now it came back. As they were taking him outside, Simon had turned to me. The expression on his face was one of pure love. "Kyra, go," he had said. "Leave Cyprus. Do that for me. Go." And it occurred to me that maybe what he meant was that he wanted me to live.

The thought startled me. My body righted itself.

His knees rose up like pillars. Evening stars dotted the sky. He wasn't directing. He didn't say anything. He picked up a twig and turned it slowly.

I didn't want to say anything about it, at least not yet. It was too new a thought, that Simon had wanted me to live.

I turned to Andreas.

"I know about betrayal," I said quietly.

"Then we both know," he said, "to be careful."

Which is exactly what we didn't do.

———

That night I couldn't sleep. I thought of cathedrals, walls like a thin skin, filtering light, letting it in. I turned on the sheets, the count of stitches, the weaving together of threads. There was something different about this man—a kind of freedom, a latitude I had never felt before in my life. I turned my head on the pillow and willed myself to sleep.

. . .

In the first light of morning, I went into Anna's room. I used to do this when we were children, climb into bed with her, my older sister.

"I'm scared," I said.

"Of what?" She turned, half asleep.

"I don't know."

Now it seems prophetic. Because I really didn't know.

I'm trying to go back to how it was then, climb into that walled garden, that summer. Because I didn't see over the wall.

We found a clearing at the top of the woods, the ground flat, the bay on one side, the sea on the other, a grassy spot between ledges of rock. We spread a blanket and took off our clothes, laying them on the hot rock. The woods smelled of wild gardenias—a startling smell. Like nakedness is startling, the first time. We were seeing in the way that painters see, washing our eyes. We had undressed each other, unhooking, unzipping, watching, waiting for the flinch of retraction—but I thought, but I wanted, but you promised—and finding—no—flesh—yes—and beauty, yes, and that gesture, the readiness, the nakedness, and yes, the knowledge that now we could wound each other. Would this become another story about wounds, exposed now to the sun, healing over, scar tissue, to remove the scab, break the bone again, the surgeon skilled, tight-lipped, determined this time to set it right.

"Lie down," he said to me, with a gentleness that is just now unbearable. "Lie still. Wait. Let it happen."

And I did.

Maybe it was the smell of wild gardenias that led us to forget what we both knew, about wounds. Or maybe it was the discovery that there is such a thing as a wild gardenia—

He ran his finger along my body, touching first my shoulder and then following the line down along the round of my breast, across my belly, through the valley of my groin to the length of my thigh and leg.

"Breathe," he said. I was holding my breath and then the smell of the gardenias came into me.

"You are so beautiful," he said, looking into my eyes.

I did not see the shadow, the wingspread blocking the sun. The air was thick with summer. I couldn't see.

When he said "now," it was like the flowers—wild, delicate, startling.

Afterward we swam on the ocean side. The wind that day came from the southwest, bringing miles of blue sky: summer blue, fair blue, angelic blue, the bluest blue, and the water blue-green, tinged with gold.

On the way back, we picked huckleberries, our teeth turning red-blue from the stain, and when we got back, we talked about that—the huckleberries.

I had done what I had vowed never to do. I had opened myself to another man. And it was a mistake.

Anna didn't think so, not that first morning when we talked, not through that whole sensuous summer. If you can accept that something as cultivated as gardenias can grow fresh in the wild, without brown edges or a sickening smell, then this too could happen. I didn't think it was a mistake at the time.

One night after a performance, we made up a game called change the ending. You choose a story and then find a point where some-one can do something to turn the action in a different direction. Andreas went first. He chose *Tosca*. "What if Spoletta, Scarpia's agent, is a member of the resistance, a mole who has tunneled his way into the highest echelons of the police, to Scarpia. Then, when Scarpia writes the order for the mock execution, telling Spoletta it would be as they had done once before, with Count Palmieri, Spo-letta recognizes the name, Palmieri, and knows that the count had really been shot. Before giving the order to the sergeant, Spoletta erases Palmieri's name. When Scarpia asked Spoletta, do you understand, meaning the part about Palmieri, he understood completely. But this time the execution really will be fake. Spoletta subverts Scarpia's intention. Cavaradossi lives and Spoletta leaves with the lovers. It's a victory for art and love, and for the resistance.

"Your turn," he said, delight in his face. The game at once lighthearted and serious.

I didn't know any opera other than *Tosca*. My mind went blank. And then I remembered the line Andreas had recited here that first day, from the Player's speech in *Hamlet*. I would choose Ophelia, not the mad scene but before that, when she and Hamlet are together and her father and Claudius are spying on them. I had played Ophelia once in school and I remembered the lie. What if she told the truth when Hamlet asks her, "Where is your father?" What if instead of lying and saying, "He is at home," she points to the curtain Polonius and Claudius are hiding behind and says, "Right there." Then she and Hamlet would leave and go to Wittenberg together.

"Bravo," he said. "You see, there is always a way."

In the mornings, when I walked the beach, he would often be there with Jesse. There was a stream that cut through the sand, and at the beginning of summer it was full, water rushing through. Jesse loved it. He built elaborate waterways, moats and canals lined with strips of kelp. I showed him how to make drip castles and decorate the walls with seaweed and shells. One morning he found a shark's tooth and we made up a story about a shark. It was a nurse shark, and he attended the people whom the other sharks had wounded, even though he hated the taste of blood. "That's not real," Jesse said, his eyes scanning our faces. "No," Andreas said, "but it's a good story."

"Tell me about your mother," Andreas asked one day. I had been working all morning, trying to speed up the construction crew. It was very hot. They broke early for lunch and went off to swim.

"My mother was part Gypsy, or at least that's what she liked to think, because she never really fit into Viennese society. One time when she was young and in Rome, the Gypsies stopped her. They wanted her to come with them, they said she was one of them. She didn't go. But she told her mother what had happened and asked if it was possible. Her mother, who was always honest—she wouldn't necessarily tell you things, but if you asked her, she always told the truth—said it could be true. My mother had been a wild child. She had dark hair, green eyes, and olive skin. Which was odd because most of her family was blond."

"Like you," he said. "But you're also wild."

"Maybe it's Gypsy blood. I like to think of myself as something of a wildflower, like my mother. Later her mother told her that she'd been adopted. My mother hadn't thought to ask."

Anna was making lunch.

"You know, the thing is I feel a freedom with him I've never felt with a man before," I said.

She put the knife on the counter and turned to face me.

"In what way?" She wiped her hands on the dish towel and sat down.

"You know, it's odd, but I thought Simon saw me. What I realize now is that he was with me, we were with each other. But that's different. It's not my sense with Andreas. I'm thinking of that day in the church when I had brought in drawings for the Act Three sets and he looked at them and then looked at me, with an expression on his face that I can only describe as awe. As if up to that point he had thought I could be helpful, but in that moment he saw me as an artist. I mean, I know this sounds pretentious, but I don't know how else to say it. He saw me as myself. And now . . ." I looked out the window. I wasn't sure I could talk about it. How I felt seen by him when we made love. As a woman, but then that sounds like a cliché.

"I think you need to listen to this," Anna said.

My back arched. I didn't need her to tell me what I needed to do.

"I mean the vow," she continued, "it was a tribute to what you had experienced together, you and Simon, but the vision of this city, I would have to say, is yours."

Something in me balked. But it was true. It was like a kind of psychological suttee. Throwing myself on the fire. Suddenly the light seemed too bright.

Our mother used to say, Listen to your feelings. Feelings don't lie. I thought it was true, but too simple.

When I sat on Anna's bed that first morning after Andreas and I had made love, I said falling in love again was like a fire on the beach. You think it's been extinguished, and then you discover it's burning again. Except now it seemed like starting something new.

"Maybe it is," she said, a faraway look in her eyes.

Anna and I had debated living with men versus not living with men. Anna thought that for men, sex was a stand-in for emotional closeness. With Tony, her question was, could they be more intimate if they didn't have sex? I said the question was absurd. Like tying your hands behind your back. Sex was the road to intimacy with men. Anna was skeptical. I had watched her with her boyfriends. I always felt something was missing, something I wanted with a man. More intense, more complete. She called me a romantic. I didn't think that was true.

Anna loved playing with Jesse. When he was annoying, it didn't faze her. She taught him seven-card rummy and casino, bought books of riddles, told knock-knock jokes. She would spend long evenings with Abe, bringing a bottle of red wine and sitting for hours playing cards and listening to his stories. "I'm a simple man," he told her, "a butter-and-egg man." That had literally been his business. His wife? He said he had gone to Olympus and

brought back a goddess. That had confirmed one of Anna's theo-
ries: men idolize the women they love, they don't see them as
human. It spells disaster, she said, because sooner or later they
discover they are human. You should have been an academic, I
told her. She said it was a fleshless occupation. She preferred to do
therapy, dig at the site. But that too was artificial. In many ways,
we were looking for the same thing. Something real that we could
believe in.

It was an amazing summer. As if from some other time. Scientists
were talking about global warming, the hole in the ozone layer.
The previous year, in August, suds had appeared in the water of the
bay, as if the washing machines of the world were draining into the
sea. Tiny jellyfish, like tapioca seeds, floated amid the bubbles, and
when you swam you got stung. Everyone went out and bought
Adolph's meat tenderizer, even the vegetarians. You sprinkled it on
and it took away the sting. But this year the water was clear. No
suds, no jellyfish. August brought a string of hot days. We made
love in the clearing after we swam, our bodies still cool from the
water, and afterward we swam again. It was as if the earth had
healed, like they say the ozone layer can repair itself.

By the end of July, our life had taken on a rhythm. In the early
mornings, we went to the beach with Jesse. "Kyra," Jesse asked
one morning looking straight into my face, "are you going to
come and live with us?" His eyes were wide. He wanted a mother.
Or maybe he just wanted me. I said that wherever I lived, we always could play. I thought it was true. Andreas didn't say anything. He was experimenting with new projects, what to do next.
He and Peter had various plans for the future. Andreas had
brought me into Jesse's life. I was sure he wouldn't have done this
without thinking. Jesse had lost his mother; it would be cruel for
him to get close to another woman and then have her disappear.

When we dropped Jesse off at the small playgroup that had
been formed for the summer, Andreas went home to study scores
and I went over to the site. At noon, we swam. Cormorants sat on

the rocks in groups of four or five, like a committee. Some of the tech crew were spearfishing, and the birds watched them with consternation. The days were still long, it seemed that the summer would go on forever. At low tide, you could see through the water, green where it was shallow, then shades of blue.

In the afternoon, Andreas worked with his troupe. Often I sat in and watched. On the weekends, after performances, we would go to the theater and improvise plays, using bits of costume, dressing each other for the parts. I gave him a purple robe, he gave me a crown. He had come into my kingdom, joined my project. Together, we would find a way. A path had opened in front of us and we had taken it. It was a summer of hope.

At the beginning of August, he had to leave for a few days, and then there was a week when I was away. Other than that, we were together. At night, the crickets were loud. We slept in his cabin, our lovemaking extended, our bodies stretched out on the sheets. We talked about the future.

I don't know what else to say, except to tell you how it happened.

In French the word for tide is *marée*. Yet the French speak simply of the sea. *La mer monte* and *la mer descend:* the sea rises, and the sea falls. Our bodies are like the sea, our cells bathed in salt water. And maybe the French are right. You don't have to talk about gravity or the moon, but just about the sea, the way it comes in and then goes out.

He left.

And then I really didn't know. What was real. What I had made up. Like we made up those stories. What had happened, what I had only imagined had happened, or wanted to happen? Anna tried to help. She did her best. I feel badly about what I did to her, about not telling her. But I couldn't. I just couldn't. I could hardly tell myself. I feel worse about having involved her in the way that I did, without her knowing what she was doing. But then in a way I didn't know either, until the last moment, what I would do. I don't know what I thought.

It was Peter who told me that Andreas was leaving, that he had an offer he couldn't turn down. In Europe. I didn't know what to think. What was I supposed to do? Say fine, that's great, I'm really happy for you? What?

Peter said that Andreas was going back to Budapest to start his own troupe.

I should have listened to those operas. The ones he liked all ended badly. I was mesmerized by the stories and the music, or maybe by him. But I didn't listen. Maybe I believed we could improvise and find a way out.

In the end, a fight. We were standing under a pine tree, the cones stubby, naked, looking strangely exposed in the first light. I had gone for a walk, come out near his cabin. He was standing in the middle of the clearing, alone.

He turned when he heard me.

"I was thinking about *Pelleas and Melisande*," he said. "It would be perfect here. It's set in a forest."

"I hear that you're leaving," I said. "Peter said."

His lips turned white. "It's not certain yet."

"Why didn't you tell me? Did you think I wouldn't know?"

It was as though he were another person. He didn't answer. Mute. He saw the anger in my face.

I walked off, got on a boat, went to the Vineyard with Tony to get some seedlings. I didn't know what I was doing.

Andreas came over that night. Anna was out. He said he wanted to talk. He said he had not known how to tell me. He said he wanted to explain what had happened.

I looked at his face. He did not look like himself. He started to speak, his story sounded convincing. If I listened to it, I would lose myself. Something else was true. What he was saying did not make sense.

Outside the night was cold. Venus, bright in the western sky, beckoned through the window. Suddenly the house felt crowded. "What are the plans?" I asked. I sounded like my father. That was always his question.

I took my jacket and went outside.

He followed.

"I couldn't tell you," he said. "I knew you'd be upset. I don't want to go. I want you to know that. I have to do this. I told you that Irina and I had started a company, but they shut it down. She joined the dissidents because she wanted me to have a company, be able to do my own work. You know that having my own company is something I've always dreamed of." He stubbed his foot against the dry soil, loosening a clod.

How could you not tell me?

How could I tell you?

Did you think I wouldn't know?

Something was wrong. The rhythm between us had stopped. Fear pooled inside me. I tried to start again, find the beat—shock it into motion, like they shock hearts.

I was furious. That much was clear.

"I had hoped . . ." he began. "I had hoped that you would— that knowing me and knowing also what has been between us, you would—"

"I would what?"

I knew this was not the way. I could not stop. A river of anger rose, crested, spilled over the barriers.

"I am trying," he said. "I'm trying to talk with you. I didn't know that Peter was going to say something. I wanted to tell you myself. It was something I thought you would understand. But it is fruitless when you . . ."

Without fruit.

We came to where there was a flat rock on one side of the path. He sat down. "There is no point in continuing this way," he said.

"Do you want to destroy everything? What do you want me to do? Give up my dream? I wouldn't ask you to do that. I would understand."

"That's not the point," I said. But what was the point? It suddenly seemed hopeless.

"What do you want?" he asked, exasperation edging the question.

I felt I was being led into a trap. What do I want? What does it matter what I want? My heart was racing. There was nothing for me to say, nothing more to say. I thought of Cordelia, Lear's daughter. When Lear asks her to say how much she loves him, she says nothing.

"Nothing," I said.

He said nothing.

I felt the ground shift under me. Frantically, I grasped at logic. "Because if . . . if I . . . if this means anything to you—"

"You know how much you mean to me," he interrupted.

But he didn't mean it anymore. He didn't sound like he meant it anymore. The rhythm was off. This was only making it worse. He was leaving. He hadn't told me. He didn't want to tell me. Because I would be upset? Is that a reason?

"You act like a stranger," I said. Once he had been a stranger. But then he had become something else, something intimate, my lover, more like a husband, joining me in that space we had made for ourselves at the top of the clearing where the wild gardenias grew, small delicate flowers, white skin, so thin you could see through it, and the faint pink at the throat. What do they call that part of the flower where the pistil and the stamen are? Lie with me, he had said, arms and legs entwining, until our bodies . . . I would not lie.

"If you are going to leave, then leave." Abruptly I turned away, heading back to the house.

———

There is a day in August when you know that summer is over. It happens each year. The water turns dark, loses transparency. The currents have shifted, the wind has changed direction. The fall term would begin soon. If I could take myself back into that life, that structure, that order. I had been interrupted, lost my boundaries. *Interrea,* in the middle of things, he had come. And now he was leaving. Where there had been a whole, now there was a hole. The opposite of dependence was independence. This was the new world.

Anna had gone over to play cards with Abe. She said that when Andreas came in, he stomped into his room. They had asked, he had said he had to read Maeterlinck's play. It was the story of Pelleas and Melisande, the basis for Debussy's opera. When I heard this, I was astounded. I don't know where he found the concentration, but maybe leaving me didn't really matter to him.

I had been with Andreas when he found the book of Maeterlinck's plays in the stacks of Widener Library, the air cool, dusty, quiet on that hot August day. He had come into Cambridge to meet me. It was the end of the week when I was away. I had sent him a postcard, "I am alive and well and living in C major." The postcard had a picture of a boat with white sails. I remembered the game about changing the ending and signed it, "love, Iseult." He came the next day.

That night it had been so hot. We sat in my apartment reading the play. He was planning to stay in Boston. They would do *Pelleas and Melisande* at Peter's theater that winter and bring it to Nashawena next summer. He and Peter were planning a cycle of operas. He wanted to do a read-through with the singers before they left the island. The lamp drew a yellow circle of light around him. He read aloud, turning the pages.

Golaud, the widowed grandson of the old King Arkel, is hunting in a forest when he comes upon Melisande, weeping over the loss of a crown that has fallen to the bottom of a well. He brings her back to the gloomy castle, and she becomes his wife. But she is much younger than Golaud, the age of Pelleas, his half brother who also lives in the castle. Pelleas and Melisande are drawn to each other. One day they are sitting at the edge of a fountain. She is playing with her wedding ring and it falls into the water. When

Golaud asks her where the ring is, she lies. He becomes suspicious, observing her with Pelleas, seeing their childish play. He lifts his young son Yniold up to Melisande's window to spy on them, but Yniold tells him they are standing apart in the room, silent, gazing at the light. Then one night Golaud comes upon them clinging to each other by the fountain. He takes out his sword and kills Pelleas. Melisande is terrified and runs away.

Andreas looked up. He had come to the part about the question, the part he had been waiting for. In the final act, Melisande is dying in childbirth. Golaud besieges her, he has to know about Pelleas: was theirs a guilty love? Leave her alone, the blind old king, Arkel, says. Leave her alone, she is dying.

Tears ran down Andreas's face as he read. And then he stood up and closed the book.

Anna said that on the night of the fight, when she was sitting with Abe at the kitchen table, Andreas suddenly stormed back into the room and picked up the phone. He was calling British Airways to make his reservation. She tried to say something, but he cut her off. "It's better if you stay out of this," he said.

Later, Anna and I picked over the entrails, the endless argument, the tired explanations. What was the name for what he had done? We went over and over the metaphysics of relationship, but underneath all the words, all the names, there was a sickening feeling that in the end it didn't matter, because the physics, the reality, was clear. He had left. He hadn't told me first, himself.

"He's in love with you," Anna said.

I didn't believe it. I wanted to believe it. Maybe it was true, because, after all, he had to go, it was like keeping a promise, he had said. That wasn't the point. He said that he had tried to tell me, there was no realistic alternative on the horizon. Peter had not been able to raise the money, the plans for Boston had fallen through. Words, it was just words.

Anna and I were walking down Mass. Avenue. Nashawena had become unbearable, and I thought it would help to leave for a few days. Now I had to go back. The builders had questions. They were waiting for me to return.

Without speaking, we headed for Au Bon Pain, a place both of us hated. But at least we could sit. The conversation was dizzying. "Come," Anna said, her face creased in concern, "let's sit here. What do you want to have?"

"What are you going to have?" I asked, distracted before I even finished saying the words. What do you want, what do you want to have, what do you think, how are you feeling? I felt numb. That was a solution: I would become numb. I had read that people in shock often go numb. I would will myself to have no feelings. Put them away, in cold storage. I shivered.

Anna returned carrying a red tray with two cups and two croissants. Orange juice and spinach and feta?

She waited. "That's fine," I said. "Thank you. That's really fine."

"Do you understand what I am saying?"

I wasn't sure.

"I don't think he has left you, he has just left. I think his feelings for you are real."

Real, reel, reeling. I was reeling. Here, with you. But not. The hard knot of reality. Not here. Literal-minded. I worked with concrete, with the concrete. It was my nature. That's why I'm an architect. We had lived together as husband and wife. I thought that meant. But then he said. Was he a guest, short stay-over, small romance, bittersweet, orange berries in the fall. The fall, after the fall is the winter. Traitor. That sharpened things, brought them into focus. I picked up the croissant and took a bite. It was slightly overdone. The ends where they circled around were charred. I decided not to care. A beginning. I bit through to the spinach and feta. It was hot. And surprisingly good.

4

I STAYED ON NASHAWENA WITH ANNA, THE ISLAND QUIET IN LATE fall. Greens and blues had given way to browns and reds. I discovered a bog of cranberries on the far side of the marsh. Construction was winding down. The first phase of the project was completed. The structure of the weave was becoming clear, warp and weft accommodating a range of surfaces and functions, open spaces and enclosed. The enclosures on the south side had a lived-in look, a warmth enhanced by the low, horizontal sun. The second phase would start in the spring. Some of the infrastructure was already in. Practical problems beckoned. For the island settlement to inspire a different way of inhabiting spaces, this was only the beginning. The permeable boundaries, the mesh of materials, and the porosity of sight and light and space, were designed to encourage an interweaving of activities, changing conventions of public and private, art and industry, shifting categories as well as boundaries. Some artists had come at the end of the summer. The fishing community would be moving in. The experiment was under way.

The letter came in late September. At the end, Andreas had said he would write. Emmanuel Santos brought the mail from the post office in Cuttyhunk, and he must have noticed the long white envelope with Hungarian stamps, because he hovered after handing me the assortment of letters and bills. "Is everything okay?" he asked. He was the caretaker, a person who takes care.

I took the thin envelope to my room and closed the door. I stood for a moment, my pulse speeding up, a feeling of trepidation. What would he say? I settled myself on my bed, bracing myself with the pillows. A single sheet of paper, typewritten on both sides. Breathe, I told myself, but in the end it didn't help.

Kyra, kyra, kyra, kyra,

I never knew before how much your name is music until I have been saying it over and over all through this time, and it means opening, the beginning of the mass: Lord have mercy. Which is what I would ask for if I could still believe in a merciful God.

It has been almost an hour since the first paragraph. I have been sitting here listening to Brahms, the sextet you liked, seeing your face, looking at the things in the apartment which are touched with you, the books you read, music we listened to, seeing you not just here but everywhere, your laughing face turning suddenly to me while we're walking along the beach, the back of your head on the boat, your hair catching the sunlight, the particular grace of your step hurrying down the path to meet me. Yes, well . . .

I have found this last month how strongly true it is that a drifting relationship between us is impossible. We have both said it countless times, and it is inescapably true. I am not even remotely tempted toward it. All my fantasies and considerations and concerns are centered around the question of a marriage. And in my current state, marriage seems very distant and unreal.

In one of the awful conversations, I said something about parting from each other and the possibility of a re-meeting, and you said there can be no re-meeting, that we have a relationship and that we will always meet in the context of it. I'm not saying any of this well but please allow for frenzy and piece out my imperfections in your mind. I have been trying to think about that and what I meant. I think what I meant was the possibility of meeting in the context of the same relationship but in the context of a new order in my head. I am saying all this incomprehensibly. I would tear it up and start again but it would be the same.

Let me say what has to be said: I don't know in what context I could see you. The drifting is impossible. I am past the point where I can accept your love on any terms other than permanently, and I am not at the point where I can accept it permanently. I must work out of this alone and in full recognition of the possibility that I may never succeed. It seems necessary to me that we not see each other. I believe that you must structure your world without me.

I love you in more ways than I knew existed. I want your world to be full of beauty and joy. I love you with a terrible hunger, and tonight the world seems altogether unbearable. I don't know how else to say it, Kyra, my darling, my beautiful darling love. a

It made no sense: I love you, we cannot see each other. I read it over and over again. Still it made no sense. I love you with a terrible hunger, you must structure your world without me. A wave of vertigo, the world upended. I lost my bearings. I tore the letter into pieces, but by then I knew it by heart.

I stayed away from Felicia and Peter. I think they stayed away from me. When my period came in October, the stain of blood seemed irrevocable. It's over. Finished. Simon's spirit returned. I wrote the paper for the journal, did the reading lists for my spring courses.

The young fishermen from New Bedford had formed a collective. They were developing a more ecologically sustainable relationship with the sea. Richard Livingston had met with them to discuss the move to Nashawena and becoming part of the new city. He would finance the move, help find support for their fishing project. There were practical issues to consider in relocating their families, but they were young and idealistic and willing to try. Plus the support was not inconsequential.

We wanted a mix of commerce and artists in the town, and given the island setting, the fishing industry was ideal. The Wampanoags had planned to build a scallop factory on the Vineyard but had run into opposition there. I was urging them now to consider Nashawena. For the artists there was studio space and quiet. A Montessori teacher, an idealist with exquisite materials, came with the intention of setting up a school. Integrating the caretakers, the Santos family, was eased by the fact that the fishermen were all at least part Portuguese. Emmanuel and Grace donated kale from their garden, and kale soup, along with Portuguese sweet bread, became a staple of our Sunday night meetings, with discussions continuing until everyone's heart-mind was at ease.

Grant, the head of the building crew, had been in the navy. He had learned to shift his weight with the roll, and I sought out his company. His daily rhythms and attentiveness to detail steadied me. "Let's go over to Cuttyhunk to eat," he said one day, picking up my need for distraction. "How about we get lunch at Mandy's down by the pier?" It was the only restaurant open at this time of year, but Mandy was a great cook. We took Grant's boat across the channel, his blind black Lab riding with us. He never asked about Andreas, I didn't say anything. But it was obvious that he knew.

I thought I had found my sea legs. But then on the Sunday after Thanksgiving, it snowed during the night. I realized that I had to leave.

I took the small ferry over from Naushon the next morning, leaving our boat there and picking up the car that we kept in Woods Hole. The gray strip of road led my eye to the vanishing point. Had Columbus wanted to sail over the edge? Had he imagined the moment of falling, ships tumbling, sails billowing, he and his crew sinking slowly into an abyss? White fields bordered the gray, wet road. Black-brown trees monitored my path. At school, the monitors' faces were solemn. Keeping other children in line, they had become old before their time. I swerved to avoid a dead skunk lying in the middle of the road, its stark black and white startling against the white-grays of snow and sky. I breathed in and let the breath out slowly, reciting to myself the things of this world. Road, skunk, trees, morning. The car smelled of wet wool. It was Monday.

I had left a note for Anna: "I'm going to Cambridge for a faculty meeting." It sounded innocuous but I knew it would worry her. Why? What faculty meeting? Aren't you on leave? The university prized money and distinction. My design studio had been bracketed for the fall. It would be offered instead in the spring. Still, I was needed. The department assistant had called to say that the chairman was hoping I could come for this particular meeting. The academic dean would be attending. It was important, she said, drawing out the word.

I drove across the Bourne Bridge, passing the sign of the Samaritans offering help to souls tempted by a watery death. The canal sliced through the land. See what men can do. The snow deepened on the other side of the bridge, and the woods became denser, inviting. The road kept receding and reappearing. If I drove straight on, I would arrive in time to get coffee. The meeting would be an oasis of boredom.

———

Ian sat at the head of the table. He was chair of the urban design department, a ceremonial position that suited his sense of formality. Like a tribal chieftain, he kept a distance, measured in inches as if he had swallowed a ruler. If you stepped one inch too close, he would move back. I tried it, fascinated by his precision.

Once he had told me a story about the Yoruba. We had been in the midst of a departmental crisis at the time, having hired someone whom no one could stand, who had been chosen to keep someone else out, who had slithered in past all procedures. He had promised to give, but instead he took: money, everyone's patience and time. We had been crossing our fingers, hoping Northwestern would choose this man as dean. Recommendations were written, praising him highly. Phone calls were returned. We held our breath. Ian had said that when the Yoruba want to get rid of their king, they bring him a bowl of parrot eggs. Once the king receives the gift of the parrot eggs, he knows he is dead.

The meeting was under way when I arrived. A streak of color in the room because Nancy had come, wearing a red suit. She was the new academic dean, responsible for overseeing the curriculum. She was known for her efforts to enhance the work of the faculty with an eye to improving the quality of instruction. When I entered, everyone looked up. Ian caught my eye, signaling welcome. I sat down to his right, in the empty chair. He moved over an inch.

Doug was presenting the new curriculum, his red hair framing his fish-white face. He had taken the lead in designing the department's new program. He was going to be the next chair. Erik sat next to Doug, Craig at the corner. The infield was ready. No one was out. Yet.

I turned to Nancy. Did she want to play? The room reeked of tedium. Doug droned on.

The new curriculum did not sound new. This was going nowhere. I caught Nancy's eye.

She glanced back, her short dark hair elegantly cut. I pushed my hair away from my face. Maybe it was time to cut my hair. Widow in mourning. I brushed away the thought.

"Just a minute," Nancy said. "I thought you guys had gotten the grant from our difficult donor by promising to integrate culture in an integral way." Clumsy, but to the point.

"Before beginning a new program, we have to figure out first how we will evaluate it," Craig said. He was the doyen of research, a master of statistics. Evaluation his game. Evaluate what?

I looked at him. Two could play.

"I realize I've been away, but I don't understand what you've said. I agree with Nancy. This doesn't seem new." My voice was guarded, steady, one word after another leading me into the discussion. Ariadne entering the maze.

Ian was dozing, the dormouse at the tea party. In the face of conflict, he could be counted on to fall asleep.

"I'm serious, you guys," Nancy said, her red suit asserting her deanship. "The entire faculty voted on the revision. There was a consensus that we needed to broaden our offerings. I was counting on you to take the lead." She scanned the room. It was like school. It was school. Everyone looked down. "You have the strength here to do it," she continued, meaning all of us. I looked around, unconvinced.

I brushed a white speck off the sleeve of my black sweater.

"With the experience you have in cross-cultural design," she said, looking at me, "you can lead the way in including the architecture of non-Western peoples as more than a slide show." She meant sideshow, but had held back from implying that this was a circus. To call other cultures non-Western was problematic enough. It was like calling Christians non-Jews.

Craig looked amused. A little action in the middle of the morning. A psychologist friend had made the observation that meetings were the academic equivalent of social life.

Ian sank further into his chair, his head folded over his gray sweater. Doug looked at Nancy through unblinking eyes.

I decided to become her ally. The girls against the boys. "It seems to me that we are only reinforcing a series of hegemonic assumptions," I said, using the jargon, the word *hegemonic* having become a four-syllable way of saying *bad*. They stared at me.

"I thought we had agreed," Doug cleared his throat, "on the outlines of what seems to me an exciting new plan." He was putting himself on the line. "We'll begin with basic design and then add courses on the history of the city with examples illustrating how different cultures have approached the idea of the city or designed their villages, like you have done, Kyra, with the Akha." He looked pleased.

It sounded good. It's just that it wasn't true. What he meant was that I would teach a seminar on the Akha, and they would include a week at the end of the term on "different" cultures. It was like having the one woman in a department teach a course on women and changing *man* to *human* in the rest. The city, which was after all our subject, was itself part of Western culture.

As children, we had played a game: rock, paper, scissors. This was a variation: hut, village, city.

Ian woke up. "Our goal is to integrate a cross-cultural perspective into the basic principles of design."

Doug nodded. "What we have worked on so hard last spring and this fall is to put together this program. Now we need to go ahead and teach it and evaluate whether or not it achieves our goal. Erik suggested that we use students' portfolios for the evaluation. We can involve the students in this process, which would also be instructive." It was as if I had never spoken.

"There is something called the repetition compulsion," I said. "As in all roads lead to . . . I may be missing something, I've been away, but this seems to me like window dressing or what some would call political correctness. The basic assumptions about urban design remain unchallenged. The focus on evaluation is a diversion, which is not to say that the students shouldn't be involved or look at their portfolios with culture in mind. It's like the reference to the Akha. It sounds exotic, respectful, but do you have any idea what it means to enter the Akha way of seeing the world?" I stopped. "You would have to experience it before you could teach it."

"I would like to think we can arrive at consensus," Doug said, his voice earnest. "Can you say, Kyra, what you see as the problem?"

I had just said it. To do what Nancy was asking us to do would mean to reexamine our assumptions about what is a city, and recognize how culturally driven our approach has been to what we call "basic design."

If I got angry, they would say I was angry. And nothing I said would have any effect. If I did not get angry, nothing would happen. I could see how they wanted to leave it. We now have a course on the Akha, we have a woman in our department. What more do you want?

"It's not as if we've never talked about this before," I said, my voice rising, there was nothing to lose. "If we're serious about integrating culture into our teaching of design, the implications are radical. We would need to bring in an anthropologist, someone who has thought seriously about the problem of holding different ways not only of designing a city or constructing a building but of seeing the world. What we're proposing now is indistinguishable from what everyone has been doing. It's like holding a bazaar. If we go on this way, we'll lose . . ."

Erik looked up.

Loss, that gets them. My friend David had been delighted by a paper that opened with the sentence "Loss has been found." I looked at my watch. I would go to my office and call David. He and Sarah had gone to Cape Town for the week to be with her father, who was undergoing surgery.

Nancy looked discouraged. She reminded people about the donor. "She's serious about this."

Erik said we could not let ourselves be led by a donor's agenda. It violated the spirit of academic freedom. A peroration followed.

"The best predictor of the future is the past," he concluded. It was his stock comment at search committee meetings when a candidate who showed promise had not yet published. Condemned to repeat. "We know of similar efforts to satisfy donors that have been well intended but have ended up as disasters"—a stab at Nancy. She didn't flinch. "I'm afraid our funder may be disappointed, but our students need jobs."

I saw it. The closing. Craig looked at his watch, Erik stared out the window, Doug picked up the signal, Ian cleared his throat.

I looked at Nancy. She met my gaze. She shrugged her shoulders. It was useless.

Outside it was snowing again. Footprints led in both directions, some toward Kirkland Street, where the clock on the Busch-Reisinger Museum said twenty to twelve. The meeting had ended early. The snow swirled around me. Across the street, Memorial Hall, monument to the Civil War. Snow landed on the ledges of red brick, veiling the building like a shroud. I remembered that I had intended to call David, but it would be dinnertime in Cape

Town now and probably he and Sarah were out. The footprints on the sidewalk were like the inlaid brass feet on subway platforms, showing the way. One pair veered off the curb. I followed them into the street, crossing the wet black asphalt, picking up the trail on the other side. It led up the steps into Memorial Hall.

I stood in the cave of the entrance. I didn't know anymore why I had come to Cambridge. To wrench myself into the familiar? A lecturer's voice droned through the closed doors of Sanders Theater. Muffled, words indistinct. Only the tone of authority came through. Sentences coming to a dead stop. The voice then picking up again, rising into the sentence and then falling into conclusion.

I was here. It was Monday, halfway through the day. He was there, in Budapest, behind the iron curtain. This building was a monument to war, to the aftermath of war. After math, there is . . . what? Science. I reached for logic, the blade that sliced. To cut through this universe, this university, to see into the core. I looked up into the dark spaces above me. The Victorian building had no ribs, no outward manifestations of inner structure. The lecture ended. Sporadic applause. Bravo. I thought of Tosca hurling herself from the battlements of the Castel Sant Angelo once she realized that her Mario was dead. Scarpia had fooled her into trusting him. The execution was not mock, a mocking of trust. She should have known.

The doors of the lecture hall opened. Students poured out, pulling on coats, shifting their books, righting themselves, and heading outside.

I went to my office and called Felicia. She was home, making a little lunch. "I'd love some company," she said.

I stomped the snow off my boots and walked into her embrace. "Here, take off these wet things." She brushed the snow from the front of her dress. "Are your feet dry?" I felt like sobbing. I handed her my jacket and scarf. The house held the stillness of snow. She had set two places at the dining room table. "It isn't much," she said, bringing a salad and a plate of cold meats.

"Paula's away, but I warmed up the soup that she left. It's one of her specialties, beans and barley." Paula had been with Felicia for years.

Two delicate white cups, porcelain ringed with gold, rattled on their saucers as she set them down. Steam rose into my face. "She puts meat in it and carrots—everything good." She was watching me carefully. "I hope you like it." I dipped the round silver spoon into the milky broth.

When we first came to America and stayed with Felicia, her spacious house had welcomed us with quiet dignity. It was like walking into the Europe my parents had fled. Felicia wore stockings every day, even when she was not going out. She and Leo had left Berlin at the last possible moment, in 1939. He was in the diamond business, had contacts in New York. Her diamond ring refracted the light from the chandelier.

"How is your project going?" she asked.

I told her about the fishing community moving in. The artists as well. "I was very sorry that I couldn't get there to see *Tosca*," she said. She went to the Dolomites every summer, even after Leo died. Together they had helped set up the Window Shop in Cambridge, run by refugees who had brought with them the secret of Viennese pastry. The Mozart torte was Leo's favorite. Felicia served it each year on New Year's Day.

Suddenly I knew I had to go back to Nashawena. It had been a bad idea to come to Cambridge. She watched me carefully as I finished my soup and helped myself to meat and salad. "Take a little more," she said, indicating the roast beef with her fork. "The iron will be good for you. You look pale."

I had thought I wanted to talk with Felicia, but the house felt oppressive. Where was the ground that he had not stood on? The earth was falling away at my feet.

I drove back along the Southeast Expressway, trying not to see, trying not to recognize what was happening. In one sense, nothing was happening, it had all happened, or nothing had happened. I was losing the tenses. I watched the gulls, like birds in a penitentiary, soaring over razor wire.

.   .   .

When I got back to the island, it was almost dark. Anna and Tony were sitting in the living room, leafing through seed catalogues. They had made a fire. I sat next to it, grateful for the warmth. Anna looked at me sharply.

"It's okay," I said. And I thought at that moment that it was. The house wrapped itself around me, and I sank into its comfort. The light of the fire intensified as the windows turned black.

"Would you like a glass of wine?" Anna asked. I could see she was concerned.

"No, I'm really okay now. I mean, yes," I said, meaning the wine.

Tony stayed into the evening, his presence reassuring. There were people around me. I was not alone. We talked about whether to grow bok choy.

When Tony left, Anna pressed me. Why had I come back so soon? Had something happened in Cambridge? I couldn't tell her, couldn't put it into words. I fished the mail out of my purse to distract her. There wasn't much. I didn't say I had gone half-looking for a letter from Andreas. I couldn't talk about it. Not even with her.

The spring term did not start until February. That left two more months. I thought I would concentrate on finishing the island project. Now that people were living there, there was lots of activity. I would watch the community as it formed, see how they adjusted to the spaces, how the spaces affected their way of living and working. But my heart wasn't in it. I can see now that it had been a mistake to involve Andreas in this project. Everywhere I turned, I came upon him.

Anna saw that, but I think I distracted her with my anger. She may have seen through that too. She would join me in berating him. The general point intrigued her: just when you thought someone was going to do something new, you discovered that in fact they were doing the same old thing. She said this happened all the time in therapy. But it was important not to give up.

Tony was hanging around, and I could see Anna hesitating. I

thought it was in part because of me. She had dropped her theory about sex versus intimacy. Now she said it didn't have to be a choice.

When I said I was going to stay at the shack on the ocean side for a while, that I wanted to work there because of the view of the sea and because I really needed to be alone—it was partly because of her. She had turned forty. The possibility of children would soon be foreclosed. She and Tony would be great parents. They raised oysters and vegetables. Why not children?

That's what I told myself.

A writer had occupied the shack the previous winter and brought in a Jotul stove. In the beginning, the shack was a good place for me to work and offered a kind of sanctuary. I was reaching the end of my design work on the project, I thought I would start something new. The gray weathered boards, the door that secured with a clasp, the pulsating warmth of the stove. There was a ritual to living there, feeding logs into the stove, securing the door each time you walked in or out. I put my drawing table under the windows so I could watch the sea, and the days fell into a rhythm. The good light for working ended mid-afternoon. Anna would come around and we would walk the beach while the light turned gold and the sun sank into the sea, leaving a trail of pinks and reds. Usually I ate with Anna and Tony and listened to James Taylor with them. We didn't talk much. Then I would walk back and fall asleep.

I decided it was a good time to paint my room in the house— change the color while I was away. Tony offered to do it for me; there wasn't much going on in the hatchery and nothing in the garden, so he had time. I moved my things out, carting a box of books and papers to the shack and leaving the rest packed up in the hall closet, where I also put my clothes.

Do you want to know how it happened? I mean how it actually happened? Obviously I had thought about it. When he left. As a way of punishing him. In lieu of killing him perhaps. A kind of dumb show in a way. But then I was also thinking that I might be pregnant, that maybe I would have his child, because my period was late, and that occupied my mind for a time. I was involved with the end of the building season and the people moving in. Also, I was numb. And maybe it was the quiet of the shack, the sense of paring life down to the core, that led me to reflect on what had happened, like someone coming out of shock. Which is why I think it was so hard that day when I went to Cambridge. Because it was as if I had no skin. I had lost my shield.

And then it was really one day. I was finishing the last of the drawings, sketching the landscape, putting in the wall to mark the eastern end of the site, filling in the stones one by one. And then I heard the word *stone* and thought of the day when we had skipped stones and talked about the saying "A rolling stone gathers no moss." He said that in his experience, if you kept moving, you would not sink. It was the story of his life. But I didn't hear it then. Like I didn't see that Anton was consumed by jealousy, that it was a competition and he had to prove he was more of a man than Simon. Like Scarpia with Cavaradossi. The ending of *Tosca* was familiar, I had seen it happen: Simon, a man, taken out and shot.

I suddenly saw what I had resisted seeing. He had said it right at the beginning, that he would keep moving. And I didn't hear it. I thought he would stay.

The world spun, the angles shifted. Suddenly it was clear. He knew from the beginning that he would leave me. He had said it. I had fooled myself.

I got up from the table. I had to see. I had to see now what was the truth.

In Greece, there are women who can read the bones of the dead, tell from the shape of the bones how they lived, where they stood in the community. I took my red jacket from the peg by the door and headed out into the wind. The ocean was opaque, slate gray, revealing nothing. I turned and let the wind carry me away from the sea.

Anna was sitting at the kitchen counter when I came in. She looked up, surprised.

"I've finished," I said. "Done. Completed the drawings. Now it's a question of waiting for the weather." I didn't want her to come too close. I regret now that I had to involve her, but it turned out she had moved my box with Andreas's letters and the postcards and the *Tosca* things out of the hall closet and I didn't know where she had put it. Tony was painting. I checked the color. Lemony in the graying light. "It looks great. Thank you so much for doing this."

"Why do you want those things?" Anna asked. She was standing beside me in the doorway. I moved away.

"Because now that it's over, I want to get rid of them, burn everything. I'm taking the old drawings for the site to the dump, and I thought I would take them too."

"Great," she said, unconvinced.

But I had drawn a cordon around me. There was no opening for her to enter.

She told me where she had put the box. I retrieved it and headed out. I hadn't taken off my coat.

Going back, I was walking into the wind, feeling the brace of its resistance. It stiffened my resolve. Now I would see. Now I would know how it had been.

The shack felt too warm, as if the stove were engulfing the room. I opened one of the windows behind the table, but everything started to blow, so I quickly shut it again and took off my sweater. The box was full to overflowing: when I removed the cover, papers spilled on the floor. I didn't realize there was so much. Good, I told myself. Evidence. Now I will see.

Do you know how sharp anger can be, how cutting, like a knife? When it is dulled, everything blurs, like paints running together turn a dispirited brown. I started in anger. I was going to burn his letters. I started reading them, one by one. The postcard from the aquarium with the lion fish on it that said, "Beware of lion fish!" The note he had left on my windshield one day. "Only a beautiful woman would park here." And suddenly

I was back in that time, as it was at that time. And it seemed real again.

So then I lost my ballast. I had started burning the letters in the stove, and then I was fishing them out, half-burned. One was still on fire and it caught the ends of my hair, making a horrible smell. I dropped the burning paper onto the floor and put out the fire in my hair with my hands. It was getting toward evening, and the room took on an eerie glow. I watched the flame eat away at the edges of the paper, leaving a gaping hole surrounded by black char. Good. For a moment, everything righted.

And then I came to a folder with the things from *Tosca*—the program, the notes that went back and forth, and then among the papers, the knife. It was a steak knife, not a stage knife. He had brought it to rehearsal one day when he felt that the stabbing had become mechanical. He wanted Tosca to feel the weight of a knife, its sharpness. She had seen it as a means of liberation—to kill Scarpia. What she hadn't seen was the trick. When Scarpia gave the order for what he said would be a simulated execution, telling his agent to do it as they did with Palmieri, she didn't know that Palmieri had been, in fact, shot. The execution would not be fake. The free-conduct passes were useless.

I hadn't seen it either. I thought it was real—the possibility of love and freedom. And then it was not. I had been tricked. Was it clear from the beginning, and I just didn't see it, didn't listen, didn't take the story seriously, didn't think I could be in that story? Voices from childhood came back: "You don't listen, you will see."

All the signs pointed in one direction, like cormorants on a rock. Without thinking what I was doing, I began to move the blade back and forth across the skin of my wrist. It made a little slice, at the surface of the skin. It was like watching the gills of a fish, blood pulsating just at the surface.

I became transfixed. As in a dream when you are in the dream and also watching yourself in the dream. I threw the *Tosca* program into the fire and watched it burn. The one he had signed "love, A."

The sketches of the sets were more complicated. I was so angry that I had ever agreed to do those sets. I cut the drawings with the knife, slicing them into strips, and then the knife slipped and I cut myself more deeply. And then I was in another place.

I watched the blood flowing and found it oddly comforting. The steady flow of red blood. A visible testament to my heart. That I had feelings, that I could bleed. That my heart was pouring itself onto this uneven floor. I took the knife and began cutting deeper along the line I had made in my wrist. I looked into the wound, trying to see the structure of the cells. I leaned forward. The ends of my hair dipped in the blood. I will write in blood, I thought wildly, with my hair. So people will know. The strands of my hair stuck together. And then another image crossed that one, of hair over my face, over my eyes, a screen of hair and blood, sticky, red in the sunlight, because it was noon and we were making love and I had my period and my blood was all over him. His eyes gentle, falling into mine like stars. We had fallen into each other precipitously, without thinking.

I took the knife. I had to cut through the surface. I had to see inside, to see, to feel what was real.

When I woke up, the light was ancient, yellow like parchment. I thought I had left this world. The white walls of the room were silent, cool in their silence, giving no clue. I didn't know where I was. My mind began flipping through rooms I had slept in, houses we had lived in, summer places. It was too bare to be a hotel. And then I remembered.

The shack hot and steamy. The fire. And I saw my wrist, bandaged.

PART TWO

1

I SANK INTO THE CHAIR AS IF I'D LET GO OF A ROPE.

"You can begin wherever you want," she said. She smoothed the folds of her skirt.

I looked around the room. Eaved ceiling, white walls. Brown couch nestled against one wall. A painting of a blue door over her chair. My eye settled on her face. A small woman, mid-fifties. A delicacy to her features. Her eyes keen, like a bird.

"If you want to begin with silence, that's fine. We'll get the feel of each other in this room." She settled in, fixing her gaze on the middle distance.

When she came to see me in the hospital, her presence was calming, dispelling the din of carts and trays, nurses coming in and out. The silence was restful. I hadn't intended to kill myself. She didn't seem alarmed. I heard her voice in the corridor insisting I not be put on medications. A hush of conversation, footsteps dispersing.

The clock on the desk said twenty to six. Ten minutes had passed. Could I really be silent here too? I looked out the window. Snow falling steadily through a cone of streetlight, days getting longer, the hopefulness of January. The plants on the desk waited, drawing nourishment from the artificially warmed winter soil. The visibility would be bad on the drive home.

Ten to six. She shifted in her chair. My body stiffened. I would take her at her word. Her glance swept my face. Kind eyes. This birdlike woman of infinite patience.

The door on the opposite wall remained silently shut. I could pick up my bag and leave. Or could I? The question was absurd. The hands of the clock moved imperceptibly. Time running out, like sand in the hourglass on the shelf next to the stove, my mother waiting, the white of the egg solidifying, three minutes. The light in the room intensified. One lamp next to her chair, the other on the desk beside me. Outside, the quiet of snow falling, spreading a clean sheet over the ground. Any footstep, and the darkness underneath would become visible.

She raised her eyebrows, as if reading my thought. The clock said six, hands straight up and down. Stick figure in a child's drawing. Mentally, I added arms and legs, a face and a nose. The figure was running.

"It's deceptive," I said, "this time of the year. The light is lengthening, but still the winter has hardly begun."

Her face suddenly alert.

I turned to the window and stared into the blackness.

"Is that why you cut yourself?" she asked. "To see into a darkness?"

"I had to know." My voice sounded edgy, defiant. I turned to face her.

"What didn't you know?" she said.

"What was true. What was real."

"With Andreas?"

It was odd, hearing her say his name. Oddly comforting. Most people avoided it in my presence.

I nodded.

"It felt true to you, at the time?"

Tears surprised me.

"And you stepped with your full weight into that truth?"

The tears welled, spilled onto my face.

"And then you found yourself all alone."

I wept, letting the tears run down my cheeks. I had stepped

onto ground I had sworn never to walk on again, and it had given way under my feet.

Her eyes filled with tears, and for a moment, the truth seemed simple.

Of course it wasn't simple. I had betrayed everyone. Simon with Andreas, Anna by lying to her, myself. And then there was Richard, who had given me the commission, the students who counted on me, everyone involved in the Nashawena project. My feet tangled in a skein of regret. If only I had kept my vow and stayed with Simon, if only I had seen through Andreas, seen who he was. If only I had stayed with Anna and continued as we had been living. If only I had killed myself.

"Do you do this," I said, meaning her tears, "with all your—" I hesitated. What did she call them, patients? Clients?

It was the end of the hour, time running over, six twenty-five.

"I usually try with people to give them their space and not intrude. But I see that with you it's more important for you to see what I feel," she said, stumbling over her words, "and something in your story must have touched something in my life because my tears surprised me. So the answer to your question is no, I don't usually cry."

I would come on time—waste not, want not—fold my coat over the wooden chair next to the desk, and then sink into the well, the circle of black leather. The lamp on the cabinet beside her suffused the room with yellow light, intensifying the gold of the rug. Field of gold, cloth of gold. She sat in her chair waiting, listening, inserting questions, quietly unsettling. One day she laughed. I had said, "You know, this therapy, I mean, look at us, two women meeting in a small room, the slant of the ceiling, the flat of the floor." "There," she said, "that's an example." She had spoken about my architect's eye. "And you?" I said. "How do you see it?" She paused for a moment. "I don't see so much as listen."

She told me she was a cellist, her ear tuned to the sound of the bass line. I looked at the rug, gold in the late-afternoon light.

Henry the Eighth and the king of France, meeting to negotiate their peace on the field of the cloth of gold.

A tide came in, the wash of desire drawing my life into the orbit of her—this woman I barely knew with her short hair and long skirts and odd name. Greta, she was called. A character from Grimm. Regretta, Anna said one day, unable to resist. Lines from a poem ran through my head: *Look she said this is not the distance we wanted to stay at—we wanted to get close, very close. But what is the way in again? And is it too late?* A suck in my stomach, an undertow of fear.

The clock on the desk marked the hour, its tick barely audible, expectant. Anything could happen in the next minute, or the one after that, until then suddenly the hour was over and I left, bewilderment overtaking me as I descended the two flights of enclosed stairs.

I had been talking about my mother. When she went to the market, open in the center of town, she would bring us back treats, reaching into her pockets, her fingers enclosing the secret. Which hand? We had to guess. When she called my name, her voice extended the syllables, Kyra, rolling the *r*. She taught me Hebrew phrases—*lilah tov,* good night, *boker tov,* good morning, and her favorite from the Bible: *Ani l'dodi, v'dodi li,* I am my beloved, and my beloved is mine. I was her youngest child. She called my sister, Anya, the three of us rolling down the hill at the side of the house, our faces flushed, the smell of wild thyme. Anton was away at school. Thorn in her side, son from her first marriage. A mistake. The atmosphere of the household lightened. It was before the political trouble began. I hadn't seen what was coming then either, I said.

Greta looked at me quizzically. Was that true?

The hour ended. At the bottom of the staircase, light streamed in through a pane in the door. The house was silent, moving toward evening. What was she doing now? Making notes about me? Watering her plants? Waiting for her next patient? Or was I the last? Was she waiting for me to leave so she could come downstairs and start dinner? The door on my right leading into the kitchen was shut. Once when I had come in the morning, I saw a man sitting at the kitchen table reading the newspaper. The kitchen window was level with the landing outside the door. I stood for a moment watching him, the graying hair, the ease in his body, the quiet absorption. Everything about him said husband.

"Today is her birthday," I said. It was March, and the light was strong. "My mother would have been sixty-three today." Greta's face blurred. I bent down to retrieve the letter I had salvaged, grateful for the curtain of my hair. Words, imprinted in memory, rushed up, dizziness overtaking me. I fished around in my purse for the envelope and then placed it in my lap, waiting for the turbulence to settle. Greta had her inquisitive look. Shadows of tree branches played on the wall behind her. Where was the branch to catch hold of? The door beckoned. I could just put the letter back in my purse and leave. It was what they call an option. "I brought a letter," I said. She didn't say anything.

The plants on the desk reached into the light. It was the first day of spring. "The coming of spring," my father would say of my mother's birthday, "born on the equinox." He had cleared his throat, resisting the impulse to repeat once again the explanation, sun midway through its journey; he launched instead into the poem he had written for my mother that year, "Once more on this occasion, I raise my voice in celebration, of you my beloved, my dearest Katya," his voice thickening as he said her name. She glanced shyly at us, her children gathered around the table, each bringing something we had written or made for her, she who had given birth to us.

Forgetting the Kleenex on the table next to me, I wiped my eyes with my sleeve.

It was the first year I was away at school and I was spending the Easter break with friends. I had written her a letter, sent it to my father to read at the table on her birthday. When I got back to school, an envelope was waiting for me in my mailbox, buried under flyers and college announcements, my name carefully scripted, a legacy of her European childhood. I took the letter and went to my room.

"Do you want to read it?" Greta asked, her voice spreading calmness. A surface I could walk on. I unfolded the paper.

" 'My darling Kyra,' " I began, the air in the room suddenly still. I glanced at Greta, her face intent. " 'Your birthday letter made me so happy. Papa read it at the table and we all laughed at the part where you described the travel.' "

I don't know what I had expected—that I would be overcome with a paroxysm of grief? Instead something lifted, my mother's voice guiding me now like a beam.

" 'I was of course relieved to hear that you arrived safely and I trust that you were careful about what you ate and drank only bottled water.' " The uncanny had turned into my mother. " 'I missed you, my dearest, your lively presence at the table, and yet in my deepest heart, I rejoiced to think of you on holiday with your friends. I could picture you swimming in the sea, and I too remembered the trip we took in September before you left for school, just the three of us, you, Anya, and me. It was one of the highlights of this last year. Anya had made me an album of her photographs and we spent yesterday afternoon before she left looking through it, including the ones from the trip, the little beach we found with the island to swim to and the simple lunch place where they made the best fish.' "

I took my feet out of my shoes and folded my legs under me. " 'Papa said to send you a big hug and kiss from him and to tell you he will write soon. Freddie is sitting here right beside me, wagging his tail because he knows I am writing you. He says he misses you and is waiting for you to come home and take him to the beach, which we do not dare to do now that they have put up a sign saying "No dogs." Charlotte said that you shouldn't give people's names to dogs but I explained that Papa wanted him to have an English name since he is an English dog. She said it wasn't English, which is true. I said maybe we should have named him Yam, for the sea, like the Israelis do, naming their children for the sea or the dew, to make a clean break with the past.

" 'We have had an early spring and I am trying to get the garden in, along with all the other things. Anya left this morning and the house is very quiet with just Papa and me and Freddie. If the food in the college is not fresh, you can go and buy yourself something in the market. Try to remember to eat some fruit every day. This afternoon when I go into town I will stop and ask Mr. Panopoulos if he can mail you a box of fresh oranges, which I think he will do since he knows me for so long.

" 'It is a gift in life to have a passion and a blessing to be able to pursue it as you are now doing. It is what I pray for, that you should have this always. Take care of yourself, my darling. I send you a million kisses.

" 'Your loving Mama.' "

Greta's eyes were glistening, her face lifted in expectation.

"So you know what love is," she said quietly.

I startled.

"What do you mean?"

She raised her eyebrows.

"That you know."

I took a deep breath, air rushing into a space that had opened inside me. I remembered the Israelis, shedding their past, naming their children Yam for the sea or Tali for the dew, and then I remembered Tali, the soprano. I turned my arm over to look at the scar. It had faded, a thin white line like the crescent moon.

"But if I knew," I began, "then"—I was flailing around, reaching for logic to steady myself—"then I wouldn't be here. I wouldn't have made that mistake. I would have known what was true."

She paused for a moment, her face reflective.

"Maybe that's why you're here," she said, a Buddha reciting a koan. "Because you knew."

I unfolded my legs and put my feet back on the floor.

"Look," I said, not knowing where to look—at her, at the door? "What's the point of this, since you will leave too? I get stronger, you go."

Greta hesitated a moment.

"We have to stop now," she said quietly.

I folded the letter, placed it back in my purse, put on my shoes, picked up my coat. Outside, the light glared back at me. All I could think of was the word *disarray*.

April was consumed by an argument about therapy that seemed to lead nowhere—Greta tense, stiffening in her chair. I could see her willing herself not to be drawn in. But I was after something, something I wanted with her that seemed essential. Something about truth, about her feelings. "It doesn't line up," I said. "And he was a mistake."

One day I looked at her right hand and imagined a cellist's bow moving steadily back and forth across a single bass note: you know. I smiled, in spite of myself.

"People," she had said, "are very good at winning at their own games," a reminder that I could defeat her.

The spring term was shapeless, no Thanksgiving, no Christmas lights, winter ignoring its official stopping point, a game without a referee. In endless faculty meetings, we argued about the curriculum, two teams forming, like color war at camp. Who would capture the flag? I had lunch with Emma, a friend in Visual Studies, and she said the same thing was going on there. "It's the academic sport," she said, biting into her melted cheese sandwich.

I thought of telling her about Greta, but instead I asked where she got her boots.

Greta told me she would be taking two months off in the summer. "Great," I said. I told her I would be on Nashawena, that I had no intention of coming into Cambridge in any case. Hand in glove. Then May came with a string of warm days. The lilacs bloomed, transforming the air with a sensuousness I assumed the Puritans would have found alarming. Greta brought cut branches into the room, standing them in a tall vase on the floor next to her chair.

My dreams were filled with houses. I would wander from room to room. Sometimes she would be in one of the rooms and I would come in, but then others would enter, making it impossible for us to talk. We would go in search of another room, looking for privacy. One night I dreamed that I went into one of the Newport mansions and the pipes had burst. A large Persian rug was covered with a sheet of ice. I was eating more, sleeping better. Looking in the mirror one morning after my shower, I noticed the pale skin of my face under my eyes. The dark circles had disappeared.

In June it rained steadily, day after day. The term ended. On the day of commencement, David and I skipped the morning ceremony. "Ludicrous," he said as we passed the bloated state official, costumed in black, staff in hand, rushing to take his place at the head of the procession, the faculty arrayed like birds of plumage in extravagant yellows and purples and blues and crimson. We turned toward the river.

"You're looking well," David said, glancing appreciatively at my summer dress, yellow-and-white striped, sleeveless, the scar now almost invisible. Anna was right about vitamin E. David checked his watch. The degree-granting ceremony at the Design School wouldn't start until noon. A friend of his had opened a coffee shop near Boston University. Perfect. A walk, coffee, another walk, and then we would be in the mood to cheer our students and greet their parents before calling it a day.

We followed the dirt path along the river, a scattering of mothers with small children playing on the grass, stray gulls overhead, messengers from the sea. We crossed at the B.U. bridge, found the shop—"Joe," the sign said simply. Pine tables, Mexican tiles, espresso machine gleaming, Bach playing in the background, piano and cello sonatas. I thought of Greta.

"What's happening with the project?" David asked. Construction at the site had been suspended until I was ready to oversee the work. "Take whatever time you need," Richard had said, kind, reserved, making space now as he had when we first came, when we also needed time to get our bearings, to find our way. "Not much," I said.

"Then why don't you come to Rome with us, stay for a few weeks. It would do you good to get away." He had won a fellowship to the American Academy in Rome, Sarah was going with him, they would stay for the year. "To Rome?" I said. "No thanks." Friends. They invite you to go with them.

Joe, David's friend, brought the coffee himself, an outline of a leaf etched in coffee on the surface of white foam. He joined us, pulling up a chair.

On the way back, it started to rain. David was amused. It never rained on Harvard commencement. "See, Kyra," he said, "it's the universe speaking, time for a new city. You'd better stay and get to work."

By four in the afternoon it was pouring. The maple trees had leafed, spreading a tent over Greta's street, turning the light green. The sewers were overflowing and the neighbor children had built dams with stones, flooding the sidewalk and wading barefoot through the water. I had changed into jeans, put on Wellingtons and an old yellow slicker.

Greta looked up as I came in. She was holding her appointment book in her hand.

"I need to ask you if you can make a change and come at ten in the morning on Monday instead of our usual time."

Why? I wanted to ask.

She was wearing stockings, a pale yellow silk jacket, heels rather than her ballet flats. Had one of her patients graduated? Someone curable? I meant to sound ironic but the voice in my head sounded hopeful. A young woman with an eye for color and style, like me I thought, looking ruefully at my jeans and drab rubber boots. I could have been seven years old.

I said nothing.

She waited, fiddling with a paper clip.

"It's okay," I said, shrugging my shoulders.

She made a note and closed her book.

"We have three weeks now until the break," she said, like dropping a stone into a pond. She waited for the ripples.

What did she want me to say? "Please don't go"? And then she would leave anyway. It was absurd. "Go now if you're going to go"? That was a thought.

Or I could leave first, leave her sitting alone in this room. She would get up, turn off the lights, close the door, go downstairs, call a friend maybe, go out for coffee, or have tea with her husband, a suddenly free hour, like a snow day, I thought, the memory bitter.

That night I dreamed I was climbing down a ladder and suddenly two rungs were missing, leaving a gap. The ladder led down into a boat, and I wanted to get in the boat, or felt I had to get in the boat, but there was no place to step. My foot dangled in the air. I became terrified and woke in a panic.

The dream seemed obvious to me. The night Simon was killed, we had left in a boat. If we hadn't gotten into the boat, we might have been killed as well. Our parents had disappeared. It was why Simon had wanted me to leave. They should have gone too.

"What about the ladder?" Greta asked. It was Monday. I had told her the dream.

I looked at her, puzzled.

"You know," she said, "in every dream there is a navel, a knotted place where it opens into the unknown."

The feelings in the dream came back. Terror, panic. I looked at the clock. It was time to stop.

"We can come back to this on Thursday," she said.

"To what?"

She said, "I have the feeling these days that whatever I say is wrong."

I glared at her and left.

On Thursday, I was talking about the project and plans for the summer when Greta said, "I'm thinking about that dream, about the ladder, and wondering if it's telling us something about the summer and the break in therapy, just when you were starting to get down into it."

Her words grated. She wanted me to talk about my feelings about her leaving. Talk about yourself, I wanted to say. How do you feel? Weren't you getting into it too?

"I'm thinking that maybe we have to go back down that ladder and find the missing rungs. Where you put your foot out and there was no place to step. Two rungs were missing. I will be away for two months."

She sat back.

"Is this the leaving cure? A Roman therapy?" I asked, thinking of David. He would get the point.

I had told Anna that it didn't make sense. You go to therapy to work through your feelings about people who have left you, and then the therapist leaves you.

"That's the point," Anna said, peeling an onion, wiping her eyes on her sleeve. "You can work through your feelings, talk about them rather than hurting yourself." She put down the knife and looked at me pointedly.

"That's not why I cut myself," I said. "What's the point of therapy? To introduce the toxin like a vaccine, gear up your immune system so you become impervious to being left. Leaving? So what?" I walked out of the kitchen.

"It's part of life," Anna called after me, "like death. You learn to accept it."

I came back in. "You've completely missed the point. There was nothing natural about Simon's death, or for that matter about Andreas's leaving. It was a shock. Unnatural. It came out of the blue. He said he was in love with me, that he had never felt this way about anyone before."

"Maybe that was it," she said.

"What?"

"Maybe he left because he had fallen in love with you." She gathered the little squares of onion to one end of the board and slid them into the pan, turning down the heat. "Maybe it was because of the strength of his feelings for you."

"That doesn't make any sense." What she said was precisely what I had thought, which is why I cut myself, I wanted to say, because my feelings had come back, so strong, overwhelming, and I needed to see beneath the surface, to know if they were about something real.

The smell of onions cooking filled the kitchen.

"Actually, I agree with you," she said, crossing to the table and taking the dead flowers out of the vase. "About therapy." She took the vase to the sink and ran the water. "To invite relationship, encourage trust, and then work through the grief over its ending, or as they would say, the termination. You're right. It makes no sense. It's why I can't do it anymore." She threw the flowers into the garbage.

"I feel that I'm not getting through to you," Greta said, rearranging herself in her chair, "or rather that we've managed to talk about the break on some surface level that might just hold the relationship through the summer."

"Like the skin that forms over milk when it cools?" I asked her, deliberately provocative. Milk, mother. Her response was predictable.

"I'm wondering about the ladder, the ship in your dream. I am leaving, maybe you want to come with me and can't because of the missing rungs. I am leaving for two months and you feel left, suspended in midair."

An invitation into a maze. Whatever I said always led back into my feelings, my problem. What about her feelings? Was the separation no problem for her? I thought of Andreas. He had no problem leaving.

"But you know," she continued, "you know how to move in the face of impasse. This is part of your history as well, and it may have been one of the reasons you became an architect. Because you have an eye for how to build things."

It's true. I do. Something inside me released. The child got up and left. I took her place. It occurred to me that I could bridge the summer by writing.

There was something I wanted to say, something I wanted to convey to her that I hadn't managed to say. I was an academic, or at least I could pass for one. I would write it, show her what she hadn't seen. What I hadn't found a way yet to say.

She worried that this would take me back into the feelings that had led me to cut myself, at a time when I would be alone with them. I reminded her that I would be with Anna, that I would not be alone.

In the end, she gave me her phone number in Wellfleet, telling me that this was where she would be, that I could call her if I wanted to, that it would be fine with her if I called. She said she hoped the summer would not be too hard, that I would have some good times. I took the paper with her phone number and left without saying a word.

———

I thought of her often during that long, hot July, how she would sit in her chair so still sometimes, like the water in the bay, except that it was translucent and she was opaque, or at least she liked to think she was. What was she doing now? I could see that she needed a vacation. Still, the structure of therapy didn't make sense. The sudden drop-offs, like falling into space. I saw her smiling, my architect's eye again.

Was she also thinking about me?

On the island, there was haze in the air, like the mists I had described to her, when the air holds the sea. The grasses stayed green even though there wasn't much rain. What was it like on the Cape where she was? The colors would be less intense because it was farther from the Gulf Stream.

At the beginning of August, Anna and Tony were going to Provincetown to meet with a marine biologist. A friend of mine had a show in one of the galleries there, and I decided to go to Provincetown with them. I wandered down Commercial Street, wondering if I might by chance run into Greta. Wellfleet was nearby. It was a cloudy day, not one for the beach. Anna and Tony finished early and found me in the gallery at the east end. The biologist had recommended a stable where they rent horses, and we decided to ride along the beach. The stable was desultory, or maybe it was the day. Tony urged me to take the black mare and I liked the knowing look in her eyes. She seemed more spirited than the rest. We filled out the forms and headed out, the horses picking up speed as we reached the water's edge. We had cantered far down the beach when the mare suddenly reared and turned, heading back to the stable, determined to go her own way. The others followed, and as it turned out, we got back just before it stormed. "See," Tony said, "she knew."

The biologist had invited us to a party. He was staying with a friend who had a house at the west end overlooking the bay, and Tony said that I might like to see the house. The friend was a musician from Cambridge. I wondered if he knew Greta. The house reached out over the sand, the deck cantilevered at a nice angle to the water. I wondered who the architect was. I picked up a glass of red wine from the bar at one corner of the living room and made my way through the crowd, thinking I would go out on the deck since the rain had stopped.

And then I saw him.

He was standing next to the rail, looking out at the sea. Like on the boat that first day when we went to Nashawena. I froze. "I don't do this," he had said then, meaning us. "I don't either," I had said, the two of us laughing because it was at once improbable and true.

He turned, and his face went white. I couldn't breathe. I reached out toward the door to steady myself and it opened. Like a sleepwalker, I stepped onto the thin wet boards of the deck.

He didn't move.

Rain dripped from the overhang. A gust of wind blew the door shut and I startled.

"Kyra," he said.

A distant bell, the clang of a buoy.

I looked in the direction of the sound.

"Kyra, Kyra," he said. Words coming through a fog.

Rivulets of water ran down my hair. I stepped away from the overhang.

He glanced at my face, his eyes drifting toward my arms.

"I'm sorry," he said.

I couldn't say anything.

"Was I . . ." he began. "I couldn't believe that I . . . I didn't want to go—" He stopped.

I steadied myself.

"Can we speak?" he asked, his face mournful.

Something inside me stiffened. No.

The lights of a boat, the sound of an engine. Fishermen returning. Too late.

"I cannot do this with you again," I said. Once broken. Not again.

I turned. Anna was standing by the door, her face a mix of attentiveness and alarm.

"I'm here only for a few days," he said.

Anna and I left the party immediately.

2

I COULDN'T BREATHE. AIR WOULD START TO COME IN AND THEN catch in my throat. I felt I was suffocating. On the boat back to Nashawena, running lights red and green, Anna put her hand on my arm. "What did he say?" she asked. I wanted to tell her but I couldn't.

Instead, I thought about Simon. The summer before he was killed, we had taken our bikes to ride down the coast to the beach at Protaras. I was wearing my new white pants over my bathing suit. I had forgotten about the chain. We hadn't gone very far when the cuff caught and I fell, my leg attached to the bike, the white cloth gripped in the greasy links. I dragged the bike to the side of the road and stood there, holding back tears. My pants were ruined. Why hadn't I rolled up the cuff? Or used a clip, as I used to at school? I hadn't thought about it because that summer I was wearing mostly skirts and the day was so sunny, like a day when everything will be fine. I was standing there in the heat, an appendage to my bike, when Simon, who had been riding ahead, turned and saw me, and raced back, taking me in his arms and asking the one question I hadn't thought to ask: Kyra, are you hurt?

· · ·

Peter was busy with a new production, but he came over to Nashawena the last week in August. The director this summer was doing *The Tempest,* but I had kept my distance. We sat together at the back of the amphitheater, darkness coming earlier now. "*Come unto these yellow sands—*" Shakespeare's words broke through my gloom. The actor playing Ariel was tiny, her body elastic, her voice enticing. I settled into the magic of the play. "*Curtsied when you have and kissed, the wild waves whist.*" Peter leaned toward me. "It's perfect here, to do *The Tempest* on this island." But it was later, in the fourth act, when Prospero said to Ferdinand, "*You do look my son in a moved sort, as if you were dismayed,*" that it came back. Not the island and the vision but the house, the deck, the thin boards, Andreas standing at the far end, chairs and table wet with rain. "*Our revels now are ended. These our actors as I foretold you, were all spirits and are melted into air, into thin air.*" Tears ran down my face. Peter put his arm around my shoulder, warmth radiating into the place that was shut. "Do you want to talk, Kyra?" he asked.

Quietly we got up and left.

There was a flat outcropping of rock above the theater, off to one side. Peter draped his jacket over one of the stones. We sat, watching the actors in the distance, their voices reduced to a blur of sound. "Are you cold?" he asked. A white moon lit the sea. I shook my head. "He told me he saw you," he said quietly. The word *dismay* came back. "*As if you were dismayed.*" I began to weep. "I was the one who told him," Peter said.

I picked up a stick, the ends frayed, and began to peel the bark, staring into the whiteness.

Peter took a deep breath. "He couldn't believe he would hurt you so terribly by going."

I broke the stick in two. "That wasn't it," I said, my voice rising in defense. Of what? My pride? It wasn't about him, what he believed or couldn't believe. It was that he had treated me this way.

The play ended. Applause. The actors reappeared. More applause. Then the stage lights went out. Below us, the audience dispersed. Boats waiting at the dock. Stagehands gathered up the props.

Peter spoke softly, his Dutch face solemn, lines down the sides of his cheeks like a woodcut, moonlight accentuating the hollows. "He said he had written to you." He had. Over a month after he left that letter, the long white envelope with Hungarian stamps. *A drifting relationship between us is impossible. We have both said it countless times, and it is inescapably true.* I suddenly felt cold. *All my fantasies and considerations and concerns are centered around the question of a marriage. And in my current state, marriage seems very distant and unreal.*

What state? My mind took refuge in trivia. He told me once of a woman he had met. We were walking around Fresh Pond. She had asked him what he did, and when he said conductor, she said, "Train?"

I turned to Peter.

"When he heard, he wanted to come," Peter said, "but Felicia told him it wasn't a good idea. You had just left the hospital. It might reopen the wound. And fortunately, nothing terrible had happened."

I stared at him in disbelief. Nothing terrible?

"I meant, you hadn't actually . . . He thought that in person, he might be able to explain."

"Explain what?"

I didn't mean to get into an argument with Peter.

"I'm sorry," I said.

"It's okay," Peter said. "It's really okay."

He bent his head and massaged the back of his neck. Then he let out a deep breath.

"These things are never easy," he said, "or simple."

For a moment, he sounded like Greta.

"Abe is in the hospital," he said. "Abe came here for the summer to visit his sister. He brought Jesse with him since Andreas's new company was touring in Europe. Edith noticed that Abe was forgetting things. She worried Abe was losing his memory. She was afraid he might get lost. It wasn't safe to leave Jesse with him. She arranged for Abe to go into McLean for tests, and they decided to keep him for observation. That's when Andreas came to the U.S. To see Abe and to take Jesse with him back to Budapest."

"And Abe? How is he?"

"Not well," Peter said. "They used to call it senility. Now it has a fancier name."

"He was such a sweet man," I said.

"Still is," he said.

The cold of the rock had penetrated through his jacket, and I was shivering.

"We should go," I said.

———

Greta stood up when I came in. It was the Thursday after Labor Day and the weather had turned hot. She was wearing white linen pants and a knitted blue top, her face tanned, looking younger. She extended her hand, a bit formal, but still I was glad to see her. My body relaxed, the touch reassuring. The room, the couch, the chairs, the plants, the painting of the blue door, everything was the same. I placed my new leather tote on the floor beside the chair, a symbol of my resolve to move on.

"So?" Greta said, scanning my face.

"I saw him," I said, realizing in that moment that I had been waiting to talk about it with her.

I began the story but something was unsettled.

Her face was alert.

I remembered a dream. "Last night, I dreamed I was in a car with a man. I was driving and we had to cross this open terrain to get to the border. There was no road. I looked down at the gearshift to see if there was four-wheel drive. When I looked up a man was standing beside the car, his face menacing. I tried to lock the doors but the buttons kept popping up. I started to panic. 'Ignore him,' the man sitting next to me said. I floored the gas and the car jolted, then sped across the open field. At the border, a sign said, 'Free State.' "

I looked at Greta. She was waiting.

"The man in the car," I began, "I think it was my father, but maybe it was Andreas. He was wearing a leather jacket. I couldn't see his face. The other man standing by the car? My first thought was Anton, but actually he looked more like Simon, his face distorted with rage. The road we were on was shaded, trees hanging over the pavement. Like willow trees, except that doesn't make sense because it was a darker green. The summer my father was teaching me to drive, we found a road lined with trees, a long, straight road with very few cars. The border?" I laughed. "The sign says it all. I guess it's a dream about finding a free space, escaping from menace. I certainly know about that."

"Crossing a border," Greta added. "But this time a man is with you, and it's a car, not a boat."

I could see where she was heading. She wanted to talk about Andreas. Had I learned something this summer in seeing him?

I told her what had happened. He had said he was sorry, he wanted to know if he was the cause, he said he wanted to talk. Peter's words came back: "He couldn't believe he would hurt you so terribly by going." How could he not have known?

"Did you say anything to him?" Greta asked.

"I said 'I can't go through this with you again.' "

She looked at me, an island of calm.

"What are you thinking?" I asked her.

"I will tell you," she said. "I'm thinking about your question, what is the opposite of losing? It is a good question for us."

I stared at her face. She had turned into a sphinx.

"He sent me another letter, written right after Provincetown, but since he mailed it to Cambridge I only got it this week."

She raised her eyebrows.

I took it out of my purse and read: "*Okay, Kyra. I think what you said is true. I think a lot of other things are true too, but that's all one. What you said is true.*" There was a space, then another

line. *"I apologize very sincerely. I will not be irresponsible again."*
It was signed *"a."* Which would have been enough, but there was
this other paragraph at the bottom. *"Oh darling, I wanted so to
break this curse. You touched me in a place of me and showed me
a vision that made me want more than I have ever wanted to
break out of this hell with you and for you. I think you are the
most beautiful person I will ever know."*

Greta's face was impassive. She wasn't going to fill in for me.

I looked at the clock. Time was running out.

"A miasma of sorrow," she said.

I looked up the word in the dictionary. It meant bad smell.

I was feeling better. Something had settled. The earth maybe,
under my feet. On Nashawena, summer stretched its long fingers
into September, reaching way past Labor Day, the midday sun
hot, the water calm. The Gulf Stream rolled in from the west, diagonal waves sweeping the beach. Then a hurricane spewed its
fury into the sea, somewhere off Georges Bank, and Anna and I
went down to watch the walls of greenish-brown water crash on
the shore. Rocks were moved, and a gull with a broken wing wandered dazed across the sand.

"It looks like me," I said. "Not now, but it was how I felt."

Anna had known. In that uncanny way women cycle together,
bodies falling into rhythm with one another, like the moon and
the tides. She had come over to the shack that day, sensing something was wrong. Later, it was she who found Greta, sent her to
see me in the hospital.

"About Greta," I began. Greta had said that the order of the
universe, what I had thought to be the necessary order of the universe, had been shaken by the work we were doing.

"That's what therapy does," Anna said. "It dislodges you.
Freud said that it deepens the darkness so you can start to see
what has faint light to it." She had been in therapy, all therapists
had. I wondered about Greta—when she was the patient, had her
world been shaken? People get anxious, Anna said, when some-

thing pulls them beyond the frame they're used to seeing things through. You can't be engaged with someone unless you're willing to take that risk.

I thought about Greta. What risks had she taken?

"Your anxiety is rising," Greta said to me one day when I was finding it hard to breathe, "and the question now is, do you have to restore the old order?" It sounded quaint, the king is dead, long live the king. She had become the therapist, taking on that order, enforcing its regulations, speaking its language, we have to stop. The therapist has to love the patient, Anna said, otherwise it can't work. But if you love someone, I said, you don't leave them.

I watched the waves inch up the beach. The tide was coming in.

"It's confusing," I said. Greta had taught me how to listen, to pick up the voice that speaks in dreams. But within her, I sensed a reserve. As if it would be dangerous to come too close. *Lay your sleeping head, my love, Human on my faithless arm.* That was Auden. The poets knew. He also knew about war.

———

At the first faculty meeting of the year, the dean introduced the new professors and visiting faculty. The room was filled, attendance mandatory, absence punished by death, David would say. He was in Rome; his replacement for the year caught my eye. A landscape architect from Tehran. Her hair was spiked, silver bracelets circled her arm. A mix of elegance and irreverence. I liked her at once. Her name was Roya. It meant *dream,* she explained over lunch after the meeting.

She was a swimmer, she had grown up by the Caspian Sea. We decided to swim each morning in the Indoor Athletic Building. Dank corridors, ancient lockers, but the pool was okay. Afterward, we went out for coffee at the Italian place in the Square. "What's wrong with the students here? They seem so docile," she asked one morning, releasing her wet hair from the woolen scarf. "All they read is what's on the reading list." In Iran, the students had been Marxists, intellectuals, they read everything they could get hold of, they had been at the forefront of the revolution. "But then"—she shrugged her shoulders—"the government closed the universities." I spooned the foam from my cappuccino and pictured Roya wrapped in black. "That's when I cut my hair," she said.

I went to see Abe at the beginning of October. I felt strong enough to do it, and I had always liked him. He was staying with his sister, Edith. His tests were inconclusive. "Maybe it's just a little hardening of the arteries," he said. A winsome smile. The Europeans knew about aging. It happens. It takes courage, my grandmother had said. Abe was planning to go back to Budapest. He showed me a letter from Jesse. *I am missing you too, Opapa,* Jesse wrote over a picture he had drawn of the two of them holding hands. A P.S. was scrawled at the bottom, *Papa says that maybe we could get a dog.* I mentally noted my skepticism. Abe's eyes sparkled. "It's something Jesse and I have talked about."

We played gin, and Edith brought a plate of raspberry-filled cookies to the table. As far as I could see, there was no problem with Abe's memory. He put down his cards. "Gin," he said, discarding the five of spades that I had been waiting for.

I didn't want to bring it up, but he did. "Kyra," he said, "I've been thinking about you. I want you to know that I'm sorry about what happened. You know that he lost his wife, Jesse's mother. It was a terrible thing. So many terrible things. They leave a scar." He pushed the cookies toward me. "Here, have one of these. They're very good. Edith makes them. Maybe you would have some coffee, or tea?" He looked in the direction of the kitchen. There was more he wanted to say.

"In Budapest, we thought we were safe. No one was prepared for what happened, but we should have known. Andreas was just a small boy, younger than Jesse, when the Nazis began rounding up the Jews. He thought we would protect him, and we did, thanks in large part to my wife. But I also had contacts, the people I delivered eggs to were well connected, and then one of the farmers took us in. I think Andreas thought he would always be protected. He has a mission in life. He wants to resolve something. You have to understand that. He feels it's a debt he owes to his wife, to do his work in Budapest. She had fought for that, for him to be able to do that. And when that debt is repaid, which is what he's doing now with his opera company, then he would be ready"—he cleared his throat—"to start a new life." He placed his brown-speckled hand over mine and squeezed it. "Take it as you will. It's an old man's wish."

I told Anna I had seen Abe. Roya had come to Nashawena for the weekend to see the project, and we were in the kitchen. I could see that Anna liked her too. Tony was away for a few days, so it was just the three of us in the house. Anna was making pasta with clams. Roya had brought pomegranates and was slicing them for dessert. I finished chopping the parsley and carried the board to the stove. "Ready?" I asked, inhaling the garlic. "Not quite," Anna said, stirring the clams into the sauce. I watched the edges of the clams curl. Roya moved to set the table. "Should I use these plates?" Anna nodded. "So how was Abe?" Anna asked. She fished a strand of linguine out of the boiling water with a wooden spoon and handed it to me. "He seemed fine," I said. "He wanted to talk." She raised her eyebrows. I bit off an end of the pasta. "Almost." "We have a bottle of Pinot Grigio in the fridge," she said. Roya offered to make the salad dressing, "if you like it with lemon." She picked a lemon from the blue bowl on the counter, tossed it to the ceiling, and caught it with a grin. A cloud of steam rose from the sink as Anna drained the pasta. I opened the wine and lit the candles.

Anna lifted her glass to Roya. "Welcome."

Roya raised hers. "In Farsi, we say *salamati*. It means good health."

It was Friday night, the end of the week. We had not had much traffic on the way from Cambridge to Woods Hole. Roya and I had gossiped about colleagues. With her penchant for saying whatever was on her mind, she had extracted information from the most steel-faced, including the architecture chairman, who was apparently on the verge of leaving his wife for a neurobiologist. At Woods Hole, dusk had settled in. The low white building of the ferry terminal, a line of cars waiting for the ferry, dock workers in their red shirts, Venus bright against the gray of the sky. We took the small ferry, Roya ecstatic. She had been longing for the sea.

I handed her the bowl of pasta and clams.

Anna, stirred by the arrival of yet another refugee from the world's political insanity, was waxing on the dangers of the current administration, Reagan in the White House, reading from a script as if he were still in the movies, the idiocy of Margaret Thatcher, the absurdity of Star Wars, not to mention the real wars in Nicaragua and Mozambique. "If there's one thing I know as a therapist," she concluded, heaping pasta on her plate and searching the bowl for hidden clams, "it's what violence does to people."

"That's what Abe was talking about," I said, "how it leaves scars."

"It's hard not to be pessimistic about the world," Roya said, twirling the linguine around her fork. "In Iran, there was hope with Mossadegh. He was nationalizing the oil industry, instituting reforms. But then he was overthrown by your CIA."

"Not mine," Anna said. She carried two passports, one Cyprus, one U.S., the hedge of the dispossessed. I had let my Cyprus passport run out.

"With the revolution," Roya continued, "we had hope again. We got rid of the Shah, but then the fundamentalists took over." She shook her head, a dangle of silver, her earrings lit by the reflected light of the candles. "My family left, went to Rome. People were executed, there was no recourse, and now it's almost impossible to get out of Iran." Her face was flushed. "This is the conversation I've been missing," she said. "In Iran nobody talked about anything but politics. Here people talk about anything but."

"No one seems to know what to do," I said, distracted. The conversation with Abe had been unsettling. At the time, I had felt numb. It was just more of the same. I remembered the sentence from Andreas's letter, the one he sent just after he left. *I am past the point where I can accept your love on any terms other than permanently, and I am not at the point where I can accept it permanently.*

"I heard an interesting lecture yesterday," Roya said, putting down her fork. She had changed out of her black slacks and silk blouse into soft gray pants and a long white sweater. "Each week when the *Harvard Gazette* comes out, I choose a lecture on a subject I know nothing about and just go. This week, I went to hear a psychoanalyst who was speaking at the Beth Israel Hospital. It was the something something memorial lecture and the title caught my eye: 'When the Problem Comes into the Room: Turning Points in Psychotherapy with Women.' "

Anna looked up, intrigued.

"I took the shuttle bus across the river. I'd never been to the medical school. It's odd, at these lectures I never see the same people, each time it's a completely different crowd. The week before, I'd gone to a lecture on Indian burial grounds at the Peabody Museum. Everything was dusty and dim, a scattering of people in browns and khaki. They all looked like anthropologists. Here, everything was brightly lit and the auditorium was full. Doctors in white coats, nurses, men wearing suits, women in dresses. I was glad I had worn my Italian boots. The woman for whom the lecture was named had been a psychoanalyst, obviously revered, and the speaker had an impressive list of degrees and honors. At first I thought the lecture was going to be dull, but as she went on, her face became animated and it got more and more interesting. By the end she held that whole group in thrall.

"As a medical student, she'd been intrigued by the process of healing, by the body's ability to heal itself and also what got in the way. As a psychoanalyst, she saw the same thing. People came to therapy, she said, because there was something they wanted to heal, and therapy was set up to facilitate that process. But she had come to see that there was a problem in the very structure of therapy."

I caught Anna's eye. This was our conversation.

"She said that she noticed this especially with her women patients. She spoke of a woman she called Alice. At a point in her therapy when change was in the air, Alice began to complain about the therapy relationship. She said it was an oil-and-water relationship, like selling indulgences or a kind of prostitution, love or sympathy in exchange for money, the whole thing run by the clock.

"The speaker, the analyst, said that at first she had seen this as a resistance on Alice's part. She had been trained to expect resistance from people at the moment when they begin to envision the possibility of change. But Alice had dug in her heels. There was a problem, she said, and it wasn't just her problem. And here's the interesting point."

Roya picked up her wine and took a sip.

"With Alice and also with other women patients, this analyst had come to realize that the impediments to healing were not just internal. Living in this world, women have learned to adapt to structures not of their own making, and this adaptation has to be confronted and challenged. That's when the problem comes into the room.

"She said that some change has to occur in the structure of the therapy itself, some action has to be taken in the relationship or in the arrangements to demonstrate to the woman that she has the power to change the situation in which she finds herself. If the patient does not initiate this change in the structure, then the analyst has to question why this woman is being compliant, or complicit. For the therapist, this also means questioning his or her own investment in the structure, her complicity in maintaining it.

"She was a tiny woman who seemed very calm. Not the kind of person to gird herself for battle. I could see she was taking a risk. Some people in the audience were clearly uncomfortable with what she was saying. It meant challenging the existing structure of therapy, seeing it as a problem that must be addressed, especially in treating women. The woman next to me began sorting through her purse, but there was an electricity in the room."

Roya looked at us, waiting for a signal to go on. Anna nodded. I was rooted to my seat.

"The speaker told a story about a British analyst named Winnicott. A minister had come to ask what he should do when people brought their personal problems to him. Should he talk with them or refer them to a psychotherapist? Winnicott told the minister that if he found it interesting, he should speak with them, otherwise he should refer them. The audience laughed, but she was serious. She said that however difficult or disturbing she found these moments of challenge from women patients, which often precipitated a crisis in the therapy, however on the spot she personally felt, she always found herself interested because the problem was a real problem. And in retrospect, it often marked a turning point in the therapy, opening the way to healing. In other words, in the patient, it was a good sign—that she challenged the structure of therapy.

"She concluded by drawing out the implications of what she had said. It is a mistake, she believed, to separate therapy or the problems that bring people to therapy from the society or culture in which it is taking place. Ultimately, the process of change has to extend beyond the individual and affect the family structures, the religious and political structures that are implicated in people's suffering. I hadn't known what to expect, but it struck me as a revolutionary talk."

"Who was the analyst?" Anna asked, passing the salad.

"I don't remember her name," Roya said. "Dr. something, but apparently she was also a musician."

I looked at Anna.

I had argued with Greta before the summer about this very issue. *Structure* had been my word, my "architect's eye" as she called it. At the time, I thought she had dismissed it as my resistance to doing "the work" as she would put it, the therapeutic work I needed to do. Had she taken what I said to heart? Who was this Alice? It sounded like another name for me.

Anna raised her eyebrows as if to ask, was I going to say anything? No.

We ate our salad in silence.

I hadn't told Roya about Andreas. I hadn't told Anna Abe's wish.

I got up to clear the table. The pomegranates were waiting. Would we go now, like Persephone, into the underworld of love? For each seed eaten, a month in Hades, according to the myth. I opened another bottle of wine.

Night had settled into the room. Outside it was pitch dark, the island still. No moon, no wind.

"Let's talk about love, really," I said, bringing the wine and the pomegranates to the table. I downed a glass. "What is love?"

"It's strange," Anna mused, "psychoanalysts have written about so many things, and yet no one has really dared to write about love." She finished the remaining wine in her glass and poured in more from the new bottle.

"Let's not talk about psychoanalysis," Roya said, her eyes glistening. "Let's say what we know about love."

"Kyra's the expert"—Anna nodded toward me—"but she's just been burned, so you have to be careful." The wine was going to her head.

I bit into a slice of pomegranate, the red seeds releasing their juice. I reached for my napkin to blot the stain, the scar on my wrist almost invisible. I didn't think Roya had seen it, and whatever her travels through the university, no one seemed to have mentioned it to her. It was hardly the subject for a public lecture, a mix of anger and satisfaction now rising about Greta. What right had she, if it was her? Yet it seemed she had heard me, taken it in. "You can't do this work without love," she had said one day when I pressed her about her feelings. "Why not say 'I'?" I had said.

"Okay, I'll start," I said, putting my napkin down. "People used to think of love as the oldest of the gods."

"Chaos, earth, and then love," Anna said. "That's Hesiod."

"Who?" Roya asked.

love. He experimented with what was called wild analy-
got into all sorts of trouble. But me—I'm not a wild per-
d unlike my sister, I've never been what you would call 'in

rearranged the seeds on her plate, mixing the colors, her
guarded, incandescent. Had she been too much the older

smiled as if reading my thoughts.
candles had burned down to the wicks. Anna began to
n old ballad she used to sing on her guitar. Quietly, she
words: "*The roads they are so muddy, we cannot walk
, so roll me in your arms, love, and blow the candles out.*"
s of smoke rose from the pools of wax. "I've said more than
nded," she said, getting up and heading for the drawer
e we kept the candles. "It's Roya's turn." She pressed the
candles into the melted wax and lit them.
oya held the pomegranate to the light. "Eat the pomegranate,
ammed said, for it purges the system of envy and hatred."
sucked the seeds into her mouth.
Me? I always thought love was a trap, and for many women
as. I wanted freedom. Not marriage or children. My dream
this, to be an architect, to work with the landscape. I fell in
with trees and plants—their names, their colors, their shapes.
as magic. I had an image of the life I wanted to lead. I would
e passionate love affairs in different countries with amazing
ple. And I did. I have. Sometimes my heart was broken." A
dow crossed her face. "Still, it was worth it." She looked past
into the room. "I read once that if you want to be an artist you
ve to be prepared to have your heart broken. In the revolution,
ve were going to purge ourselves of envy and hatred, renounce
ssession. It was a discipline of the heart. But given what hap-
ned, I think we were mistaken about freedom. What it meant.
Maybe it's love that's revolutionary. Because it's love that frees
s."
An astonished look, as if she were amazed by the words that
ad come out of her mouth.

"A Greek poet," Anna said.

"And when you fell in love, they said you'd been smitten by a
god, or pierced by an arrow, or infused with a potion. It was a
kind of madness. Beautiful, but still . . . I know the feeling, the
sense of being overtaken, consumed."

Anna was watching me, her eyes slightly blurred. Roya's face
was lit with anticipation. I would take her dare, say what I knew.

"But I would say in a way it's just the opposite. It's the deepest
kind of knowing, and that can drive you mad. It can make you
feel crazy, but this crazy feeling is not love. Love is something you
know with someone. It's hard to explain, but you know it in your
body. It's like it happens in your cells, your cells and their cells
recognize one another. You can't make it happen or make it not
happen, which also drives some people crazy."

I edged a circle of wax from the table with my fingernail. It
broke away in bits.

"It was almost two years ago. A total surprise. *This* is happening? I tried to brush it aside. We started working together. He was
directing a play, an opera. He asked me to do the sets. It was
something I'd never done before, but I did it, and then I went
away. And when I came back, it felt inevitable. We became lovers.
It sounds trite, but everything lightened, as if gravity had released
us from its grip."

I examined the spot where the wax had fallen, the wood glazed
milky-white.

"Or like the wind at this time of year, clearing the leaves, ex-
posing the structure of the branches. I felt seen in a way I'd never
been before. And he too. We said it to each other. That's what I
mean by knowing. We knew each other. Or at least I thought we
did. Was that love? I don't know. It felt like love, but then what
happened didn't look like love."

I braced my elbows against the table and put my head in my
hands.

"He left. Suddenly, with no warning. Someone else told me he
was going, not him. Nothing had changed between us, but then
he was going. He said he had to do his work, but that wasn't it.

In this world there are many ways to work out these things. If he had wanted me in his life, he would have told me he was going, tried to work something out. But he was adamant, he had to go, and by then I was furious. He wrote me a letter, but it made no sense. *I love you desperately, in more ways than I knew existed. We cannot see each other.* I couldn't feel without feeling crazy. Then I started to go numb, and that was worse. I'm in therapy now because last December I cut myself. People thought I was trying to kill myself, like someone in an opera. But that wasn't it. I cut myself because I had to get under a surface that was crazy-making, to see what was real. And Greta, my therapist, she knew that. She said no to medications. Which was a relief. And there was this other thing that surprised me. I thought she would say 'get rid of this guy,' which is what many people told me. Get over it. But that wasn't it. If you can't feel love, what can you feel? Greta said I would find out what I wanted to do. It might take time."

I stopped, suddenly rattled. I looked at Anna, wondering if she had noticed. She was picking the pomegranate seeds from their white husk, lining them up on her plate. I hadn't even mentioned Simon.

Anna scooped up the seeds with her spoon. "I'll go next," she said, filling her mouth. I couldn't read Roya's expression. I assumed she would be in the get-rid-of-him camp. She held up the bottle of wine. I shook my head, and she filled her glass.

"I didn't know you were in therapy," she said quietly.

I stared at my hands, white against the olive-green suede of my pants. My mind was on Simon. The lecture suddenly seemed inconsequential. "You saw her," I said, "my therapist. At that lecture."

A startled look on Roya's face.

Her eyes widened, dark circles of amazement. "She was the speaker?" She paused, clearly flustered. "I should have not said . . ." she began, glancing first at Anna, then at me. "I'm sorry," she said, "I didn't know."

"I didn't either when you started, but then it became obvious,"

I said, turning to Anna, who was st
felt too exposed.

"Isn't everyone in America in thei
her bracelets.

"It may seem that way," Anna sai
litical situation, it isn't having much e

"But that's what she was saying," F
ing, "why it hasn't been effective."

Anna picked up her glass and held
the awkwardness to dispel.

"Love is what we bring with us into
"Hesiod was right, in the beginning
That's where the story starts. I loved my
loved many people, men, women, you na
versity, all the old rules were suspended.
vent love, strip it of jealousy and possessi
that we could, but love has a way of circur
Kyra said, you can't contain it, and yet it v

She put another slice of pomegranate on
sort the seeds, darker red, lighter red. They

"With Tony now, it's a sweet love. Asid
best friend." She hesitated a moment, th
"We're talking now about having a child."
child. I didn't know they were actually planni
spoon and turned it, watching the flame from
and disappear. "It's not a passionate love," A
maybe the two are incompatible. With patien
these Talmudic discussions about love. They
with me, or at least some of them would, and
felt love for them. But as they suspected, I w
them, or if I felt my feelings moving in that dire
mind myself that it wasn't really me they were
some image they had projected onto me or a n
reenact an old script of rejection and confirm tl
Then I began to question that. I started readir
Hungarian analyst who said that the physician h

We sat watching the candles burn down. Stars spinning in their distant constellations. Maybe love is the revolutionary emotion, the true freedom, because it releases something in ourselves. The thought made me sad.

We had finished the second bottle of wine. I stood up, waiting for the room to steady. "What's the old Dylan song, '*Freedom's just another word for nothing left to lose*'?" I put the bottle in the recycling bin.

"That's not Dylan," Anna said. "It's Kris Kristofferson, 'Me and Bobby McGee.' The song he wrote for Janis Joplin."

"Who was Bobby McGee?" Roya asked.

"Who knows," Anna said, "but about freedom. You can't love without freedom. That's what makes love feel so unsafe, you have to relinquish control."

We left the dishes on the counter, a red stain on each plate.

———

"I hear you've been talking about me," I said.

Greta stiffened in her chair.

"My friend Roya, the Iranian architect, she went to your lecture. Each week she goes to a different lecture, it's her way of sampling Harvard, and last week, she chose yours."

I waited, my heart beating fast.

"And you have some feelings about that?"

I laughed.

"I do," I said. "For one thing, you might ask me if you're going to quote me. I gather you talked about problems in the structure of therapy. And for another, you might have told me. I'd like to have heard what you would say."

A twist in the corner of her mouth.

"What do you think I would say?"

"Actually, I know what you said. Roya told us, without knowing that you were my therapist. She might have done so anyway, since she doesn't really believe in therapy, but that's beside the point. What I think is that you would have said exactly what you said. But the problem is not just that women need to discover that they can change the structures in which they are living. That's what my work is about, changing the structure. It's why do *you* set up this situation, this structure, in the first place. Why set up a relationship with the ending built in? You're asking women to buy this, but my question is, why have you bought it?"

She picked up a pencil, her features set. I could see she was angry, not therapist anger but really mad. A genuine feeling. I sat up straight in my chair.

"I think I see your point," she said, her voice steady. "But I have to ask, why now? Why is this coming up now?"

"Because of the lecture," I said. Because of the conversation with Roya and Anna the other night.

"I'll tell you something that will interest you," I continued, pulling off my sweater and tossing it onto the wooden chair next to the desk. Outside it was still light. Soon the time would change, the clocks aligning with the earth as it moved into darkness.

Greta removed her shawl, placing it on her lap, an island of red against the black of her dress.

"Roya came to Nashawena for the weekend, and we had this long conversation about love, Anna, Roya, and I. I spoke about love without even thinking about Simon. I was talking about Andreas, how it had been, how I had thought that was love, and then when he left, I didn't know what was real. The love? The leaving? Which only underscores the absurdity of this situation here. Because if you think about it, it's an exact repetition. Someone elicits love and then leaves. But here, the ending is built in from the start. What's the point? I'm in the same situation again. Maybe I'm not in love, but love, that's what you're inviting. You say you can't do this work without love. And if that's true, why would you end the love, the relationship? Roya would say you're just perpetuating the old system."

I thought of Mohammed, what Roya had said. Purge the system of envy and hatred.

"You know," Greta said, "you can attack me. Maybe you need to get angry at me. But it might be worth asking if you're also angry at yourself for not thinking about, or speaking about, Simon. That would show a big shift, for you to let go of that."

"That's too easy," I said. "When I realized I hadn't even mentioned him, at first I was startled, but then I had this image of myself standing on the shore, watching a piece of the continent drift away. As I thought about it, it made sense. I had already let go of Simon when I fell in love with Andreas. I just hadn't seen it."

She raised her eyebrows, indicating a question. Was that true?

"What really rattled me that night was the realization that with Andreas I had gone to a completely different place. What's the poem, '*somewhere I have never traveled.*' It was like that, which I also hadn't admitted to myself. And then after he left, I had to ask myself, was it like that? Was it the way I thought, had felt? Because then I couldn't tell anymore what was real. Which is why I cut myself. Now I have feelings for you, you say you have feelings for me. I can feel that. But are the feelings real?"

She switched on the lamp.

"Our purpose here is to understand your feelings," Greta said, "for you to know them. Then you can make whatever choices you want. To act on them, to not act on them. But in either case, you will understand what you are doing."

A clutch in my stomach, a wave of despair. I could see where this was going. It was just my problem. Not hers. A voice in my head. Don't give in.

"I just don't buy that," I said. "You speak as if my feelings exist completely apart from yours. But here we are in this small room, breathing the same air, literally taking each other in. If you're fudging your feelings or withholding your feelings, it's confusing to me, to mine. It makes it hard to breathe."

I picked up a Kleenex and put it over my nose.

She watched. I couldn't read her face.

"Roya said that in the revolution in Iran, they tried to discipline their hearts. Isn't that what therapists learn to do? But it's not something I want to learn to do."

That was the point. I had no stomach for this situation, this so-called relationship. Once was enough. Too much. I looked at my bag, lying on the floor. I had seen the effect on Anna. She had done that, learned to discipline her heart. I saw the cost.

"This is the way I know how to work," Greta said. A simple statement.

I watched the light shift on the painting of the door over her chair, the blue deepening as the afternoon waned. I had seen that door as an invitation. Now I noticed. It was shut.

"I have a proposal," Greta said, her face alert. "It's October now. What if we agree to continue until January, that gives us three months, and it will be a year. Then we can decide together how we want to proceed."

My stomach went into free fall. She had removed the barrier. What would happen would be up to us.

"I'll be away in January," I said. "There's a conference in Vienna on reenvisioning the city, and I've been asked to give one of the talks. It's the first week in January, and since that's reading period at Harvard, I thought I might stay on another week."

"Then that will be our break," Greta said, picking up her book. "It will give us time between now and then, and we can continue to talk about this."

That was her signal. I looked at the clock. We had run over. I gathered up my things and glanced at the painting. I could swear that the door had opened a crack.

3

WE HAD GONE THROUGH THE FACULTY MEETING AGENDA, AND the dean asked if there were other matters people wanted to bring up. Reckless question. Silent prayers lofted around the room: let no one speak and the meeting end early. Jerry raised his hand. He was the young recruit on the architecture faculty, a winner of prizes, a popular teacher. "What about the students' demand for more diversity on the faculty?" A shudder ran through the room.

A naïve plant lover from landscape looked up, consternation on his face: "I don't see any objection to what they're asking for. The question is, how are we going to respond, what action are we prepared to take to make this happen?" Diversity was the coinage of landscape architecture: many plants, different colors.

I glanced at the dean, his face impassive: whatever happens, may it not involve emotion.

Roya, on my left, was doodling. She sketched a woman in a chador. I raised my eyebrows. She raised her hand.

"Mike, Alex, Roya, and then Sanji," the dean intoned. He made a list on his pad.

Resignation settled over the room. Give academics a topic and they will debate it. Give administrators a question, they will form a committee. The dispirited soul on my right began surreptitiously to read his mail.

It was twenty to four.

Mike, who taught the seminar on deconstruction, began by de-molishing the dialectical oppositions and binary categories that were, like the not-diverse faculty, deeply entrenched.

The jargon landed on the sodden faces of those allergic to crit-ical theory, not to mention Mike's outfit of black sweater and jeans. Philip, the chair of architecture, in tailored jacket and trousers, got up to refill his cup of tea.

"If we are not only to analyze concepts in their most rigorous and internalized manner," Mike continued, "but also to question from the outside what these concepts hide as repression or dissim-ulation, then the presence of a more diverse faculty can only be an advantage."

Good for you, I thought. Standards weren't the issue. Who didn't want rigor? The question was, whose standards?

Mike smiled at Jerry. They were squash partners, pals. It was a love letter written in the language of Derrida.

A beam of late-afternoon sun crossed the room.

The queue moved forward.

"Correct me if I'm wrong," Alex began with rhetorical flour-ish, adjusting his small wire-rimmed glasses, "but if what the stu-dents are saying is that we should now hire on the basis of skin color, then it seems to me—"

Jerry broke in. "What they're saying is that's exactly what we're doing, hiring on the basis of skin color. White."

Alex shot back, "The only criteria for hiring should be excel-lence. Otherwise, we're talking about racism."

"That's exactly what we're talking about," Jerry countered. "Look around."

Here we go again, I thought. Last time this happened, Alex walked out.

Silently the faculty divided. If this were gym class, they would give out pinnies, or play shirts and skins.

"Please," the dean said, his expression sour. The purpose of the queue was to avoid conflict. Let a hundred flowers bloom, the meeting would end, the flowers would wither, people were busy, nothing would happen.

Jerry, undeterred, let out his sail. "There's more at stake here than noble gestures, letting in those who have been excluded. The question is, what have we lost, what has been lost to architecture and design by virtue of this exclusion, and what can we do to include it now? What is it that we are not seeing?"

Alex, tight-lipped, receded into his stony castle of excellence.

"Roya," the dean said. She put down her pen.

And now for something completely different.

I settled back to watch.

"In Farsi, we have a saying, '*Hameen yek karam moondeh.*' It means, that's the last thing I need to do. I observe you already work too much."

General laughter, a jangle of bracelets, Roya adjusting the collar of her blouse, an infusion of fuchsia in the otherwise gray room.

"But as a Jewish woman," she continued, faces suddenly on guard, "who has lived in an Islamic regime that does not value diversity, even though historically there is a strain of tolerance running through Persian culture, I have seen what can happen when one group thinks they possess the truth or that God is on their side. At least some of these students may be trying to communicate what is for them a painful experience, the feeling of being disappeared. They have come here to learn and yet they discover that what they know from experience has no significance. The question for us is, what do we want to teach them, not only about architecture but also about how to live in this world?"

A stir in the room. Some people looked thoughtful, others began to gather their papers.

The dean looked at his watch.

"I too am a visitor here," Sanji began, his voice melodic, his glasses reflecting the light. He was from New Delhi, an architect with major commissions. "There is a saying my daughter told me from one of the songs she listens to on the radio: 'You don't know what you don't know.' I will not tell you in what context she said this"—a ripple of laughter—"but maybe you will guess it was not about architecture.

"But this is not my point. My point is that if what your students are calling for is to explore, as the painter Anselm Kiefer does, the possibilities of the frame, then you have done a very good job of educating them." He smiled broadly.

I wasn't sure this was what the students had in mind, but he had cast them in the best possible light. A surge of warmth for my colleagues, the ray of intelligence in this dour meeting like sunlight in a Dutch landscape painting.

It was four o'clock.

Predictably, the dean suggested we form a committee to meet with the students and take up the matter.

Jerry, Mike, and Roya volunteered.

The dean asked Alex and Sanji to join them.

I hesitated a moment, then raised my hand, a flicker of hope trumping my aversion to taking on more work.

Roya had office hours starting at four. I headed for the river, propelled by a lightness I had not anticipated. "You don't know what you don't know." Greta would love that. The last session with her had left me unsettled. Nothing might come of the dean's newly formed committee, but what happens when two women decide to explore the possibility of changing the frame? As Greta and I had agreed to do.

The headlights brightened as the light fell, the stream of rush-hour traffic heading home. I realized that, like Roya, I was a foreigner here, although no longer a visitor. The deconstructionists would say, Explore the between. The November sky streaked pink and red. I could turn and walk in the opposite direction, toward rather than away from the sunset. I could call Roya from the pay phone at the gas station and invite her for supper. I could pick up prosciutto from the Italian store on Prospect Street and a melon from Bread & Circus. I had been remiss about swimming, had missed our coffees. Yet something impelled me to keep walking in the direction I was going. Into the darkness. I would call Roya when I got home. I would swim with her in the morning and spend the evening alone, exploring the between.

———

"Last night I dreamed I was walking on a narrow bridge over a deep ravine. Midway, the railings stopped. I turned, but the bridge behind me had disappeared. In its place was an old Roman aqueduct, the stone surface wide like the aqueduct at Avignon, but still there was nothing to keep one from falling over the edge. The height was dizzying. Both ways were dangerous. I took a step forward on the thin bridge. Now it was impossible to turn back. I panicked, and then I woke up."

Greta sat still in her chair.

"My associations," I continued, grateful for the enclosure of the black leather chair, "are to my paper, the one I have to write. The MAK, the Austrian Museum of Applied Arts, has a new director. They're planning to restore the old buildings, he has a bold new agenda. The conference I'm invited to speak at is the beginning. There are no guidelines."

I stopped, the room frozen in time.

"The feeling of panic was that I couldn't turn and go back because the bridge was too narrow, and I couldn't go forward because if there had been the slightest wind, or if I made a misstep and lost my balance, I would fall to my death." The terror of the dream washed over me. It was how I felt about the paper, frozen for fear of making a misstep, my project too narrow for a conference of this magnitude. Or was that it? A painter friend said that with each new project, you had to be prepared to walk off the edge.

I looked at Greta, saw the faintest etching of a smile on her face.

"I'm wondering about the aqueduct," she said. "They were built to carry water long distances, but they also were used to divert water."

"So going back would be a diversion?"

"You have said what we do here was a Roman therapy, you objected to the setup, the structure. I thought you had a point. I understand about the paper, but I wonder if it is something of a diversion from what the dream is telling us."

She crossed her legs, adjusting her skirt.

"Which is?"

I glanced at the spider plant on the desk beside me. It had produced a new crop of babies, hanging over the edge, out of the light.

"If you hung that plant from the window frame," I said, "its offspring would get more light."

Greta laughed, and for a moment we were two women in a room.

"Do you want me to say it?" she said, her voice playful.

I crossed my legs and eyed my low boot, the heel scuffed, the brown leather cracked and faded. In the window of the Italian shop on JFK Street, there was a pair of boots I coveted. A persimmon suede that would be perfect with my black slacks for the conference.

"That we've taken away the railings here," she said quietly.

The *we* grated. It was I who had said there was a problem with the structure, with the ending, and then she— My thoughts jolted. She had met me halfway.

Dizziness swept over me, a swell of emotion. The skin on my forehead tingled and then thickened.

"What's happening?" Greta asked.

"I don't know," I said, swallowing hard. Inexplicably, I began sobbing.

She waited until my sobs subsided. "Let's just say," she said, her voice soft, caressing, "that whatever this is about, it's connected to very strong feelings."

I looked at her blindly.

It was time to stop.

Afterward, the session replayed in my mind. The dream, the bridge, Greta coming forward, meeting me halfway. More than that, given her training. We've taken away the railings here, she had said. The sudden vertigo and then were sobbing. As if something were being purged from my body.

Anna and Tony were nesting, surrounded by catalogues on the sofa. Their winter season had begun. I found myself watching Anna carefully, looking for the first signs of pregnancy, the passing on a glass of wine. So far no sign. Greta had asked how I felt about the possibility of my sister having a baby. The question set my teeth on edge. What I would feel, I said, if she got pregnant, is what anyone would feel in my situation: happy for my sister, and then—I eyed Greta steadily—jealous. It was the word she was waiting for. I was tired of the game.

I told Anna what had happened, how the "problem of the ending" had been suspended, upended, who knew. It wasn't that therapy would continue endlessly, it was about the future of the relationship.

In return, Anna told me a story. She had gone to a conference, a meeting of psychoanalysts. It had been held at the Waldorf-Astoria hotel in New York. A fur-and-jewel occasion, she said, she whose sympathy was with the minks and the seals. The room was full, and the analyst presenting was young and recently trained, known for her work with difficult patients. The case she was presenting was of a young man who had fallen in love with her, his therapist. He wanted to know if they could become lovers once the therapy ended. "And I can't remember her reasoning," Anna said. "I mean, how she reasoned it out in terms of his issues, but her response struck me as brilliant. What she had said to him stunned the whole audience. She had refused to close off the possibility."

"Did she really think of sleeping with him?" I asked.

"You're missing the point, which was not to foreclose anything, but I don't think she did."

"Then it wasn't an honest move on her part."

Anna looked thoughtful. "Maybe you're right, and it was a ruse, which would give it a sinister cast. Or maybe she meant you

can never really know in the present what may happen in the future, which makes it an existential statement."

We were in my room, sitting on my bed. I was brushing my
hair. Anna picked up the barrette, opening and closing the clasp.

"But that's not the issue with Greta," I said.

"What?"

"Sleeping with her."

"What would you say the issue was?"

"It's about love, the meaning of love. When it's real and when
it's not."

I took the barrette, gathered up my hair, and clasped it at the
top of my head.

"It's daring," she said.

"What?"

"To do what you're doing."

"You think so?" I wondered how she felt about it.

A light came into her eyes. "You know," she said, leaning back
on her elbows, "what I'm feeling now is that when all these other
people entered our lives—Greta, Tony, and before that, the whole
thing with Andreas—it was hard sometimes, there were times
when we weren't really talking to each other, I felt myself moving
away but that's not how I feel now."

"Me too," I said.

She smiled and put her arms around her knees. "I like it this
way," she said, "I mean us, and also your hair."

I went and looked in the mirror, my face completely exposed.

———

I knew I couldn't sit in the chair. A rawness had come over me as
I entered the room. There was another chair, catty-cornered from
Greta, wooden arms, upholstered seat. I opted for the couch, to
Greta's left against the wall, and settled into the brown velvet.

"So?" Greta said.

"So," I said.

I had always avoided the couch, averting my eyes, but it now seemed more inviting than frightening. I lay back and pulled the green chenille throw over me. The room looked different from this angle, the faint stuccoing of the walls more pronounced, the lamp reflecting on the ceiling, a circle of light and shadows, the window directly in my line of vision.

"Kyra, darling," my mother would say, "take a little rest." I had resisted her then.

I turned toward Greta. She was staring straight ahead, her face in profile looking older. Was this how she looked to the members of her trio or quartet?

I shifted the pillows and lay down fully. My thoughts began to drift. There was an advantage in not seeing her, in not being looked at. Roya had said it was painful to be disappeared. I knew what she meant. Still, this was different. I pulled the throw over my head, disappearing like a child. Where's Kyra?

Greta said nothing.

The silence took on a buoyancy, I floated on its surface, the ceiling my sky.

"I'm thinking about that dream," I said, my voice coming from a distance I could not measure. "About the bridge and the railings."

I paused.

"Two years ago, I gave a talk at Cornell. A friend I had known at university was on the faculty and he had invited me up to Ithaca. There was a job opening in urban design. He thought it would be perfect for me or I would be perfect for it, one way or the other, or maybe both, but to Anna, Ithaca was unthinkable. I decided to go, just to see. Anna said that if I wanted to go to Ithaca, why not leave the country and go to the real thing. I said it was a thought. At the time I was feeling very unsettled. It was before Andreas, before the island project got under way.

"Following the Cornell talk, there were the usual drinks and dinner with members of the faculty. The wine was good and we drank a lot. Afterward, Gabriel, my friend, suggested that we go for a walk to clear our heads. It was November, this time of the year. I had been nervous about the talk, as I am now about the Vienna paper, but it went well, and I remember feeling relieved and lighthearted. Gabriel wanted to show me the campus, high on the hill overlooking the lake, suspension bridges crossing the gorges, like in the dream. There was a harvest moon, pulsating on the horizon. We stood in the middle of one of the bridges, talking about the moon illusion, how it looks larger on the horizon than at the zenith, when he turned to me and said, 'You know, Kyra, I've always been a little in love with you, but at university you were with Simon. And now I'm with Karen.' I remember feeling sad for his wife, that he would even say this to me, whether or not it was true. But he was an attractive man and I felt a stirring inside me. There had always been something between us. And then he said, 'You know I don't do this,' and I said, 'I can't.' "

I stared at the ceiling. Andreas had said, I don't do this, but he wasn't married, at least not anymore, so it was more an internal resistance, like keeping a vow. Greta was married, she had made a vow. Had she also, like a nun, taken a vow in becoming a psychoanalyst: a vow of silence, a vow of chastity, a vow of obedience. Yet she was now bending the rules, leaving the ending up in the air.

"Where are you?" I asked into the silence.

"I'm here," she said, her standard reply.

"I mean, where are you really?"

A stir in the air.

"What is it you want to know?" she asked.

I picked at a cuticle. The heat was on, winter an impossible season for hands. I thought of Roya, her implausibly long nails. Saying maybe it's love that's revolutionary.

"Do you love me?" I asked.

The question naked in this spare room.

"I've told you. You can't do this work without love."

"Why not say what you are feeling?"

My thumb rubbed the strand of cuticle. I bit it off, my finger started to bleed.

"What do you need me to say?" she said, her voice clipped.

"I need you to be real with me."

I sat up on the couch to face her, crossing my legs in front of me.

Greta turned toward me, a flash of anger, in her eyes a flicker of fear.

Was she a little in love with me, she who had seemed so married, so settled in her life, with her bathrobed husband in the kitchen, reading the paper, drinking his coffee.

Did I feel desire for her? Could I be with a woman, I wondered.

She had said that in my work I had always taken risks, moved forward in the face of fear. I had done this with Andreas as well, but then I had panicked, which was why I was here. What risks had she taken or not taken? What did she fear?

I eyed her steadily, holding her gaze.

"What does it mean to you to suspend the ending?" I said. "I need to know from you now whether or not you mean it, or whether this is a ruse, a technique."

"Where is this question coming from?"

She picked up her pencil.

I could see it, she would write up the case, turn it into a presentation. The patient, she would say—or she could call me K., like a character in a Kafka novel—had a problem with endings. The end of the hour was always difficult for K., and as the therapy proceeded, its ending became a seemingly insurmountable obstacle. She had a history of relationships that had ended traumatically. It was inevitable that this issue would come up with me. She began therapy when she cut herself after her lover left her. She said she had to know what was real. The same question came up between us. She wanted to know if this was real.

That was the question. Was this real? But it was not only coming from my "history."

I could see how she could make a watertight case. The patient comes to therapy and repeats the trauma. Wasn't that what therapy was about? Reexperiencing the trauma? So it loosens its hold? But what if the therapy itself was repeating the trauma? How then was I supposed to "work it out"?

I stared at Greta.

She picked at a spot on her dress.

I said, "I can't work this out with you if you continue to hide within this therapy structure. You said that women have to change the structures. What about you? Or is it too much of a risk?"

The bridge in the dream, no way to turn back. I unclenched my hands.

"Is this a so-called brilliant move on your part, leaving the ending in suspension to see how I will react?" I said.

She would become apocryphal, like the analyst in Anna's story who would not rule out the possibility of an affair, the one who refused to rule anything out. In theory.

Greta's eyes moved quickly from side to side, as if searching for guidelines.

No rails.

"I am not you," she said in a voice so naked it went down my spine. "But with you now I have taken a risk. I don't know if it was wise."

She sat back, receding into herself.

I unfolded my legs and lay down.

Outside the window, the sky was an unsuspecting blue, the color of angels, the color of virgins. The branches of the tree reached into the blueness, wind sweeping away the last vestiges of the year that was coming to its ending, the Roman calendar timed to coincide more or less with the solstice, moment of turning away from darkness and into the light, the stars reminding, shining, remember, remember the light, remember that once there was light, long light stretching endlessly, like sand flats at low tide.

"What is it you want to end?" I wondered aloud.

She reached for her bag, which contained the apparatus of endings, her book, her bills, ladders of escape. I wanted to climb out the window onto the tree, sit astride one of the branches and ride into the onrushing night, away from this house, looking for the window of another house, a different house, where the talk was not of endings, of the necessity of ending.

"But I'm not talking about endings," she said, removing a Kleenex, blowing her nose.

The words barely made their way through the barriers,

whistling, high-pitched sounds, drowning, confusing, love, misleading, leading me into temptation, into wanting now, yet again, what must not be given, what cannot be given, what will be taken away, forever and ever, amen.

Unless?

"Do you want to play this out with me now?" she said, her voice no longer stripped.

"Me? It is not my game."

Ending? I will have nothing to do with ending. If you want to end it, end it. I saw red.

"I see what you do," I said. "You sew your heart into someone's psyche, using wide, basting stitches so that when the time comes, when the therapy is finished, you can easily cut the threads. And then sew your heart into another."

"Why don't you ask me? Why do you tell me?" Greta said.

"Because you tell me one thing and then I see another. I need to know from you now if this time you mean it. If this time you are in it for real."

"It is real."

The thin air of the winter evening, the moon rising, pale crescent of white light in an inky blue sky. Star light, star bright. Wishing, once again, dangerously wishing. Reaching like the leaf-barren arm of the tree into the elements of your presence, long moment, breath-holding time, to see if you, if she wants to turn with me toward the light of a new season, the lengthening light of winter a harbinger of spring.

I got into my car and turned on the engine. The Eva Cassidy cassette rewinding, spinning. The voice began, *You'll remember me when the west wind moves among the fields of barley, you can tell the sun in his jealous sky when we walked in fields of gold.*

I turned the corner onto Beacon Street and pulled over to the side, tears streaming down my face. *In his arms she fell as her hair came down among the fields of barley, will you stay with me, will you be my love?*

4

I spent Christmas in Gmunden with my mother's cousin Lily. They had grown up together. Lily would come to visit us in Cyprus, but my mother never went back to Austria. I understand, Lily said. I could never again live in Vienna, but the Salzkammergut, the lake district—she closed her eyes and let out a sigh—it's different.

Outside, the Trauensee, the lake where she and my mother swam as girls, was still visible in the fast-falling light.

Lily's face was longer than my mother's, her blue eyes darker, her features had a woodcut angularity. Your mother was the beautiful one, she had said the last time I had seen her, at Simon's and my wedding, the comparison very Viennese. Who was the smarter, the more beautiful? It was a legacy my mother had refused.

Her husband, Hans, was making a Stroganoff for dinner. He gave me the onions to slice. "It's good for the jet lag," he said, handing me a board and a knife. "They don't know how the onions work, but they do." He smiled, warmth radiating from his face. The bowl holding the onions came from the local ceramics factory, the mossy-green glaze, the swirl of the spiral pattern, the clay itself almost like porcelain, part of the history of this region, clay and salt, mountains and lakes. Hans had named the lakes on the way back from the airport in Salzburg, German words softened by the lilt in his voice, the light in his eyes.

I had finished my paper for Vienna the night before I left Cambridge, its sentences reverberating like the thrum of jet engines. I sank into eiderdown and slept without dreaming, the window open, mountain air filling the room. In the morning, snow had silenced the world.

For a week, it was the three of us, a mix of familiarity and strangeness. We had been in one another's lives but I had never been alone with them. Lily was an eagerly anticipated visitor in our childhood, arriving with chocolates and presents. My mother and she lingered over coffee, speaking German. *Shoene tochters,* beautiful daughters. She beamed at us, promising to play after they finished their coffee.

I wanted to talk with her now about my mother. I think you will find this visit interesting, Greta had said, the word noncommittal. Yet she had come forward as the therapy ended. At the last session, she lit a candle. A birthday, a *yarzheit, Shabbat*? All three, she said, a shyness in her face. A beginning, an ending, a wish for peace. When you come back, we'll see where we are. I watched the candle flicker. What did it mean for her—to suspend rather than end? Outside it was December dark. When it was time to go, I thought of blowing out the candle. I remembered Anna's song. *So roll me in your arms, love, and blow the candles out.* Greta took one of the marble eggs from the collection on her shelf and gave it to me. It glowed in the light, swirls of deep yellow and white, a line running down along one side. I held it, solid in my palm. Thank you, I said, for everything. I'll miss this, I said, and smiled, tears running down my face. I'll miss this too, she said. For a moment I was puzzled—but you do this, end therapy, all the time, I thought. It was part of her practice.

Lily wanted to know what Anna and I were doing, what our lives in America were like. She and Hans lived simply, ran a small travel business. Their passion was walking, hiking in the mountains. You will see, she said, her face coming to life.

She and Hans declared that I needed first to rest, "just for one day or two." Lily needed to finish preparing for her sons and their families, who were arriving for New Year's. The room they had added onto their house, a small winter garden, was filled with presents. I felt Lily watching me, making a decision.

The next night at supper, there was a box next to my plate. "These are for you," Lily said. "I kept them for you and Anna, as well as for myself. They are the letters from your mother." I drew back, as if I had been handed her ashes. But this was a living presence. "I would have sent them to you, but I couldn't part with them." Her eyes teared. Had Anna known about this, would she have come? I waited until supper was over and took the letters to my room, to read them alone.

I expected the family news, descriptions of daily life familiar from the letters she wrote us. I anticipated the impact of hearing her voice, the immediacy of her speaking. It was her candor with Lily that surprised me. *Dearest Lily, I am so grateful for your letter. This has been a difficult time, one of the hard times in a marriage. I feel very alone now, especially with the girls away at school. Mischa says nothing is wrong, but I know this is not true. Do try to come in April, even if just for a few days. I am longing to talk in the way that we can, holding nothing back, and the sea air will be good for your health.*

Had my mother lived, would she and I now talk in this way?

It was late when I folded the last of the letters back into its blue envelope and turned off the light. Sentences floated in the darkness. *I am worried now about Kyra. I will tell you more when you come.* I knew I wanted to talk with Lily, but now I had a new sense of the possibilities of that conversation. I didn't think I'd be able to sleep. But then I dreamed about my mother. I was in a room, a large, bare studio. The door opened and she came in. "We have to talk," she said. "But honestly," I said.

At breakfast, Lily announced, "This is Kyra's and my day," glancing at Hans, who was reading the paper. What she meant was she was taking the car. She had picked out a walk, a place for lunch, my feet snug in the hiking boots she lent me. I had added a second pair of socks.

We drove into the mountains, the sky blue, more snow forecast for late in the day. Shorn of husband and household, Lily became more energetic, her voice freer, her body lighter. "I was always sorry, Kyra. I wasn't able to help you more during that terrible time, especially after your mother died." Her eyes focused on the road. "I have always felt simpatico with you." She glanced at me. "I once thought of studying architecture myself, but then Hitler came." Her voice choked on the name. "I too have known disruption, upheaval, loss. It is my hope now that we can become friends."

She parked the car, and we followed the path through a snowy meadow, Lily setting a fast pace. At the edge of the woods, the trail narrowed, went through a birch forest, and then climbed steadily until we reached the lake, its frozen surface glistening, the sun high in the sky. I opened my jacket, also borrowed, Lily took the water bottle out of her rucksack. The physical exertion overcame the shyness I felt after reading the letters. She was my mother's friend and, yes, she had given me the letters, but I wasn't sure on what grounds we would talk. I was afraid she still saw me as something of a child. I wanted her not to hold back.

"It was intense for me, reading those letters," I said, my eyes fixed on the lake.

"I would think so. Your mother was a remarkable woman. I have never experienced that kind of a friendship with anyone else. We could talk with each other about things deep in the heart."

"I saw that," I said. "I was a little envious. I didn't know women of your generation would speak so openly about their marriages."

She laughed, her eyes mischievous. "That's the naïveté of each generation, to think they've invented love and sex. But in some ways I think we may have spoken more openly about the usual problems of life. We assumed them, so we could speak about them. We knew what real trouble was, and your mother had more than her share of that."

She meant Anton, my half brother, and also the political crisis, first Hitler, then on Cyprus. To go through that again was too much. Austria, shrouding itself now in neutrality, had tried to put a good face on a bad history. "It doesn't work," Lily had said, "but at least we don't have war."

She capped the water bottle, and we followed the path around the lake. I knew about my mother's childhood, I said. But I never really knew her as a woman, except as a child knows things. I was away at university, and then I married. I assumed we had all the time in the world.

I wanted to know about my mother's marriage, but it turned out I already knew. "They were in love with each other," Lily said, "no doubt about that. They went through some hard times, everyone does." I could see why she had shown me the letters, there was nothing in them to hide. It was the closeness between them that was special. I had that with Anna.

We had reached the end of the lake. The path followed the shore. Clouds gathered in the distance. "There is a chalet just a little farther, on the other side of the lake." She knew the couple who ran it. "The food is simple but good, and it's a place where we can talk."

She chose a table next to the window, looking out on the lake. "Have the schnitzel," she said. "It's the real thing." Lily ordered two glasses of Riesling.

I took a sip. My head tingled. I decided to plunge in.

"In one of the letters, my mother said she was worried about me. Do you remember what that was about?"

Lily hesitated, her face clouding. Had she forgotten or was she unsure whether to say?

"My mother is dead," I said. The word sounded finality. "I think it would be fine with her for me to know. We were always close. She told me there was nothing I couldn't tell her. I think now the same would apply to her."

Lily searched my eyes.

"It was about your marriage. She felt it was too soon. She wanted you to have more experience of life."

A dart.

. . .

We had been on the beach, the day unseasonably warm. I wanted to swim. I took off my sweater and shirt, unclasped my bra. A look of consternation on her face. I thought it was about swimming. I hesitated, my breasts soaking in the sun. It's hot, I said, unsnapping my jeans, suddenly self-conscious. I had started sleeping with Simon. I wondered if she could tell. What do you think of Simon? I asked her. He seems very nice, she said, her voice flat.

"Was it Simon?" I asked.

It was hard to breathe.

Lily put down her fork.

"Your father thought highly of Simon, embraced him as a son. She saw this, and she worried about Anton. I'm sure she would have spoken about that. But she also had other reservations. She wasn't sure he was right for you."

Not right for me? Did she question my judgment, she who claimed never to judge? You will know, she would say. I had fallen in love, it was the first time, I knew how I felt. My face went numb.

"She cherished you, Kyra, maybe a little too much. She had encouraged your gifts, and she wanted you to have the freedom to explore them. Simon was a very impressive young man, ambitious. Your father saw that and helped him. It would be easy to fall in love with him. She worried, though, that he would constrain you, not in some horrible way but in the way of such men. She thought you needed more time, more experience, before you would know what you wanted in life. In her eyes, you were very young."

"But it was a shared ambition," I said, needing Lily now to see how I saw it. "It was a vision we held in common, mine as much as his, to create a socially transformative architecture that would sustain and nourish democratic values. This was something we deeply felt. I believe in it as strongly now as I did then. It's my life's work."

Of this I was certain. Still, something was troubling.

. . .

A conversation with my mother in the kitchen. She was making lunch, I was peeling cucumbers at the sink. Long green shapes. Are you using a pessary? she asked out of nowhere, the word quaint. They're called diaphragms, I said. Had she found it in my drawer?

You know, Kyra, Greta's voice now, I cannot help but wonder about your relationship with Simon. It's easy to idealize someone who has died and forget how it really was. I've never heard you talk about any difficulties between the two of you.

With Simon, once, I was on a lake, like this one. We'd gone on a hike, taken a picnic. I spread the cloth on the ground. It was early spring, the ground covered with cowslip. He said he imagined us doing this someday with our children. We had just been married. I said someday maybe. He said soon. He wanted five children, God willing, he said. It was superstition. He wasn't religious. He lay back on the cloth, admiring the sky. I unpacked the sandwiches. One, I said, or at most two. He sat up. Kyra, he said, I've always wanted a large family. Just think what our children would look like, his eyes taking me in. But not really. You don't listen to me, I said, it's all about you, what you want. He said that's not true. It is, I said. Listen to yourself, you don't hear how it sounds to me. Five children, can you imagine what my life would be like? Hurt crossed his face. I thought that was something you wanted, he said.

"Coffee?" Lily asked. "They make an excellent strudel."

I scanned her face.

Was there more she hadn't told me?

"How did she feel after the marriage?"

Lily put her hand over mine.

"She hoped you would wait to have children."

. . .

The night before I left Lily's house, the run of the Gloecklers took place, a ritual dating from pagan times, said to chase away the evil spirits. Streetlights were turned off, the sound of cowbells approaching, and then men dressed in white shirts and pants, wearing traditional Gloeckler caps—huge paper sculptures built on wooden frames, lit from the inside by candles. The candlelight and the sound of the cowbells worn on their belts were intended to call the good spirits of the coming year and scare the bad spirits away. We stood in the cold night, Lily and Hans, their sons and their families, watching the dancing caps move down the street. We followed them down into the town square, men converging from all directions, falling into the prescribed formations, which was called "running the figures." The celebration ended with singing. It was January 5, the night of Epiphany.

If there is magic, if there can be hope here, in this lakeside town in upper Austria, this was its expression. Hundreds of hours had gone into making the sculptures, the requirement being each design can be used only once. I turned to Lily and saw my mother. What would she have made of this ritual? Multicolored caps lighting the night like stars, beauty mixed with superstition, the number of men in each group must be uneven. Yet here was this family, united rather than riven, gathered rather than scattered, everyone miraculously alive. I let out my breath and watched the heat of my body evaporate in the cold night air. What Lily had said about Simon was something I had known—that he required a kind of submission to him, subtle, but there. Still, it didn't change the fact that I loved him, deeply and genuinely, and I always would.

———

In Vienna, the contorted faces of Egon Schiele's self-portraits stared back from the walls of the Albertina. David had come from Rome to meet me, and we had gone to the museum. "Look at the women," he said. Their naked bodies defiantly sexual, their eyes challenging the averted gaze. I looked back at David, the delight in his face, and maybe it was the joy of his presence, but I was finding the city a wonderful surprise.

I had imagined Vienna gray and filled with Nazis. Instead, I saw statues of women reclining on pediments, figures perched on roofs, domed churches, skaters in the park in front of the Rathaus, its Gothic spires filigreed against the evening sky. People stopped to give us directions, taking off their glasses, putting down packages to examine the map David and I helplessly extended. The sleek trolleys running along the Ringstrasse were more a child's fantasy than the ominous streetcars of World War II movies.

That night we went to the opera, David in a tux, I in my long velvet skirt, vestiges of formality, like the Staatsoper itself. The opera house, bombed during the war, had been rebuilt and regilded. David looked crisp in his penguin suit, his scrubbed face glowing with anticipation. *Così* was his favorite. Just wait for the trios, he said. As we settled into our seats, I thought, This hall is everything Andreas detests, the orchestra pit a moat between singers and audience. I brushed away the thought and opened my program. *Così fan tutte, ossia la scuola degli amanti* (*They're All Like That, or The School for Lovers*). The conductor appeared, the audience settled, the overture began, the curtain rose on an all-white set. A blank screen, the age-old question: would the women be unfaithful? Still that question, after all that had happened. I turned to David. He was entranced. I had read the synopsis in English, the opera was in Italian. I liked it better in a language I didn't understand.

The next morning, we followed Prinz Eugenstrasse to the Upper Belvedere Palace, now a museum. I wanted to see the Klimts. In the room to the right at the top of the stairs, *The Kiss* dominated the far wall, its length majestic, the experience of the actual painting startling after the endless reproductions. I stared transfixed, unsure of what I was seeing. The man's head was bent toward the woman, his hands caressing her face. The tenderness

of his kiss was set off by the rigidity of the gold garment envelop-
ing them. The audio guide pointed out the squares on his side of
the gold, the circles on hers. Trite. And then I saw it. He was completely encased, only his face and his hands visible, the garment
enclosing him like a sarcophagus. But she? "Look at her," I said,
my voice rising in astonishment. "She's with him inside there, and
also not." Her bare arms wove in and out of the gold, the shape
of her body, the pattern of her dress, clear. On her side, the cover
was transparent. You could see she was kneeling, and her feet—
they were bare and sticking out completely.

I rewound the audiotape and listened again. The guide had
missed it, or chosen not to see it. "Look at her hand," David said.
Her arm was draped around his neck, her fourth finger crooked
in a casual gesture. "He's trapped in that gold glitter; she's all that
he has in there with him. She's in it with him, yet she's also outside it." The kiss, his kiss, became heartbreaking.

I turned to the opposite wall, a painting of Adam and Eve. Her
eyes were wide open, his were shut.

Something was coalescing. The artists had seen it. In the Albertina, the naked men in Schiele's portraits looked haunted, their
bodies exhausted. In *The Kiss,* a man trapped in opulence was
reaching for human contact. Klimt's Adam had closed his eyes to
the knowledge Eve was offering him. If the audio guide was any
indication, it was forbidden to see this.

David bought a book about Klimt at the shop and read it to me
over lunch at a Greek taverna, located improbably across the
street. The specials on the board outside sounded enticing, but the
owner insisted on overriding our choices and choosing for us,
providing a bottle of wine to distract us from the cost.

David turned to the pages on the university paintings. Klimt
had been commissioned by the Ministry of Culture to design three
ceiling panels representing Philosophy, Medicine, and Jurisprudence for the ceremonial hall of the new university. The theme, set
by the academics, was to be the triumph of light over darkness.
Yet Klimt had shown the darkness, not the triumph. We stared at
the illustrations: detached, mythical figures representing Reason,

Science, and Justice surrounded by twisted chains of naked bodies drifting in a void. At the center of *Jurisprudence,* a naked victim of the law writhed in a nest of snakes. In *Medicine,* a headless nude floated in space, her pelvis thrust forward, her outstretched arms suggesting crucifixion. The paintings had created a scandal, dividing faculties in the manner we knew so well.

"Listen to this," David said, reading aloud from the text: " 'Representatives of the university demanded that if the figure in the Medicine painting had to be female, then it should be clothed, or if it was unavoidable that it be naked, then it should be a male figure instead.' " He closed the book.

"It would be one thing," he said, "if Law or Medicine or Philosophy or the university had stood up to the Nazis, but that's not what happened." The commissioning of the paintings had coincided with the election of a blatant anti-Semite as mayor of Vienna. The emperor, Franz Joseph, held out for two years, refusing to ratify the election, but in 1897, he gave in.

I worried about my presentation. "Sweetheart, you'll be fine," David said. "Just remember Klimt. They showed him what they thought of his murals, he showed what he thought about them." *The Kiss* was a late painting, its perception of the situation of men and women haunting.

We divided the check, registering our gullibility but deciding in the end it was better to have trusted and lost than to go through life withholding and suspicious.

The conference started after lunch on Thursday, banners hanging from the front of the MAK proclaiming its mission: Art, Architecture, and Design. The nineteenth-century building stood at one end of the Ringstrasse, just before it curved around the park. The Baroque façade was predictable, but the high-columned, open main hall had more of a Renaissance feeling, arches lining the sides, a balcony ringing the space from above. Despite the size, it had the intimacy of a cloister, the open area light and airy, filled with chairs in place of a garden. I saw colleagues, old friends from school, people I'd met at other conferences, the atmosphere friendly, informal. Richard Livingston had arrived from Boston, his blue blazer an anomaly among the hip black outfits, which were more New York than Boston, more European than American. I was happy to see him. The design crowd and the urban planners had gathered in Vienna, the center of Europe, what better place to reenvision the city? I was glad I had bought the persimmon boots.

Georg Naumann, the museum's new director, a trim man with the sharp eyes and quick manner of the Viennese, opened the meeting. Art functions as an investment in and a prophecy of the future of society, he said, and he was determined that the future not repeat the past. Monuments of barbarism, like the antiaircraft tower in a Vienna park, could be turned into international centers, showing contemporary projects. The city itself, the crucible of civilization, must be reimagined with architecture leading the way. The museum would be a central forum for resistance against the widespread loss of meaning pandemic in contemporary popular culture.

A heady vision. I looked around the room: there was a minimum of skepticism. The conference itself, I realized, was an act of resistance.

"How will this happen?" Naumann asked. A flurry of attention. "This is our task." He smiled, much applause, high energy in the room.

I left after the coffee break. Too many people, too many conversations, my head was spinning. My talk was scheduled for the next morning, I needed to settle into myself. On the way back to the hotel, I stopped at a drugstore and bought some bath oil, green with algae from some remote sea. I would read over my paper, soak in the tub, spend the evening by myself.

At five-thirty, the phone rang. Dripping, I answered it, David on the other end. He was afraid I would spend the evening worrying, so he had leaned on the concierge, who produced two standing-room tickets for the Musikverein. For seats, he said, you must wait for someone to die. It was a Vienna Philharmonic concert, Mozart arias, a Chopin concerto. I put on my black slacks and sweater, adding the jade necklace Lily had given me, and met him in the lobby. It had started to rain, and the concierge, after a mini-lesson in German—house is *haus,* mouse is *maus,* here is *hier*—smiled broadly and offered an umbrella. We took it and headed out.

The standing room was at the back, behind a railing and in front of a graying mirror, the purpose of which was obscure. The hall itself, aside from the gilding, was strictly wood, seats included, a requirement for the acoustics. Gold statues of women lined the sides, weight-bearing women, slim, holding up the first tier. We squeezed in among the standees, finding a place in the middle. I opened the program. It was in German, the concierge not around to help. Three Mozart arias, the third from *Così,* followed by the Chopin, then intermission, with a Schumann symphony to end the evening. The pianist for the Chopin was young, a new star. The soprano I had never heard of. Yet it was her voice I would remember, clear, unencumbered, her singing effortless, the phrasing exquisite. A young, dark-haired woman in a blue dress, a visitor from another world. And maybe it was a premonition, because after the Chopin, during the intermission, when we were discussing whether or not to stay, leave, whether we really wanted to hear the Schumann, I saw him coming toward me, toward us. David, a soldier on guard, having spotted him first, was standing close beside me.

"Kyra," Andreas said.

My face froze.

He stood there, motionless, as in a dream.

David took my hand. The intermission crowd was pressing around us. We were blocking the way to the bar. We moved off to one side.

Andreas followed, his eyes darting between us.

"I'm David, Kyra's friend," David said, steadying the situation. "We've met."

A flicker of recognition on Andreas's face, memory registering. He cleared his throat. He opened his mouth as if to speak, then swallowed hard. His eyes on my face.

Chandeliers glittered. On my left, the wide marble staircase. He followed my glance.

"If you're leaving now, will you join us?" he said.

Us? I thought, suddenly stricken.

David tightened his grip. My hand turned cold.

"The pianist," Andreas said, "he's a friend." His voice was toneless. "We're going out for supper." He scanned my face. "Will you come?"

And maybe it was the openness of the question, because determination rose to fill the hollow that had formed inside my chest. I had seen the resolve in David's face when he told me he was planning to stay on in Italy, not go back to Cambridge. A similar resolve formed inside me. I would hold my ground.

I looked at David. He would take my cue. If there was anyone I trusted, it was him.

"Let's go with them," I said, heading down the stairs.

The first bell sounded, the intermission was ending.

The rain gusted, blown by the wind, changing directions. I was freezing. The pianist, a red-haired Hungarian, high from the performance, a fidgety energy, talking nonstop about the Chopin, the conductor, the decision made at the last moment to pick up the tempo. David adjusted the umbrella, a sail in the wind. I thought of the soprano, her effortless singing, stunning in her dark hair and blue dress. A wave of self-consciousness. What was I thinking? This was hardly the moment for a confrontation, my new boots now stained with rain.

Andreas glanced in my direction, the pianist commanding his attention. What was he thinking? A quiet supper with friends?

The narrow street opened into a square behind the Albertina. The Schiele women, their stare defiant. If you look at me, I'll look back at you. No need to speak. It was a plan.

Easily executed, as it turned out, because as we headed into the café facing the square, the three men fell into a discussion of music. Supper was ordered.

I went to the restroom, my hair spilling out of its clasp, curling wildly. I stared at myself.

Breathe. The morning warm-ups, Mika's voice coming back. Let the breath fall in. The *Tosca* rehearsals. What did it mean to be unfaithful? It meant to betray someone you love, to betray trust. Is it true, *Così,* that all women are unfaithful? Aren't all men unfaithful too? Air rushed into my body, solar plexus, sacrum, inner sun, sacred space expanding, oxygen circulating, coloring my face. I unlocked the door and went back to the table.

The food had arrived, and the conversation had turned to politics, the ins and outs of the music world, the pianist, now flushed with wine, clearly counting himself among the ins. Andreas glanced at me. I looked back at him steadily. His face was distressed.

"You can't leave Vienna without eating Sacher torte at the Hotel Sacher," the pianist announced, his wide face beatific, oblivious to the undercurrents swirling around him. He was leaving the next morning. And Andreas? I chose not to care. Either it would or it would not happen, the delayed conversation. As for the torte, David was game. We left the café, the hotel was just around the corner.

"This rain," Andreas said, "it's unrelenting. Budapest and Vienna, they're crime scenes." Then why did you go back, I wanted to ask. I said nothing.

We settled into the bar, the blue damasked walls gloomy, stifling. The waiter brought the tortes. Andreas picked up his fork, misery radiating from his body. Nobody said much of anything. I looked at my watch. It was almost midnight.

The pianist was leaving. David's eyebrows formed a question: did I want to go or not?

I looked at my wrist, the scar imperceptible in the dim light. You can go, I signaled.

Once you choose a path, my father had said, you must follow it. At the time, he was talking about Simon. It was just before our marriage.

David left with the pianist. Andreas leaned forward, his elbows resting on the small table. He put his face in his hands.

My eyes swept the bar, empty now except for us.

"What can I say?" he said, the sound of his voice coming over a long, rough road, a letter arriving maybe too late.

He looked up, a fleeting hope in his eyes.

"What can I possibly say to you now? You were right. All I could think of was my work, my mission."

He twisted his napkin, then bunched it into a ball and put it aside.

"I thought then that you would understand. You also have work you're devoted to."

He picked up his fork, put it down, searched my face.

"I've said this to you before, that terrible day last summer in Provincetown. It was raining then too. I couldn't believe I would hurt you so terribly by going."

My shoulders tensed. Me hurt? What about you?

I scraped the remaining chocolate from my plate, the taste bitter.

If I wanted to leave, this was the moment. Outside there would be air.

He read my thought.

"If only this rain would stop, we could walk. It would be easier then to talk."

He looked around, distracted.

"This bar is like a bad opera set."

He moved his plate to one side, put mine on top, clearing the space between us.

"I'm working on *Pelleas* again. Do you know the scene by the fountain where they are alone together, Pelleas and Melisande, and she loses the ring that her husband had given her?"

It was beside the point. Or maybe it was the point.

I didn't say anything.

"The concert tonight," he continued, his eyes fixed on my face, "during the Mozart, the aria from *Così,* I felt your presence. It was completely improbable, but I knew you were there. Then I saw you, standing a few rows in front of me. I was in back, leaning on the mirror. Did you feel it?"

I didn't answer.

"You know, at the end of *Pelleas* when Melisande is dying, the old blind king tells her husband to leave her alone. Is that what you want me to do?"

Did he think I was dying, like his dead wife? Or was he talking about Simon?

I broke my silence.

"Look, I don't know these operas. I don't care about these operas. You wanted me to come to supper. I came. Can you just say what you want to say?"

He raised his eyebrows, lines crossing his forehead like railroad tracks.

He took a deep breath.

"When my father became ill last summer in Boston, Jesse came back to Budapest with me. It was the first time we'd been alone. There was a woman who came in when I was working, but otherwise we were by ourselves. He would ask me these questions."

A shadow crossed his face. He waited a moment. It passed. He continued, his eyes softening, his voice more present.

"One night when I was putting him to bed, he suddenly sat up and stared into my face with that serious look he has: 'Papa, do you love Kyra?' I couldn't speak. Then he said, 'I miss Kyra. I want to go back to Nashawena.' "

Andreas looked away, his eyes wet with tears.

It was too naked, this moment. I suddenly wanted to get away. I remembered what Anna once said to me about men. When they open like this, it's so unguarded, almost too exposed. It's hard not to rush in and cover them, cover for them. Before they cover themselves. I wrapped my coat around my shoulders and waited.

"I've started to reread *Crime and Punishment*," he said, his voice retreating into himself. "And what the beginning of the book seems to be about is the terror of having absolutely no place to turn."

He swallowed, then picked up his spoon and turned it in the light. A gesture I remembered from a long time ago in Cambridge. It was the beginning then. Reflected light, like watching the moon.

"I've thought about my inability to have opened up all of the horror to you and cry it out, wondering what it would have been like if I could have, and even now it seems wrong that you should have to bear that."

He put down the spoon and searched my face.

"By now it will be clear to you how fragmented I feel. I'm saying nothing but whirling words. I will stop."

He looked around. No waiter in sight. David or the pianist had paid the check.

I started to get up.

He reached out and touched my arm. My gut registered danger.

"One more thing," he said. I sat. "I don't know what this could possibly mean to you now, but I love you, Kyra. I think the vision we have seen I will not see elsewhere, that the richness of the life we could have is not given lightly or often."

A crack, a spine responding to an adjustment, vertebrae aligning, falling back into place.

I bowed my head. When I looked up, he was standing.

In the cab on the way back to the hotel, he said, "If it's all right with you, I'd like to come tomorrow and hear your talk." My mind went blank. I turned, his face somber in profile, staring straight ahead.

I turned to look ahead. "It's fine," I said.

———

During the night, the rain turned to snow, falling steadily now, buildings blurred, the city muffled. Before leaving the hotel, I checked my bag one last time—my paper nestled in its folder, the box of slides—and glanced at my reflection in the lobby mirror. For a moment I didn't recognize myself. The face was too naked, like a nearsighted person without glasses who stared back at me, dazed. Tendrils of hair curled around my face.

I turned up my coat collar and went outside.

Trolley bells punctuated the stillness. I would walk, focus my concentration. Still, the images sped through my head, the bar, his face, *I love you, Kyra.*

The light turned red. I was in front of the café where David and I had eaten the first night. I shook out my hair and went inside. A rack of newspapers, all in German, stood beside the glass case filled with morning pastries. The cheese strudel caught my eye. I found a table by the window, ordered the strudel, chose mélange from the list of coffees, and added fresh orange juice. If I did meditation or prayer, this would be the moment. I closed my eyes. Words from an architect's manifesto I had come across and copied that summer into the front of my journal: *I am an architect, a constructor of worlds, a sensualist who worships the flesh, the melody, a silhouette against the darkening sky. I cannot know your name, nor can you know mine. Tomorrow we begin together the construction of a city.*

I opened my eyes. The mirror on the far wall reflected the gray light, underneath a row of heads bent over newspapers and coffee. A face disentangled itself, rose, came toward my table, arched eyebrows, cleft chin, unmistakable smile. Sid, my architect friend from New York.

"Do you need quiet or do you need a friend?" His eyebrows arched higher. "It's a real question."

I thought for a moment.

"Both," I said, removing my coat from the empty chair.

He took the coat, found a hook on the wall, retrieved his coffee, and sat down. "Hello, you." He reached out his hands for mine and squeezed them. "It's been a long time."

I smiled, my face tight.

"Nervous about your talk?"

"A little. Seeing you helps."

"It was *basheert,* meant to be. I looked for you last night at the drinks party, but you'd vanished. Have you ordered?"

I nodded. He released my hands.

The waiter arrived with my breakfast and proceeded to re-arrange the table.

"I'll have one of those," Sid said, pointing to the strudel.

The waiter hovered, thin face solemn.

Sid tried in German. The waiter interrupted.

"Would you like also the juice?"

He nodded. The waiter left.

"So catch me up," Sid said, extending his legs into the narrow space alongside the table. "The last time I saw you, you took me to an opera rehearsal. How's your friend the conductor?"

I steadied the strudel on my fork.

"Actually, he's here. He's coming to the talk."

He waited.

I said nothing.

His strudel arrived, flakes of pastry dotting the plate, falling onto the table.

"So, did you go to Thailand?" he said, swallowing a mouthful. "Did you have your baby?"

We laughed. "She's almost two."

I opened a packet of sugar, poured it into my coffee.

"We've moved to Brooklyn. The only thing we don't have is a dog. Otherwise, it's much the same. Still fighting the city, working on projects. And you?"

"Still working on the island project. But you don't want to hear about it twice."

"You'll be brilliant." He cleaned his teeth with his tongue, finished his coffee. "They'll love you. They always do."

"You too," I said.

"You see, we would've made a great team," he said, his eyes playful, teasing. "You should've come to New York with me. Besides, you'd love the city."

"Look at my hair. It's wild in this moisture." I raked it back with my hands.

"It's European hair, a little blond for Vienna. Still, you look great." He stared for a moment, narrowed his eyes. "Something has changed, it's in your face."

"Maybe it's Vienna," I said, reading his watch across the table.

"No, it's more inside."

We left a generous tip, "for having to clear two tables now," Sid said, helping me on with my coat.

The hall was filled, students draped over the balustrades. The first talk of the day, Changing Architecture, was a call to arms: "Architecture carries the potential to create peace and force war." Yet Vienna with its Enlightenment buildings had welcomed the Anschluss. *Grüss Gott,* the Viennese greeting, had turned into *Heil Hitler.*

I rifled through my paper, the pages in order. I would go back to the beginnings, the fundamentals of space and housing, places remote from this history, a coastal island, the mountain villages of the Akha. The first speaker was reaching his conclusion, his face flushed. He removed his glasses, blue eyes fixing the crowd. He wound up: "Changes in architecture directly affect society. We live now in an epoch of extinguished utopias; the age of conquest, it seems, has finally come to an end. We must envision a new way of thinking, contrasting with the old."

After I was introduced, I rose and went to the podium. I stood for a moment, taking in faces—David in front, Richard beside him, a woman with a lively face in the fifth row. I would not look for him. I put the paper aside and spoke. "The city has been called the belly of civilization, inextricable from the history of culture and war. As architects, we are conscious of the physical environment, less attentive to what is unconscious or hidden. I start from the premise that the spaces we live in shape our inner worlds."

A glass of water stood on the podium beside me. I took a sip, scanned the audience. So far they were with me. I clicked the button for the first slide.

Nashawena appeared on the screen behind me, a stretch of green surrounded by blue. The indoor lights dimmed, the snowy day a blessing. The colors intensified, the audience settled.

"My project is set on this island, thirty miles off the coast of Massachusetts. Virtually uninhabited, it was a blank slate, a tabula rasa, an opportunity for an experiment in design, a settlement which, if promising, could be taken to a larger scale."

Slides of the cliffs, the harbor, Quicks Hole, hills dotted with sheep, the project site. The mood in the room became quieter. I pushed back my hair.

"I was inspired by the Akha, a hill tribe living in northern Thailand, who believe, like the builders of the Gothic cathedrals, that the spiritual world infuses the material world. For the Akha, everything is porous, permeable, not only the walls of the buildings, the transit of light from outside to inside, but every aspect of life. There are no boundaries between inside and outside, no concept of what we call the individual. The soul resides not in the body but somewhere in the vicinity of the body."

A series of slides showing Bear Mountain village, the Akha houses, each with its center pole, the repeating patterns, everything organized around the relation of center and periphery. "When a baby is born, the umbilicus is buried at the center pole of the house, and when someone dies, their soul is called back to reside there." The weathered face of a priest, calling back the souls of the dead.

"You could say this is a tribal people living in a hilly setting, but inscribing their spirit world into the design of their villages, they have resisted the topography, the divisions between higher and lower, inside and outside, that have led to various forms of repression and alienation."

A momentum was building, faces intent.

"My question was, could this approach to design inspire a new model for cities, responsive to the kinds of dislocation that have plagued the modern world? I am thinking of the contrasts between neighborhood and ghetto, houses built under expressways, people cut off in various ways. As Peter Eisenman has said, the 'supposedly happy home has become unhomely, it is exactly where terror is alive—in the repression of the unconscious.'

"On Nashawena, my intention was to create opportunities for something new to happen. I conceived the settlement as a weave, like a fabric thrown across the island, the roofscape irregular in silhouette, evocative of its shallow, broken contours. I began with an open grid of structure from which to hang or attach the enclosing elements, some fixed, others mobile."

Slides of the buildings in various stages of construction, the amphitheater a cascade of surfaces for sitting and viewing. "I envisioned pools of solitude as well as continuities of public and private, a fluidity of inner and outer rhythms where the architecture would resist the patterns of living that have led repeatedly to war, such as the setting off of higher from lower, or sharp demarcations between inside and out. I wanted spaces that would encourage people's aspirations without linking ambition to being at the top. Structures and materials that would challenge conventions of control and authority by evoking an experience of life as fluid, flowing from one person to another, one activity to another."

I ended with a slide of Carthage, a model of the ancient city reconstructed, the name itself, "new city," carrying a vision of possibility. It was the road not taken—history followed the Roman way, the path of conquest and empire. It was also a nod to Richard, a look of appreciation on his face.

"My hope has been to convey a possibility, on a small scale, of changing the frame. The city I envision is not on a hill but on water, not towering but fluid, like life a place of renewal and exchange."

It was over. I rubbed the back of my calf with my boot, standing on one leg, like a crane. The word *crane* danced wildly in my head—a bird, and also a machine for building, the natural world, the material world coming together in a single vision.

Georg Naumann was standing beside me; he waited for the applause to subside. "We are open now for questions," he said.

I scanned the room and saw him. He was standing near the front, off to one side, leaning against a column. The look on his face was one I remembered from the *Tosca* rehearsals when a singer exceeded his expectation. "I love it," he had said, then.

The small of my back released. I placed my foot on the ground.

"Thank you for this wonderful talk." It was the woman with the so-alive face, her accent Viennese. "I'm intrigued by your project. Would you tell us where you are now with this experiment?" It was the part I had forgotten. I filled it in. The fishermen and the artists moving in, the question pending as to whether the design of the spaces would invite the openness and the civic culture needed for democracy to flourish. That would take time. "I'm trying to have patience, it's not my forte."

"This I understand," she said, flashing a smile.

Technical questions followed: the materials used, zoning restrictions, elevations, wetlands, water supply. People wanted to know more about the Akha, what it meant for the soul to be located not in the body but in its vicinity. "Think of permeability," I said, "transit across what we perceive as fixed boundaries, freeing the soul to wander without getting lost. It doesn't mean losing oneself but having a more fluid experience of one's existence. What we would call a self is to them more a river than a fortress."

A gray-haired man rose, an architect from Toronto. "In listening to your talk, I found myself wondering what you wanted to ask from the world."

The room was silent.

My mind flooded, went blank.

He continued. "You remind us that terror is alive in the repression of the unconscious and suggest that perhaps there is an architectural position that might clear the air. I remember feeling that way, but at this time in my life, it's simpler. I chose to be an architect because I wanted to build. You clearly have a similar motivation. You found inspiration in the Akha, but it seems fair to say that they can only exist where they are, in this remote place hanging off these mountains. Their simple way of living allows them to understand their spirits. You are trying to translate this, or perhaps use it as a metaphor, but in order to build it becomes necessary at some point to work within our social system. It's nice to work on an island but . . . I won't finish the sentence."

I took a drink of water.

"I know what you're saying, but you have to start somewhere. The island was a gift. A place to experiment. And I guess I believe that if you can show a possibility concretely through building and people can see it, it has a chance of making its way into their imaginations, so they begin to see differently. Like with a painting. Before they tell you why it can't work, they see how it could work. And then it can, potentially, enter the realm of social consciousness."

There was a stillness in the room, then a flurry of hands.

"I'm afraid that will have to be the last question," Georg said, "if we do not want to miss our lunch. Thank you, Professor Levin, for a most stimulating presentation. You have provoked us to think about space in a new way. The *Akhazang* will stay with me, along with the spirit of your project. We resume at two."

People rising, approaching the podium. I gathered my things.

"Kyra."

I turned.

He waited for me to focus.

"I loved it," he said, his voice gentle, sure.

I swallowed, met his eyes.

He looked at me, head tilted to one side, and smiled.

"Let me take you to lunch. I'll tell you all the reasons why."

Sensé, my mother would say: He has wisdom about how to do things.

"I just need . . ."

I turned to the people in front of me, David standing off to one side, watching. He would understand.

I turned back to Andreas.

He nodded. "I'll wait," he said.

. . .

"Let's walk," I said. "I need air." I wrapped my scarf around my neck, letting the snow fall on my hair.

We crossed the Ringstrasse, his hand light on my shoulder.

This was too easy, the rhythm too familiar. My shoulder stiffened. I shifted my bag.

At the entrance to the Stadtpark, the flower-stall woman braved the snow, shielding her roses and long-stemmed tulips. "Later," he said to her. He wanted to buy me flowers, he said, but we were heading now into the park.

The path led down beside a pond, frozen at one end. Ducks swam in the open water. Statues of composers sat on stone seats, heads capped with snow. "It was riveting," he said. "My attention never wandered, and the slides were just right. The talk was beautifully crafted." He looked at me and smiled.

The conference receded, adrenaline drained from my body, leaving me light-headed. Beyond the pond, a bridge crossed the shunt of the Danube that ran through the park, thin metal railings, the patina pale green. We stood in the middle, watching the channel, water flowing between crusts of ice and snow, stone walls containing the river, beside it a path, carved balustrades, steps leading down. I looked at Andreas, his face solemn now. I steadied myself.

A muscle in his cheek twitched.

"I had to go back," he said quietly, the words dispersing. "I'm sorry." In the distance, a tall white building, modern, a bland rectangle. Behind it, roofs of the city, a church tower, the silhouette of a crane.

"Maybe later I'll understand more why I did it in the way that I did, without talking it over with you." He picked up a stone, threw it hard into the river.

A man walking a dog looked up, then disappeared under the bridge.

"There is this I want to say."

He paused, looking into the distance.

"My soul lives in the vicinity of you."

My vision blurred, I swallowed hard.

He turned to face me.

"I realized this listening to you this morning. You gave me the words."

"It's from the Akha," I said. An image of the priest calling back the souls of the dead.

"Yes," he said, brushing the snow from my hair. "Kyra."

He took off his gloves, a shower of snow.

"There's one more thing, here in the park where no one can see us."

He kissed the top of my head, took my face in his hands, pressed his lips against my forehead, raised my chin, searching my eyes. "It's okay if I do this?"

He kissed me, softly at first, his fingers reading, distant signals, the sound of a buoy, safe channel, I opened my mouth, tongues exploring. A surge of feelings, and then we were floating. We turned our faces up to the snow.

We crossed the bridge, walked down the steps and along the path to the end where a ramp led up.

"I can't deal with a restaurant," I said. "All I want is hot coffee and a sandwich."

We were standing across from the ugly hotel.

"If you'll settle for soup, I'll make you lunch." He was staying with a musician friend, a person, he said, who existed on soup. The apartment was only a few blocks away.

It turned out to be homemade, a spinach soup. He heated it up, cut slices from the loaf of dark bread. I took off my boots, dried my hair with a towel. An old Viennese apartment, large windows, the furnishings elegant but simple. A round marble table, the piano at one side, behind it a wall lined with books and scores. I settled into a chair.

"Lunch is served," he said, "such as it is." He brought the soup to the table, opened the wine. "There are no guarantees, but we have to celebrate. You were magnificent. And now I'll tell you more of the reasons."

He thought for a moment, picked up his glass. "Let's take a chance and drink to us."

The wine, the hot soup warmed my body. I took off my sweater, adjusted my blouse. I was wearing the necklace Lily had given me. I touched it, the jade still cool.

He put down his spoon, leaned back and studied my face.

"To begin with, I loved that you waited at the beginning, took in the audience, and then spoke directly to us. And it was so clear, the slides meshed with what you said, your descriptions enhanced what we saw. It was like a pavane, a dance, the way everything unfolded. The island, the Akha, you had your own *zang*. I'd never seen a presentation like this before. It was, to use one of your favorite words, translucent. The light passed through you, through everything you said.

"I found myself thinking about Jesse, about this time with him. It had that quality, his openness to the world led me to see how I had boxed myself in. I had been caught in a past I had been trying to free others from. Listen to yourself, I said one day. And it's true, I hadn't been listening."

He picked up a slice of bread, buttered it.

"You know, Kyra, what I said to you last night about being fragmented. I've been working in so many different places, trying to assemble a company, raise the money, do my work. But it isn't how I feel now."

I wasn't sure that was it. Still, something inside me turned.

"Coffee?" he asked.

He brought the cups to the table in front of the sofa. The tulips hung over the sides of the vase. I leaned back, propping my feet against the edge.

"You know that singer you liked last night—that's how you were this morning. The talk itself was fluid, the flow seemingly effortless. There was a clarity in your face I hadn't seen before."

"A lot has happened."

"I know," he said.

I hesitated a moment.

"To me as well as to you," I said.

I told him about Greta, the conversation with Lily about Simon.

"There are things I knew, but couldn't allow myself to know. With Simon."

I picked up my glass, put it down.

"Here's what I didn't let myself admit. That it wasn't perfect. He wanted many children. I needed to do my work. He would say, it won't be a problem. I receded into myself. And then he died."

I let out a breath.

Andreas sat quietly, taking it in. Then he drew in his cheeks, his face narrow.

"And with us?"

I stared at the empty coffee cups.

"The world turned upside down," I said, looking away and then at him. "When you left in the way you did, everything I thought I knew, everything I had felt between us, knew in my body, suddenly made no sense. I didn't know what was real."

His face paled, a look of pain.

"I think you know how I feel," he said. He paused, his eyes darkening, the color of slate. "I think you've always known. But then I confused you. Because I was confused. I thought at the time that our love was a distraction from what I felt I had to do, that the very strength of my passion for you would deter me from achieving my goals in the world. It's not how I see it now. If anything, loving you was a breakthrough, but I didn't see it then. If I could . . ."

He picked up my wrist, looked at the scar.

"If I could promise you anything, it would be never to confuse you again. Because you were right, it was true. It was like looking into the sun. That summer on Nashawena, there was so much sun, and something in me missed the shadows. It would be like imagining *Tosca* with a happy ending. Who would come?"

A rueful smile.

Just listen, a voice inside me said.

"Listen," he said, "I have a friend who is a botanist, a serious man infatuated with plants. This winter he traveled to the Amazon to see a flower. Because it wasn't supposed to bloom. And it did. Twice in one century."

"You're making this up."

"I swear it's true."

He put his arm around my shoulder, his hand resting on my breast. My nipples hardened.

"Come," he said.

I glanced at my watch. It was two o'clock.

I took it off and left it on the table.

"I want to see you," he said.

He turned on the lamp beside the bed.

Outside the snow fell steadily, curtaining the window.

"I want this to be everything you want," he said.

A pulse started, deep within my body.

He unbuttoned my blouse, my camisole white against the dark walls.

He touched my shoulder, ran his finger down my arm.

The room was still.

I leaned back against the wall.

He took off his sweater, his shirt, his chest winter-white.

I traced the pattern of hair, spreading out from the midline.

"You are so beautiful," he said, looking into my face, "so incredibly beautiful."

There were times when I looked at the light, fading outside the window, the glow of the lamp intensifying, spreading across his face. A language beyond words, dolphins calling to one another, swimming alongside, finding the currents, diving deep. And behind my eyes, colors—orange-reds, yellow-greens. And he then on top of me, hands braced against my shoulders, seeing in each other not a reflection but surprise. That this could happen, history vanishing, holiness entering the room.

He brought a glass of water to the bed. It was almost dark. Friday night.

He began to hum, I recognized the tune, my mother lighting the candles, the ancient melody. *Shalom aleichem.*

And maybe that was what it was about. Redemption. That it was possible in Vienna, after all that had happened, to welcome the Sabbath. I told him what Roya had said, that love was the revolutionary emotion. He smiled. "It's true," he said, "it's the emotion that allows things to turn."

We spent the night together, his soup-loving friend away from the city. In the morning, I went back to the conference and he took the train to Budapest. And because we were holding something so fragile, neither of us said anything about plans.

"I have just taken a leap off a dock," I said to David, settling in beside him. He studied my face. "But Kyra, you know how to swim," he said.

The room quieted, the speaker began, someone I knew from school. A calm came over me. The high, columned hall, slides on the screen, the voice explaining, a project unfolding. An odd sensation, a feeling at once of beginning and completion. He was heading for Budapest, I would go back to Boston via Rome.

Anna once said that the past was the best predictor of the future. And then she said to believe that was to commit oneself to doom.

I had dinner with Richard that night, he flush from the island project's reception. He wanted to talk about next steps, the enlargement of the harbor, the plans for the summer, his mind filled with thoughts of expansion. I remembered the mantra from a yoga class I had taken. I am here, in this room, with you, now.

The next morning, I flew with David to Rome, my flight paid for by the American Academy since he had arranged for me to give a seminar there. We went to Apulia to see the project he was working on with two Italian architects, integrating landscape in the way he envisioned. He would stay in Italy, give up tenure. You have to act, he said, when the moment comes. I smiled inwardly, a sweet secret. You have to move forward, he said, not back.

The last night in Rome, the three of us had dinner, David, Sarah, and I. They wanted me to come back to the academy, stay for a year. David had brought a fellowship application, spoken with someone about extending the deadline. Sarah was looking for apartments. "I'll find one with an extra room," she said. I felt like an island in a sea of plans, a person held in suspension. For the moment, I needed not to know what would happen. It was a pledge I had made to myself.

5

ON THE MONDAY AFTER I GOT BACK TO CAMBRIDGE, I SKIPPED the faculty meeting and called Greta. I got the machine. *You have reached the office of Greta Blau.* The sound of her voice. "It's Kyra," I said, suddenly flustered. "I'm back."

A stack of mail and a pile of pink message slips lined up on my desk, neatly arranged by Hannah, the assistant—her form of welcome. I had a syllabus to complete. The gray cinder-block walls drained the light. David was in Rome, Roya wouldn't be back for a week. I had offered to teach her class. I switched on the lamp to dispel the bleakness and started with the mail.

The line of Hungarian stamps caught my eye.

I fished the envelope from the pile, the sight of my name in his handwriting producing a wave of joy, then apprehension.

I took the kettle from the shelf and went to fill it, the corridor blessedly deserted.

The bathroom door opened, the sound made me jump. Hannah emerged, her round face brightening, the perennial quiver around her mouth. "Oh, Professor Levin, I hope you had a good trip. If you can get me your syllabus by tomorrow morning, I'll have it photocopied for your class."

I forced my face into a smile. "Hannah, you're a gem."

The waiter boiled quickly, the kettle switching off with a firm click. I spooned some Earl Grey into the strainer, balanced it on the rim of the cup, and poured the water over the tea, watching the color darken.

With tea in hand, I forced myself to settle into the battered arm-chair. I stared at the envelope, took a sip of the tea, which scalded my throat. I put the cup on the floor and took out the letter.

Dearest K,

I wasn't sure where to find you but I figured you would show up at work. It's Tuesday night late, less than a week, and I can't stop thinking about our time in Vienna.

The aura that surrounded us dissolves the gloom here. It contains the key to the hope of my life. There was very much that same quality Thursday night—my fragmented attempts to explain what cannot be explained, the "realities" which are no more real-ities than dirt on the hands of an obsessive, and then on Friday, your answer to it all and your affirmation of the power of love over the power of despair. The challenge you lay down to me is to accept this affirmation.

Oh Kyra, I have promised myself never to hurt you again. What you must know now is that I love you in a way I have never loved anyone before, and for reasons that you also know, it's hard to admit this to myself.

I'm listening to Schubert, the B-flat piano sonata. The last movement begins with a long G octave, the minor key, but then the melody breaks away into B-flat major. The G minor returns, again and again, but it cannot take hold. And that's how it is.

Here's a thought. In March I'm doing a staged reading of Mon-teverdi's L'Orfeo at King's College Chapel in Cambridge. There's an island off the coast of Wales that used to be a pilgrimage site and is now a bird sanctuary. Wouldn't that be a perfect place for us? You could come for the concert and then we could spend a long weekend or a week on Bardsey. A friend who is one of the trustees said there's a farmhouse where we could stay.

So that's it for now, my goddess of the moon, temptress of chiaroscuro. I see your face in that light, you in your body walk-ing across the room, your openhearted passionate look, your amused look . . .

There are no barriers other than time and distance . . .
Love, A

A mix of delight and trepidation. Chiaroscuro, he would say, dark and light, bittersweet, hot and sour. My mother used to play the Schubert sonata, the opening melody like waves rolling in, the ominous trill in the left hand.

The words, the feelings. I picked up the letter and read it again.

Greta had said come at the usual time on Thursday and we'll talk about where we are. There would be no fee.

I stood for a moment on the small landing outside her door. The sound of a cello inside the house. One of the Bach unaccompanied suites. Was she going solo now? I looked around, suddenly self-conscious. The suburban street was occupied by shrubs, the kitchen window dark. The playing stopped. I waited a few minutes, then opened the door and mounted the two flights of stairs.

She was turning on the lamps, dressed in black slacks and a white silk shirt. Concert attire or her idea of casual? She had another life. I did too. Something in me wanted to draw back. I overrode the impulse, and for a moment, we were two women in black pants, standing in the room where so much had happened between us.

Where's your skirt? I wanted to ask her. I said it and she laughed.

"I thought we were here to talk about change," she said.

When I was a child, we had a large Persian rug, bright red with blues and greens like stained glass. Every year, after the summer, the slipcovers would come off the furniture and we would gather to unroll the rug, back from the cleaners, its colors, brightened, spreading slowly over the floor. Then one year, my parents bought a new rug, deep blue instead of red. "Do you like it?" my mother had asked. I had burst into tears.

I told this to Greta and she smiled, her face wistful, her gray eyes thoughtful, watching me, as an awkwardness set in.

I wanted to tell her all that had happened, with Lily, with Andreas, with Anna, who was pregnant. I wanted her quiet attention, her questions leading me to what I had overlooked and to feelings I had not anticipated. But we had come to the end of that journey. Whatever happened now would be different in a way I could not quite envision.

Was I afraid now of what I had asked for, of being happy rather than aggrieved? Would I even recognize myself? My breath stuck somewhere between my throat and my chest.

Greta settled into her chair.

I glanced at the couch, the black leather chair, and chose the chair nearest to hers, the one with sleek wooden arms and flowered upholstery.

What now?

I looked at my hands, the ring Lily had given me along with the jade necklace, its stone emerald green. Like your eyes, she had said. She loved my green eyes. You have your mother's eyes, she had said.

Greta didn't say anything. I suddenly felt angry. Why was the burden of this on me?

Because I wanted this, because it was I who had refused to participate in what Anna had called "extermination." In spite of myself, I smiled.

"So," I said.

I took a deep breath. "My question is, where are you?"

"I'm here," she said. She placed her hands on her lap.

It's one thing to take apart a structure, another to build one. We had a lopsided history. She knew a lot about me, I knew practically nothing about her. I caught myself. That wasn't true.

"My question is, where are you now in relation to me?" I said.

She thought for a moment. "I wonder what you know about me that you haven't said," she said.

An invitation to a precipice.

I thought a moment. "I know that something in your life is unsettled."

Her wedding ring shone. I didn't think it was her marriage.

Something about her work, her music, her therapy practice? I remembered Roya's description of the talk. Greta had come to an edge in that talk, and then stopped.

"Remember the first time I came here, when I said I didn't know what was true or real, and you said, you were talking about Andreas, that it had felt true to me at the time and I had trusted that and then . . ." I swallowed hard.

"You started to cry," Greta said, "and my eyes teared up as well, and you asked me if I did this with everyone."

"Right," I said, "and you said that something in my life had touched something in yours. I knew it was true, but I didn't know what it was and I thought you didn't want me to know, so I pulled back. I think that's built in, the price of love."

Her thumb traced the edge of the nail on the fifth finger of her left hand.

"I wouldn't," she said quietly. "I wouldn't pull back."

She looked at me steadily.

"But here?" I said. Once, as a "talking point," she had said, why don't you get on a plane and confront him: say, why aren't you talking to me, why did you leave?

At the time, it had seemed an exercise in futility. Because . . .

It was what we had talked about. Freezing, going numb, receding rather than coming forward.

"What's happening?" she said.

"I was just thinking there's something more to it. I was protecting something."

"Me? Were you protecting me?"

"Maybe." I smiled. "But what I was mostly protecting is something inside myself, some deep sense of conviction. I don't even know what to call it, it's in my gut, it's what I rely on in my work. Even as a child. I always knew about Anton. No one wanted to talk about it. That night when he came for Simon, my father acted as if we didn't know how dangerous Anton was. And then with Andreas, he could have just said afterward that he wasn't in love with me, and if he had said that, people would have believed him, and then what could I say? If I said it wasn't true, I would seem pathetic or deluded, and yet it turned out not to be true. It was something he couldn't say at the time, maybe not even to himself."

The room tilted. I thought the plants would slide off the desk.

"But here, with you," I continued, "I have no way of knowing. This is for me, you say, for me to know my feelings, my thoughts, to understand why I did what I did, or play it out with you so I could see it. But you?"

"Therapy is a hothouse," she said. "It creates an intensity that has to be contained."

Her whole posture seemed to close, like a flower.

She pursed her mouth. "I've thought a lot about what you've said, about the costs of continuing to work in the traditional way. For you, given your life, the issue is so stark that you cannot help but see it as something you want to subvert, a structure to change. But I see it as well. Sometimes traditional therapy works and people are freed to move on with their lives, but sometimes a spark goes out. Sometimes people agree to what they should not agree to."

A smile crossed my face. It was what I thought. I had seen it in students, making an accommodation, swallowing the loss of what had been most alive in themselves. For the sake of what? I wanted to ask them, but they had already turned away. Because of fear, because of ambition. It's not the way, I wanted to tell them. I said it to some. If you do the work you want to do, that you believe in, then whatever happens, you'll be okay. It was somewhat naïve, but basically true.

"When you first came," Greta said, "you said that you had cut yourself because you had to see into a darkness. You had stepped onto ground you thought you could trust and you found yourself all alone. My eyes teared up because I too had taken that step and experienced the aloneness. You sensed that, and it's one reason you trusted me."

She hesitated, then added, "And I trusted you."

We sat in silence for a long moment.

It was a moment I would hold close to my heart, the quiet

room, the window darkening, summoning it up at those times when I wavered in my belief in myself as a trustworthy person.

Then she told me the story. "I think it won't surprise you, given your experience with academic politics, but it will tell you what is at stake for me in doing this with you. It's only partly what I was concerned about but it was a concern, and I needed to resolve it for myself.

"Some years ago I was working with a patient, a candidate at the institute who was in analysis with me. She was a woman who spoke her mind, an independent thinker, a little self-righteous, but she was right for the most part and she had a sense of humor. What happened was she said what she thought about the institute, that it did not allow independent thought, but she put it more pointedly in an article that was published in a psychoanalytic journal. She wrote that her institute beheads those who think independently. And so, inevitably, they went after her, not for this but for breaking some rule about seminar attendance, not conforming to institute procedures. People spoke of her as an angry patient. Her candidacy at the institute, her ability to become an analyst, was called into question. Her case was taken up at a meeting of the training committee.

"That's the part about her," Greta said, her voice taking on an edge. "The part about me is that I spoke out in her support. I spoke up for my patient at the meeting. That was considered a violation of analytic neutrality, a breaching of the analytic boundary. I was to analyze, not comment on what she had done. But there's another layer to this story."

A look of uncertainty crossed her face.

"Another analyst this patient had seen in therapy, a person with whom I had been friends, resented the fact that this woman had left her and chosen me instead for her analysis. There were all sorts of issues involved having to do with the fact that my practice was flourishing, I had more of a reputation in the community. What happened is this analyst reported me to the American Psychoanalytic Association for 'boundary violations.'"

She stopped, shook her head. Her voice had become hoarse. She cleared her throat.

"This started the chain of events that, as you picked up on, has left my relationship with the institute unsettled. To my astonishment, my colleagues, instead of supporting me, took a hands-off attitude. We're not going to decide who's right and who's wrong, they said. I felt it as an enormous betrayal. I had assumed they would protect me."

The look in her eyes, like an animal suddenly caught in a trap.

"The committee at the American that takes up these issues said that they didn't want to put me through a trial-type thing, where this other analyst and I would both be called to testify, one person's word against the other's. But the very fact that they would even entertain the belief that I'd done some terrible thing made the whole thing humiliating. In place of a hearing, they said that if I would accept six months of supervision on the case by an outsider, an analyst from New Haven, from the institute there, who was a friend, they would let the matter drop. And since I had many patients in analysis, including many candidates who were in training to become analysts, I decided to do it. But for me personally the matter has not been dropped. It's become part of a larger series of questions about what I will stand up for in my work."

There was a light in her eyes. "So on a personal level I had some understanding of what you were going through, and maybe you can now see why when others were so alarmed by your cutting, I had a sense of what you were doing. I understood how important it was in the midst of that confusion to hold on to your experience. And although the cutting itself was very dangerous, I admired your intention, your determination to see for yourself."

Somewhere in the house, a phone rang five times and then stopped.

"I want to thank you," I said, my eyes brimming with tears. "Your understanding was crucial to me at that time. Others were trying to be helpful. They were trying to tell me what they knew. But I knew something different, and it was hard for me to believe it or to put it into words. You encouraged me to trust my experience, which was huge because it was very difficult for me to do that once he had left. It would have been easier to take what seemed the moral high ground, he the betrayer, I the betrayed. And I also want to thank you for having encouraged me to look at my relationship with Simon."

There was a lot I needed to tell her. I said I would like to come again the following week, pay for the session. I wanted to tell her about my mother, talk through my feelings about Andreas and Vienna and his letter and also Anna's pregnancy, and also what happened at the Vienna conference, my quirky project accepted now, in the spotlight.

"It sounds like more than one session," she said, taking out her book. In the end, it turned out to be five, but it felt more like a gateway than a return.

We also made the beginnings of a plan.

"Let's rely on dreams to start with," she said.

We would write down our dreams, keep track of them in a journal, and in the interim time, once we were no longer meeting in the traditional structure of therapy, we would write each other on Thursday evenings, plumbing our dreams for what was emerging.

Standing, I said to Greta that in reality everything was in suspension, and yet I felt grounded in a way I never had before.

Greta smiled and rose from her chair.

We stood for a moment, silently taking in where we had come to.

PART THREE

pack
write out Jesse's schedule for Abe
leave money for Szofi
buy razor blades
pick up shirts
find the book on Atlantic seabirds Rick sent
pay bills
call Gabe

I PUT THE LIST ON THE COUNTER. REHEARSAL HAD RUN LATE. SZOFI had left dinner for me on the stove. She had made the chicken the way I like, with cinnamon and paprika. I took a plate to the living room and turned on the TV. It was the Soviet film of *War and Peace*. I turned down the sound but it must have carried because Jesse ran down the hall. He stood for a moment in the doorway. Then he walked to the sofa and climbed up beside me.

"Daddy," he said, "I like your pants."

I was wearing my old rehearsal pants. I looked down at the frayed cuffs and suppressed a smile.

"Want some of this chicken?" He nodded. I scraped off the sauce, he liked it plain.

"That's Napoleon," I said, "the one on the white horse."

"Is he the good guy?"

I pointed to Kutuzov, his round face, his sleepy eyes, his uniform decorated with stars. "He's the good guy, and he's going to win, but not yet. His motto is 'Time and patience.' "

Not in Jesse's lexicon.

Part One ended, the screen turned to snow. Jesse followed me into the kitchen.

"Daddy?"

Standing beside me in his spaceman pajamas, he looked so small.

"What?" I lifted him up.

It could have been anything, but what he wanted to know was about gravity. How it holds us to the earth.

"I love you so much," I said, kissing his head, carrying him down the hall back to bed.

In the end, it was love that held me to the earth. At first, I felt it as a betrayal. "Love life," Tolstoy had said, "for God is life and to love life is to love God." I had cast my lot with the living now, but I couldn't believe in God.

When I came back to Budapest after the summer on Nashawena, I felt I had no choice. I thought it was my fate to live here and to do my work. A Hungarian refugee who came to see *Tosca* in Boston had said, do this in Hungary and I'll give you the money to start your own company. The condition was that I do it within the next six months. It was an opportunity I felt I could not refuse. Not to go seemed wrong. My friend Gabriel offered to be my partner and handle the business side. But the ambition I had for the company, to do opera in a way that would change how people saw, was also an excuse for not seeing what was before my eyes.

Kyra standing on the deck in Provincetown—her face, the suffering in her eyes. She wouldn't speak. I hadn't seen the impact I'd had on her. What had made sense to me didn't make sense to her.

After that, what loyalty meant was no longer simple.

I couldn't be loyal to Irina now without being disloyal to a living person. I said this to Clara, Gabriel's wife, and she said, "Including yourself." I found that unsettling.

I was reading a book on memory. I picked it up from the bedside table and found my place. One must refuse the temptations of closure, it said. I underlined the words, *"Forgetting without amnesia, forgiving without effacing the debt one owes to the dead."*

I still looked for Irina in the street. Last night, she came to me in a dream. She was wearing a black dress, her face pale. A white moon reeled around the sky. "You are moving away from me," she said, "and like the wind, it's impossible to stop." "I'm sorry," I said over and over again, my voice thick with grief. She disappeared.

The dream shifted. It was indoors now. A concert hall. A woman was singing. I thought it was Irina, but the face was Kyra's. I stood off to one side listening. A voice I had always heard and never heard. Bright and clear in its assurance.

I had been impatient with the tenor tonight. I was sorry about that. I had tried to keep the irritation out of my voice. "How does hope feel to you? Where does doubt lodge in your body? When Orpheus hears the noise that will lead him to turn around, what happens viscerally in that moment?" We'd been through it many times. "It's beautiful, Nick, the singing is beautiful, but with the control you have, you can afford to take more risks." We were leaving now for King's College Chapel. We might as well be doing nine lessons and carols. On Monday in England, the instrumentalists would join us. And then Kyra.

There was one more question I had asked the tenor. "What is the sensation of joy?"

I turned off the light.

The combination room in King's College was painted deep red. Over the mantel, a painting of a man peering down from a balcony at a group of women dancing onstage, their ballet costumes scant. I wondered what Kyra would make of the painting, or would her eye be drawn to the row of high windows on the far wall?

The director of music had organized a Monteverdi festival. The invitation to perform came as a surprise. He had heard about the *Tosca* production in Boston. He was hoping to come to Budapest next winter. He came over to me now.

"How do you find the chapel?"

Kyra had arrived that morning. She had taken the bus from Heathrow to Cambridge. My friend Rick, a fellow at King's, had picked her up and taken her home to sleep since I was in rehearsal all day. He'd bring her into King's for dinner.

I glanced at the doorway and turned back to the director.

"What can I say that hasn't already been said about the acoustics? In the last act of *L'Orfeo,* the echo is shattering."

I checked the door, any minute now. It had been two months since I'd seen her.

Fear wrapped around me. What if something had happened? A bus accident? What if she had changed?

Monteverdi had changed the ending. In the original version, Orpheus runs off at the end, fleeing the Bacchantes. Two years later, when Monteverdi published the score, the Bacchantes were gone. Instead Apollo appears, descending from heaven to rescue his son from anger and grief. He invites Orpheus to heaven, to live with Eurydice in the sun and stars.

I yearned for Kyra. We would have a week.

"Do you find the apotheosis convincing, or do you think Monteverdi was pandering to his audience?" the music director asked.

"What troubles me," I said, fighting distraction, "is not the ending. All through the opera it's clear that fate can be reversed. But there's always a contingency. Here Orpheus renounces all living women. Compared to Eurydice, he says they are worthless."

As if on cue, Kyra appeared, an expectant look on her face. Rick stood beside her, the butler behind them, bell in hand.

I went over to kiss her and felt in her a reserve—was it the college? Her public, academic persona? I hadn't thought that mattered to her. I had wanted to pick her up at the airport, meet her at the bus station in Cambridge, but the timing was impossible. "I hate operas," Jesse had said one day, "I hate your work." She had said she understood.

We filed into the hall with the others, assembling around the high table. It was literally raised, on a platform at one end of the vaulted room. The Latin benediction was said. A scraping of chairs, we assumed our seats. The music director was at the head of the table, Kyra on his right. Smart man, I thought. I was seated toward the other end between the music tutor and a physics professor. I picked up the printed menu and counted the courses. There was a limit to this. The performance of the Vespers started at eight.

We followed the path around to the chapel, trailed by the group from the high table. I squeezed her hand. "Soon," I said. At the door of the chapel, we stepped aside and let the others go in. Then we moved into the shadows and kissed, the warmth of her body rushing through me. I touched her face, then her shoulder under her sweater. The feel of her skin. I longed to undress her. I thought of Jesse, only the spacemen were watching. It was freezing. I put my arm around her, and we went in. I couldn't stop looking at her.

"This is a first," she said. I thought she meant the chapel but what she said was that it was the first time we were together at something where neither of us was responsible. I wasn't directing, she wasn't speaking. It wasn't my performance or her project.

We found our seats, in the front section to one side.

The leader of the orchestra came out. A final turning, then a hush in the audience. The conductor appeared. I put my jacket on my lap. Underneath, we held hands.

If I could just keep touching her. The ghosts, were they with us here in this chapel? The fan vaulting, the stained-glass windows dark. The voices rose, resounding. We had come out of this history, the Latin words resplendent: *laudate, seraphim, audi coelum verba mea,* hear, oh heaven, my words.

I pressed my leg against hers, and her face flushed. I wanted to know what she hadn't said in her letters. We had a week, her spring break. Szofi was staying with Jesse and Abe. Gabriel and Clara said they would look in. Clara was a painter, like my mother. She looked like a Gypsy. "Read my fate," I had said one evening, holding out my hand. She had laughed. "Aren't you doing *L'Orfeo*? Then you know what not to do."

Don't turn back, that was it. Orpheus didn't trust that Eurydice was following him. How can you trust, after the earth has opened under your feet? She had been snatched away from him before, it could happen again. But maybe not.

On the night Irina disappeared, I ran through the streets calling her name, my voice echoing against the buildings. I had visions of her body bruised, her face distorted with fear and pain.

I'll slow down the tempo in the fifth act to allow for the echo.

The Magnificat began, my favorite part of the Vespers. It was not to relinquish the past but to trust the present. Kyra must be tired. The overseas flight. She had walked through the open market. Cambridge a market town. Fishmongers, vegetable and flower stalls, bright spots amid secondhand books and clothes. Monteverdi had recycled his music. The passage here was almost identical to where Orpheus is seeking Eurydice in the underworld. Kyra had gone into the underworld. I had not followed her. With Jesse, I had to pay attention—Daddy, play with me now, he would say, insist, his face dark with intention. Now, Daddy, now. He would take the score from my hands. *Esurientes implevit bonum.* I turned to Kyra. She loved the word *esurientes*. Who knew it meant hungry, she said one day when we were making love. Let the hungry be filled with good things. Let the Hungary be filled with good things.

After the concert, we declined invitations to go out for drinks. I had a concert the next night, Kyra had been on an overseas flight, we said. But the truth was, all we wanted was each other. We picked up her suitcase from the porter's lodge where Rick had left it and climbed the stone stairs to my room in King's. I wanted to look at her. I wanted to hold her. She turned on the desk lamp, I turned off the ceiling light. I wanted her. She dropped her coat on a chair. I buried my face in her hair. Kyra, Kyra, Kyra, my lips brushing the softness.

The next morning, she went off with Geoff, Rick's partner, to drive through the fens. He wanted to show her Ely Cathedral. On the way back, they would do the shopping. With Rick's help, we had made a list of the things we would need to take with us to Bardsey.

In the final rehearsal, the soloists held back. Something in me was holding back as well. The opera was semistaged, no costumes, no sets. The drama would be enacted against the backdrop of the chapel. It was about the power of music to alter fate. I believed in that. If not for music, I would have succumbed. Budapest dismal, buildings pockmarked with bullets.

We finished at noon. I went to the buttery, asked for a sandwich, chose the smoked salmon, and ate by myself.

The afternoon stretched before me. I liked to walk on the day of a performance. I turned down Silver Street and followed the path into the water meadow. Cyclists sped through the thin passageways at the sides of the cattle gates. A kite sailed in the wind, at the end of the long string a boy and his father. "It's time now," Abe had said as I was leaving. A knowing look, his brown eyes steady. There was a liver spot on the left side of his forehead. Abraham, my father. They had thought they were part of something, had trusted that they were part of something, Budapest the Paris of Eastern Europe. They didn't think of themselves as Jews. Different for my generation. I was Jesse's age when the war ended. The Soviets became the enemy. We took to the streets. I was in conservatory. The uprising, the revolution, we believed this was it, the Enlightenment, freedom. Ducks circled behind the dam. Moss on the sides of trees, a green cast, different latitude. Kyra had grown up on Cyprus, light and sun. Her parents were refugees from Hitler. Same story. She had fallen in love with the architecture of Europe, I with the music. The older generation knew it could happen again. At any second you could be betrayed. For us, to be Jewish meant to wander around the world, making beauty, trying to change things, and wondering what's safe to trust.

I crossed the road. A group of boys, their voices bright, a ball thrown high in the air. The morning I left, Jesse was in the kitchen talking with Szofi. I stopped to listen, checking to see if he was okay. "Are you married?" he asked her. "What is your work?" He knew the answers, it was a game. "Are you married?" she asked him. "Yes," he said, his voice strangely adult. "What does your wife do?" she wanted to know. And then an answer I wouldn't have dreamed of. "She's a hang-gliding instructor," he said.

To stay in the air, to trust the currents. It was time now, Abe said.

The chapel was filled, a hush, like silence in music. I lifted my arm, the trumpets began. La Musica came out to deliver the prologue, *Dal mio Permesso*, from my beloved Permessus, *amato a voi*, I come to you. And then I was inside the music. The horns, the insistent drums had issued their summons. The theme entered, first in the strings, then the soprano, evoking a world so exquisite, so measured, at once wistful and majestic. How could one not want to reside in such sureness?

During the interval, nobody spoke. We had been visited by the gods. Act Three started with hope, Speranza. The soprano voice reached through the chapel. If you are still determined in your heart to set foot in *cite dolente,* the city of sorrow. This was the place where I had held back, but now something within me let go.

With Orpheus, I would enter the underworld, persuade the boatman. *Non vivo io,* I am not living, for since my dear wife is deprived of life, my heart no longer remains, and without a heart, how can it be that I am alive?

This unhappy man, *quell infelice.* We were in Act Four. Persephone pleading with Jove for Orpheus's release. Compassion and love triumph today in Hades, the Spirits sang. A sensation rose inside me. I lost my place. It had never happened before. The singers and instrumentalists continued on their own. I was in another world. When the noise sounded, startling Orpheus, I startled as well. Everything now was at stake. Would he lose her, just as they were approaching the light? Doubt overtakes him. Was Eurydice still behind him? A cry escaped me. It registered on the singers' faces, but they kept their concentration. Heat rushed through my body. Don't, don't do it, I wanted to say to him. Don't look back. But Orpheus had turned around. The Third Spirit sang, You have broken the law and are unworthy of mercy.

The cry was a lapse, the audience must have heard it, had it lodged high in the vaulting, been drowned out by the Sinfonia? I would know later from people's faces. At the end, there was silence before the applause. Monteverdi, the architects who designed this chapel, the singers, the instrumentalists had worked their magic.

During the reception, some were reluctant to meet my eyes. Embarrassed for me, for themselves? I wished for a cloak of invisibility. How could I explain the lapse? It was unprofessional. I let it go. The performance had worked; the wines were flowing, King's had opened its cellar for the occasion. The music director seemed pleased. It's what you wanted, Kyra whispered, to feel it in the moment.

Afterward, we were giddy. We went for a walk, and standing on Queen's Road, King's behind us, I lifted Kyra into the air.

When we left King's College, it was raining. I wasn't sure we would make it, with the two of us alone in the car. Like the first time, she said, "except now there are no hedges." She looked at me, raised her eyebrows and smiled. I turned onto Trumpington Road, and she ran her fingers across the back of my neck. A wave rose through me. I placed my hand on her knee. I wanted to stop the car. We passed the Botanic Gardens, and the light turned red. Behind the windshield wipers, we kissed. When I looked up, the light was green, the drivers behind us waiting. I collected myself. At this time of the year, the ferry ran only once a week.

We circled the roundabout and turned onto the motorway. A truck passed on the right, spraying the car. I turned up the wipers and watched the blades on the glass. "I want to know everything," I said, my hands light on the wheel. Kyra took off her boots and put a foot on the dashboard. I glanced at her leg, admiring the long line of her calf.

"It was an odd time," she said. Images of her in Boston, fall, the house on Nashawena. "I was doing all the things I usually do, teaching, the project." She adjusted her foot, the angle of her knee rising. "In the mornings when I went swimming with Roya, I felt it most clearly, the sense of being unimpeded, moving effortlessly through the water. It was disconcerting. I'd catch sight of my face in a mirror and for a moment not recognize myself."

She reached back for an orange, peeled it, and placed a section in my mouth.

The citrus tasted sweet, slightly acidic. I ran my tongue over my teeth.

"But there were also times when I thought I'd lost my mind. I was doing this again?" She sucked in her breath. "I didn't want to talk about it. I knew what people would say. I figured Anna knew and would say something if she thought I was in trouble, but she was distracted by her pregnancy. I did talk with Greta. She said what she always said, which was 'You know,' so I decided I would trust that and see."

She waited for me to say something, but I'd already said it. That from now on I would not confuse her, that my spirit, my soul, lived in the vicinity of her. Before, I had said that I loved her more than anything, and then I had abandoned her. She couldn't make sense of it. I hadn't seen that.

I reached over and found her hand.

We crossed into Wales, the road signs doubled. The Welsh names unpronounceable, a profusion of consonants. "Like wild-flowers," she said, cheered by the spray of *l*'s and *d*'s, *w*'s and *y*'s. The rain settled into a drizzle.

At Aberdaron, we found a small shop with sandwiches and coffee and read the instructions: a member of the Bardsey Island Trust would meet us at the car park at Cwrt Farm and transport the luggage to the beach at Porth Meuddwy, a ten-minute walk away. Rick had lent us waterproofs, Wellingtons, kerosene lamps, flashlights, loading them into the car along with the boxes of provisions. We put on the jackets and transferred the rest into the cart.

I had imagined Bardsey as Nashawena in midsummer. The first glimpse was a shock. A desolate hump rising out of a steel-gray sea. What had I gotten us in for? When I was fourteen, my mother had insisted I join the scouts. It was unlike her. She had only disdain for such things. You spend too much time indoors, she had said, her voice unconvincing. What she meant was you have to blend in. A school friend joined with me. We shared a tent, rain seeping in under the flaps, wind beating against the canvas. On the endless hikes, we made up a game: can you think of anything worse than this?

The ferry appeared and anchored offshore. We strapped on the life jackets and climbed into the inflatable dinghy. Kyra's face was alive to the adventure. I felt my jaw tighten. The sky had darkened, the sea was choppy, the transfer to the ferry unsteady. Wooden benches lined the sides of the open boat. The crew was impatient to get under way. Spray washed over the bow.

The man on my right, glasses misted, identified himself as a member of the Bird Observatory. The spring migration has started, he said. The Manx shearwaters were returning from Argentina. They had crossed the equator, the light their signal. I looked at Kyra, her hair wet, streaming behind her. I remembered the day we stood on the cliffs at Nashawena. She had asked me if I liked edges. I had said yes, but then I had pulled back, driven by an urgency I had not questioned. My passion for her had felt like an impediment.

The boat passed under a stern wall of cliffs. Only birds. No sign of human habitation. I looked at Kyra, her face undeterred. And she was right. The boat turned south, revealing an expanse of fields, and ahead of us, a small harbor. The mountain had hidden the island's secret from all but the hardy sixth-century pilgrims, the guidebook said, and now us, descending onto the beach. I steadied myself against the sudden stillness, alarmed by a feeling of expectation. What was I hoping for?

A sculpture greeted us. An ancient king sat in the middle of the shale, his metal crown askew. With a twist of tobacco in his hand, a rum bottle by his side, he looked content. He hadn't had to deal with what we had to deal with. Just the sea, and the weather and the birds. We could be stranded here. I glared at the king. "How did you get away with sitting it out?" And then the humor of it all melted my gloom. Kyra came up with a shell and placed it on the old king's lap. A simple offering.

The fields brightened beyond the small harbor. Across the narrow isthmus to the south, a red-and-white striped lighthouse marked the passage to the Irish Sea. We followed the tractor, loaded with luggage, and headed north along the single dirt track.

Nant was at the far end under the western slope of the mountain, near the ruins of the abbey tower and the island chapel. A simple farmhouse with a low stone wall in front. We opened the gate and went in.

It was life pared down to the essentials: a cottage, an outhouse in the garden, a single spigot with cold water in the kitchen, a gas cooker and fridge, and each other.

I called her name, my voice suspended in the cold, still air.

A shyness came into her face. It was easy to miss, this moment on the edge of coming forward when she would recede into herself. I loved her hesitation, the implicit questions: Can I show you, do you want to see? Her opening of herself became a gift. "Out loud," I would say to her sometimes, wanting to hear what she was thinking. Wanting now everything. In this remote house, we were unencumbered. I drew her to me.

"Come," she said. We climbed the narrow stairs leading to the room where we would sleep. Gray light streamed through the small window, blankets stacked on the wooden chair. On the un-made bed, we made love. "It's something you have to make," she once said. "It doesn't just happen." That wasn't completely true. It does just happen, and then it has to be made, over and over again.

I ran my fingers through her hair, in this light the color of wheat. She closed her eyes, her fingers tracing my face. Like the blind make love. Knowing by touching. Seeing by feeling. Clara had said that to feel a feeling you need someone to feel it with you. At the time, I wasn't sure. Yet now Kyra was leading me into something I hadn't felt before. I closed my eyes and entered her si-lence. You need not to know, I would tell the singers, you will find it in the music. Now there was only the rhythm of her breathing. I touched her shoulder, marble-smooth. I ran my finger down her arm, the texture changing from bone to muscle, the knob of her elbow, then the softness of her skin.

Berber trackers can read fear in a person's footprints. Her fin-ger paused in the hollow at the base of my neck.

"What?" I said, opening my eyes.

"Are you afraid of this?" she asked.

"Of what?" I said. My shoulders tensed.

Don't be afraid. I was standing on a rock at the edge of the quarry. It was the first summer after I entered conservatory. A group of us had taken the afternoon off. Someone knew of the quarry. We could swim there, he said. We climbed the fence. The water was green, completely still. I hesitated a moment, my feet absorbing the heat. Don't look, just go. I dove in.

"Of what is between us."

The one thing she demanded now was honesty.

"A little," I said.

"Then let's take it slowly," she said, meeting my eyes, a mischievous smile on her face, "from the top."

My body stirred, an impulse to move quickly into the passion that would sweep us past this moment.

"Okay," I said, treading water.

"I'll tell you something I've never said before. There's always a part of me that holds back, that goes away into someplace hidden."

"I know that," I said, then added, "in myself."

"Like those old Volkswagens that had a reserve tank, just in case."

The distance between us closed. I placed my hand on the side of her breast. I stirred again, her nipples hardened.

"Not yet," she said, propping her check in her hand. "I've always wondered what it would be like to let that go."

"We have a week," I said, feeling my breath slow.

"I want to try it now, to stay with you in every moment. I'll tell you when I move away."

"Okay." I said I would too.

The air in the room was still. The whitewashed walls gave off a milky light.

I lowered myself down the length of her body and kissed the soles of her feet.

"For stepping into the new."

I can see it now as the beginning of tracking the subtlest shifts in each other's presence. We learned to follow and not be frightened when the other moved away. But it took a long time.

That night when I placed the pillow under her hips, I entered a body so unguarded, so welcoming, our eyes holding as sluice gates opened, water rushing, filling, spilling onto the white mattress pad that lay beneath us.

"It's true," she said. It was known to be true. The island was a magical place.

. . .

I woke to the alarm in her voice. "The food!"

The room was pitch dark. We felt our way down the stairs and found the boxes. I reached for a flashlight and handed it to Kyra. She held it while I wrestled with the kerosene lamp. The scouting had turned out to be useful, though not in the way my mother imagined. Or maybe it was. How to find your way across a border, escape from certain destruction.

We put the perishables in the fridge.

"Are you hungry?"

She had come back from the garden, flashlight in hand.

I looked at my watch. It was twenty past twelve.

We made cheese sandwiches and opened a bottle of wine.

The loneliness I sheltered within myself, the sadness I had treasured, thinking it essential to my work or perhaps mistaking it for a kind of loyalty—would I open this now to her as well? It was something we shied away from in each other, sensing a danger of intrusion, the possibility of violating a sanctuary. But it was our lovemaking now that felt holy.

I watched Kyra's face as she ate her sandwich, her hand lifting the thick stem of the glass. She had a rich life, I did too. Yet they had been seriously unshared.

I picked up the wine bottle and refilled our glasses. The kerosene lamp on the table between us gave off a spray of yellow light.

My father loved the morning. "A new day," he would say, even in the worst of the bad times.

It was Sunday, literally a day of full sun. The fields were ripening, the sea in the distance. I opened the window to let in the air. I would make coffee and check out the garden. I pulled the covers over Kyra and retrieved my clothes from the floor.

I found watercress growing next to the stream and brought it back, thinking it would please her. I poured a cup of coffee, intending to get out the score or one of the books I had brought. Instead, I sat in the quiet kitchen and remembered the tenderness in her face as we blew out the lamp and headed up the stairs, making love again before drifting back into sleep.

A wash of sadness swirled past me, familiar in its tinge of remorse. There had been so many losses, so much to regret. My mother's face before me, beautiful, arresting. I thought of Kyra. She was standing in the doorway. "Where did you just go?" she asked, coming over. I burrowed my face in the V of her sweater, inhaling her smell.

The watercress delighted her. We would make an omelet. She chopped the stems, reserving the leaves while I broke the eggs into a bowl, the rhythm of our lovemaking extending.

After breakfast, we set out to explore the island. There were bluffs overlooking the Irish Sea, seals on the rocks on the side opposite the harbor. Seals were Jesse's favorite, after giraffes. Kyra had brought a sketch pad, and she settled in to draw. I wandered across the narrows to the lighthouse. A bird lay dead at its base, blinded by the light. It was so hard, this question of intention, how easily it can go astray. What I wanted now more than anything was to steer a clear path.

It was harder than I thought. In the months alone with Jesse, I had spent many evenings talking with Clara. Perhaps because she reminded me of my mother, her dark hair, the swath of orange at the bottom of her long gray skirt. It was a touch my mother would have liked. My mother's paintings were small compared with Clara's, yet with the same strong sense of color, often just a single bright square or circle against a dense surface of grays and black. It was pretty much the history of that time. Small moments of intense life amid horror and gloom. I was committed now to opening myself in a way that filled me with alarm. I had no idea what might come out.

In the end, it surprised me. We were walking one afternoon. It was Wednesday, the turn in the week. Mentally I had counted the days left before we had to leave. Kyra asked what I was afraid to ask. What would happen then? My first impulse was to say I didn't know, but then I thought that might register with her as an evasion. Which it was. Maybe I didn't want to know. The thought of returning to our lives was shattering in a way that took me aback. I had my company, we were planning now to do *Wozzeck*, an opera that would challenge us, edging up to the contemporary in a way I had avoided. But now it was time. And then there was Jesse, my father. A life filled with a dailiness in which I found solace. Yet now it stretched like a desert.

"I want to be with you," I said, thinking as I said it how difficult it would be to arrange. And then I started to weep.

Dear Greta,

I'm sitting on the daybed in the small living room of Nant, our cottage on Bardsey. Outside, soft, steady rain. It's Thursday afternoon. Andreas has gone to have tea with a painter who has lived on the island for many years, something of a recluse and also an expert of sorts on old Celtic legends. I didn't think Andreas could be in the Irish Sea without thinking about Tristan, a stark reminder of how things can go wrong.

So you see, I still brood about that. And maybe especially after this week, which has been such a quiet alone time for the two of us. Here in this remote outpost of Europe, always a sanctuary from horror of one sort or another, I find myself settling into the cadences of morning and evening, the light, the latitude different from Cyprus or Nashawena, everything starker, more sharply etched, closer to the pole. Which is how it's been for us as well.

I had a dream last night, people gathering, as if from the corners of the earth, bringing with them tokens, symbols of what they'd been through, an old woman with broken sticks, seated cross-legged on the ground at one end of a circle. Except a circle has no end. Which makes me wonder if the dream was expressing the hope that there could be an end. The mementos in the dream, the stories the people had come to tell were all about war.

This house is so silent. No hum of electricity, no phone to interrupt. *I lean against the milky wall, pillows against my back, a throw over my knees. Across the room a row of windows, small panes framing squares of yellow-green fields, in the distance a shimmer of sea. The shearwaters have returned, making their nests in burrows, the nights loud with their calls, each bird guided by the distinctive sound of its mate. One of the local bird experts told us they breed on islands to secure their nests from rats and other ground predators. And we too have found a kind of safety here, making it possible to trust what is between us.*

I did not think I could do this. I did not think A. would be this naked. I watch myself move to cover it, as if to restore a shield that would protect me as well. And then I catch myself. His face, shorn of accretion, so beautiful in this watery light.

So why the dream? Why the old woman and the group assembled on grass that resembles the fields here, an expanse of flatness? Last night we fought, a serious fight. It was the first time we didn't make love. We had been talking about Abe and the way ours is a different generation. I've always found Abe's sweetness with Jesse touching, the way he plays with him or holds him when Jesse is sad or upset. As though living through such treacherous times had reduced life to its essence. I said I wanted to do that, to live an uncluttered life.

Then why don't you come back to Budapest with me, Andreas said, and I said because it would be going back. And then I couldn't quite explain what I meant. He said if we want to be together somebody has to make a sacrifice, and I said I thought he had come to question the whole notion of sacrifice, that both of us had been ready to sacrifice our lives for the sake of a loyalty that was also a reach for security, the safety of not risking loss again. And then he said that with any choice you have to give up something, and I said I knew that but it was not the point. I felt I was being trapped in a kind of logic box, like a house with halls and passageways dead-ending in small, isolated rooms. I said we had to imagine something more open and he said did I mean an open relationship, and I said I wasn't talking about sex. Then what are you talking about, he said, and it suddenly seemed hopeless.

I got up and filled the kettle to heat water for the dishes. He cleared the table and got out his score. What are you thinking about, what are you feeling, my questions pelting like rain. He looked at me. Kyra, I need to study now, just give me some space. He adjusted the lamp, turning up the flame. I wasn't the one who brought this up, I said, trying to remember how we had reached this impasse. There were two days left before we would leave. The house felt dark and small.

I took a flashlight and went out into the garden, the ruins of the abbey tower jagged against the night sky.

The woman in the dream—she reminds me of my grand-mother, my father's mother. I don't think we talked about her. She was the one who taught us to play cards, but she irritated my mother because she always wanted to win. "They're children, Mother," my mother would say pointedly, "can't you let them win sometimes?" "It's not up to me," she would say. "It's in the cards, and they have to learn to pay attention and not make mistakes." She had a sharp eye, she was the one who saw what was coming, who insisted they leave Hamburg. She had a cousin in Cyprus. She took my father and his brother with her. Her husband, my grand-father, said he would follow once he had settled his business, but then he was arrested by the Gestapo and couldn't get out.

So what's she doing in the dream? I remember a story she told me one day. I must have been ten because that was the year I had measles and then chicken pox and I was home for weeks. My mother set up a card table next to my bed, and in the afternoons when she had to go out, my grandmother would sit with me, play-ing cards or Parcheesi. I remember the light, the sun edging around the corner of the house, slanting across the board. I was waiting for my mother to come back.

She said that when my father was a boy, he had a red wagon he loved. They lived on a street with a hill, and he and his friends would pull the wagon to the top and ride it down. He was about my age, she said. One day, they went down too fast. Another boy was steering and the wagon went out of control. My father reached for the handle to keep them from going into the street, and the wagon turned over. A sharp edge of metal cut into his arm. The cut got infected. It was before antibiotics. Every night they bathed the wound. The doctors said he might lose the arm. Then slowly the wound began to heal. It was a miracle, they said. You have to believe in miracles, my grandmother said. Sometimes things look hopeless, but it's important not to give up.

I told Andreas the story. When we were children, we would look at the scar on my father's arm, the skin shiny, the edges ragged. He was lucky, Andreas said.

We were lucky too. The hardest thing for us still is to talk about sadness. To let each other into a place we had guarded. Not to move away or bury ourselves in our work, which is something we've both done. You always said I've taken risks, but this seems like the greatest risk.

This morning, we made love and made up, and then at breakfast I remembered another dream.

We were in the country and we were building a house. It was different from the one Anna and I built, more experimental in design. You need a lot of light, Andreas said in the dream, and I was surprised that he knew this about me. What's always said about my work is that I saturate my buildings with natural light. I think of Louis Kahn, "the shadow belongs to the light."

Yesterday afternoon, we talked about leaving this island. I want to be with you, he said, and then wept. Not choked crying but simple weeping because the wanting now is so raw. We both feel it. It's as though something has been washed clean by this astringent northern air.

We were standing on the beach, the wind blowing in from the sea, tears streaming down our faces. And then we looked up and started to laugh. It was low tide and seals had climbed onto the rocks, their whiskered faces looking bemused, watching us.

Last night, standing in the garden, feeling so jangled, I thought of you and the fights we had. At first it was hard for me to say what I wanted. You spoke of my fear of abandonment, and that was there. But there was more to it than that. I wanted something with you I thought I couldn't have. It seemed too risky to ask for it, so I fought with you instead. And then I took the risk. And you did too.

I wonder what you're dreaming. I hope you can read this writing. Needless to say, there's no typewriter here.
Love,
Kyra

―――――

Dear Kyra,

I want to write you this dream before I forget it. It's from last night. I'm driving through my neighborhood and I see a house I'd never seen before. It is made entirely of glass. I get out of the car and walk around it. The angles are striking. I can't see how they've managed to do it or what is holding the panes. It's very beautiful and daring. That's all I remember now. There was something about a book.

I'll just jot down a few associations: people who live in glass houses, etc., transparency, something I like in music, living in a way that is transparent. I looked up the word in the dictionary (the book in the dream?). It means allowing light to pass through with little or no interruption or distortion so that objects on the other side can be clearly seen, to be completely open and frank about things.

I thought you'd like this.

I really must go now. I'll write more next week.

Love,
Greta

Acknowledgments

While most places in this novel are real, the story and characters are fiction, imagined events and lives. My ability to envision these lives was enhanced by the generosity of Linda Pollak, who invited me to sit in on her urban design studio at Harvard, and Joel Revzen, who invited me into his rehearsals for *Tosca*. I also want to thank Kristin Linklater and Tina Packer for encouraging me to take the Shakespeare & Company intensive actor training workshop, where I learned the Linklater voice work and the text exercise called "dropping in." My guide into the world of the Akha was Deborah Tooker, then a graduate student in anthropology at Harvard, who asked me to serve on her thesis committee. My thanks to Martin Richards and Sarah Smalley for inviting me to spend a week with them on Bardsey and to Alexia Panayioutou for introducing me to Cyprus.

I would like to acknowledge information drawn from *Peter Brook: A Theatrical Casebook* (compiled by David Williams) and especially from the rehearsal log of *Carmen* kept by Michel Rostain, which opened the rehearsal process to me. I have directly quoted Peter Brook in Andreas's talk to the cast following the opening of *Tosca*, and Frank Rich's review of Mr. Brook's *Carmen* inspired the line attributed to the *Globe* review of *Tosca*. Similarly, *The End of Architecture?*, edited by Peter Noever and reporting the proceedings of a conference held in 1992 at the MAK in Vienna, allowed me to listen for the way architects talk with one another about their work. I have woven some of Mr. Noever's memorable phrases into the opening remarks at the conference Kyra attends and borrowed a question and some observations from Frank Gehry's preface for the discussion following her talk. Elizabeth Grossman, formerly of the Rhode Island School of Design, introduced me to the metaphor of weave as used by architects and was most generous in helping me to think about Kyra's project. She also directed me to the work of Toshiko Mori. My descriptions of the Akha village and their way of life are drawn from Deborah Ellen Tooker's dissertation, "Inside and Outside: Schematic Replication at the Levels of Village, Household, and Person among the Akha of Northern Thailand."

Other books that were especially helpful to me were *Tide Race* by Brenda Chamberlain for her evocative descriptions of Bardsey; *Three Islands* by Alice Forbes Howland for her descriptions of Nashawena; *Louis Kahn: Essential Texts* for his reflections on light; *The Gothic Cathedral* by Otto von Simson; *Deconstruction,* edited by Andreas Papadakis, Catherine Cooke, and Andrew Benjamin; *The Shifting Point* by Peter Brook; *Divided Cyprus,* edited by Yiannis Papadakis, Nicos Peristianis, and Gisela Weiss; *Hungary and the Soviet Bloc* by Charles Gati; and Susan Rubin Suleiman's *Budapest Diary.* I was also inspired by performances of Jonathan Miller's semi-staged *L'Orfeo* and Peter Brook's *Pelleas et Melisande,* by Normi Noel's direction of *Hamlet* (which I drew on for Kyra's part in the game of changing the ending), and by Zaha Hadid's exhibition at the Guggenheim Museum.

The lines in italics on page 122 are from Jorie Graham's poem, "Act III, Sc. 2"; the passage Kyra copies into her journal on page 188 is from Lebbeus Woods's "Manifesto 1992," a wall text displayed at the MAK in Vienna. Her quotation (slightly rephrased) of Peter Eisenman on page 191 is from "Peter Eisenman: An Architectural Design Interview by Charles Jencks" (*Deconstruction,* p. 143). The book on memory Andreas is reading is Susan Rubin Suleiman's *Crises of Memory and the Second World War,* and the line he underscores is on page 232. The English translations of *Tosca* are from the libretto provided with the EMI recording (#56304).

Thanks to the School of Law and the Steinhardt School at New York University and to the Chilmark Public Library. I am grateful to Kristin

Maloney, who found books for me on the Elizabeth Islands and let me keep them for a long time.

My deepest thanks to my editor, Kate Medina, who joined me at a level I had not imagined and brought her extraordinary ear and eye to this project with a generosity that always inspired me to go further. Her knowledge of literature and her wisdom as an editor were a writer's dream. I also owe an immense debt of gratitude to Rachel Kadish, my writing pal and an experienced novelist, who taught me a lot about writing. The precision of her ear was a great gift. Diana de Vegh's ear was also invaluable to me, and in her own way, she too was a writer's dream.

I also wish to thank the many people who were helpful to me at various stages of this work. I am especially grateful to the late Jean Baker Miller for her encouragement when I first started writing fiction; to Irene Orgel, Mary Hamer, and Normi Noel for their responses to early drafts of this book; and to Emily Hass for her exceptional help. My gratitude also to Helaine Blumenfeld, Nicole Dabernat, Eve Ensler, Peter Friedman, Jonathan Gilligan, Helga Kaiser, Julia Leonard, Bob Levine, Rob and Karen Loomis, Golnoush Niknejad, Carole Obedin, Tina Packer, Linda Pollak, David Richards, Cora Roth, Niobe Way, and Kate Wenner. A special thanks to Adrian Nicole LeBlanc for crucial swims at the final stages.

Finally, my thanks to the outstanding editorial and design staff at Random House: Steve Meyers, Beth Pearson, Abby Plesser, Robin Rolewicz, and Katie Shaw.

I have dedicated this book to my husband, Jim Gilligan, without whom I would never have written a novel.

About the Author

CAROL GILLIGAN is a writer best known for her book *In a Different Voice*. She was a member of the Harvard faculty for thirty-four years and held the university's first chair in gender studies. She is currently University Professor of the Humanities and Applied Psychology at New York University, and she lives with her husband in New York City and the Berkshires. *Kyra* is her first novel.

About the Type

This book was set in Sabon, a typeface designed by the well-known German typographer Jan Tschichold (1902–74). Sabon's design is based upon the original letter forms of Claude Garamond and was created specifically to be used for three sources: foundry type for hand composition, Linotype, and Monotype. Tschichold named his typeface for the famous Frankfurt typefounder Jacques Sabon, who died in 1580.